"Chilling . . . propulsive . . . Koepp is skilled at sharp, often humorous dialogue. . . . [A] taut, mordant thriller debut."
—*Kirkus* (starred review)

"A terrific thriller: ambitious, audacious, gory, scary, flamboyant, and funny . . . [Koepp makes] a seamless, massively effective transition from the visual medium to the literary. The book doesn't read like a modestly beefed-up pitch for a movie; it's a rich, textured, and downright impossible-to-put-down story."
—*Booklist* (starred review)

"A sensational SF thriller. . . . Breakneck pacing and nonstop action. . . . Michael Crichton fans won't want to miss this one." —*Publishers Weekly*

"*Cold Storage* is *The Andromeda Strain* on crack: chilling end-of-the-world terror infected with wicked humor. Koepp pulls it off with style. When the real apocalypse arrives, may it be even half as funny as this."
—Linwood Barclay, *New York Times* bestselling author of *A Noise Downstairs*

"To be simultaneously terrifying and hilarious is a masterstroke few writers can pull off, but Koepp manages in this incredible fiction debut that calls to mind a beautiful hybrid of Michael Crichton and Carl Hiaasen. *Cold Storage* is sheer thrillery goodness, and riotously entertaining."
—Blake Crouch, *New York Times* bestselling author of *Dark Matter*

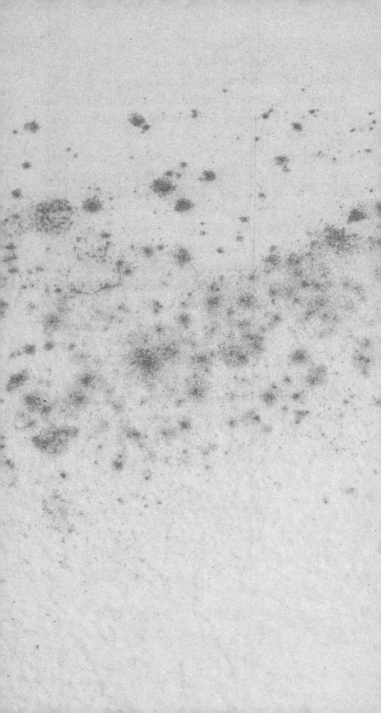

DAVID KOEPP

COLD STORAGE

A NOVEL

ecco

An Imprint of HarperCollins*Publishers*

COLD STORAGE. Copyright © 2019 by David Koepp. All rights reserved. Printed in the United States of America. No part of this book may be used or reproduced in any manner whatsoever without written permission except in the case of brief quotations embodied in critical articles and reviews. For information, address HarperCollins Publishers, 195 Broadway, New York, NY 10007.

First Ecco premium printing: August 2020
First Ecco trade international printing: September 2019
First Ecco hardcover printing: September 2019

Print Edition ISBN: 978-0-06-302334-5
Digital Edition ISBN: 978-0-06-291645-7

Title page and part opener art: shutterstock/andy_pol
Cover images © bubaone/Getty Images (biohazard symbol);
© Woters/Getty Images (running man)
Stepback image © alexslb/Shutterstock (splatter)
Author photograph by Melissa Thomas

Ecco and HarperCollins are registered trademarks of HarperCollins Publishers in the United States of America and other countries.

20 21 22 23 24   QGM   10 9 8 7 6 5 4 3 2 1

For Melissa,
who said, "Yeah, sure!"

COLD STORAGE

PROLOGUE

The world's largest single living organism is *Armillaria solidipes*, better known as the honey fungus. It's about eight thousand years old and covers 3.7 square miles of the Blue Mountains in Oregon. Over eight millennia it has spread through a weblike network of lines underground, sprouting fruiting bodies above the earth that look like mushrooms. The honey fungus is relatively benign, unless you're an herbaceous tree, bush, or plant. If you are, it's genocidal. The fungus kills by gradual takeover of the root system and moves up the plant, eventually choking off all water and nutrients.

Armillaria solidipes spreads across the landscape at a rate of one to three feet per year and can take thirty to fifty years to kill an average-sized tree. If it could move significantly faster, 90 percent of all botanic growth on Earth would die, the atmosphere would turn to poison gas, and human and animal life would end. But it is a slow-moving fungus.

Other fungi are faster.

Much faster.

DECEMBER 1987

ONE

After they'd burned their clothes, shaved their heads, and scrubbed themselves until they bled, Roberto Diaz and Trini Romano were allowed back into the country. Even then they hadn't felt entirely clean, only that they had done everything they could, and the rest was up to fate.

They were in a government-issue sedan now, rattling down I-73 just a few miles from the storage facility at the Atchison mines. They followed close behind the open-air cargo truck in front of them, tight enough that no civilian vehicle could get in between them. Trini was in the front passenger seat of the sedan, her feet up on the dashboard, a posture that always infuriated Roberto, who was behind the wheel.

"Because it leaves footprints," he told her, for the hundredth time.

"It's dust," Trini replied, also for the hundredth time. "I wipe it right off, look." She made a half-assed attempt to wipe her footprints off the dashboard.

"Yeah, but you don't, Trini. You don't wipe it

off, you kind of smear it around with your hand and then I wipe it off when we return it to the pool. Or I forget and I leave it, and somebody else has to do it. I don't like making work for other people."

Trini looked at him with her heavy-lidded eyes, the ones that didn't believe half of what they saw. Those eyes and what they could see were the reason she was a lieutenant colonel at forty, but her inability to refrain from *commenting* on what she saw was the reason she'd go no further. Trini had no filter and no interest in acquiring one.

She stared at him for a thoughtful moment, took a long drag off the Newport between her fingers, and blew a cloud of smoke out the side of her mouth.

"I accept, Roberto."

He looked at her. "Huh?"

"Your apology. For back there. That's why you're bitching at me. You bitch at me because you don't know how to say you're sorry. So I'll save you the trouble. I accept your apology."

Trini was right, because Trini was always right. Roberto said nothing for a long moment, just stared out at the road ahead.

Finally, when he could, he muttered, "Thank you."

Trini shrugged. "See? Not so bad."

"I behaved badly."

"Almost. But not quite. Seems like pretty small potatoes now."

They'd talked endlessly about what had happened in the four days since it had all started, but they were pretty much talked out now, having relived and re-examined every moment from every conceivable angle. Except for this one moment. This one had gone unspoken, but now they were speaking about it, and Roberto didn't want to leave it that way.

"I didn't mean with her. I meant the way I talked to you."

"I know." Trini put a hand on Roberto's shoulder. "Lighten up."

Roberto nodded and stared straight ahead. Lightening up did not come easily to Roberto Diaz. He was in his midthirties, but his personal and professional accomplishments had raced ahead of his chronological age because he never lightened up, he Got Shit Done. He ticked boxes. Head of class at the Air Force Academy? Tick. Major in the USAF by the age of thirty? Tick. Superb physical and mental conditioning with no obvious flaws or weaknesses? Tick. Perfect wife? Tick. Perfect baby boy? Tick. None of this could be accomplished through patience or passivity.

Where am I headed?, where am I headed?, where am I headed?, Roberto would ask himself. The future was all he thought about, planned for, obsessed over. His life moved fast, it stayed on schedule, and he played things straight.

Well. Most things.

They both just stared at the truck ahead of them for a while. Through the canvas flap over the rear gate they could see the top of the metal crate they'd flown halfway across the planet. The truck hit a pothole, the crate slid back a foot or so, and they both sucked in their breath involuntarily. But it stayed settled in the back. Just a few more miles to the caves and this would be over. The crate would be safely stashed three hundred feet underground till the end of time.

The Atchison Caves were a limestone mine back in 1886, a massive quarry that went down 150 feet under the Missouri River bluffs. They started out producing riprap for the nearby railroads and dug as far down as God and physics would allow, until the pillars of unmined rock that held the place up reached the very outside limit of any sane engineer's willingness to sign off on their safety. During World War II the empty caverns, now a sweet eighty acres of naturally climate-controlled underground space, were used to house perishables by the War Food Administration, and eventually the mining company sold the whole space to the government for $20,000. A couple million dollars in renovations later, it had become a highly secured government storage facility used for disaster and continuity of government planning, storing impeccably machined tools in a state of well-oiled readiness, set to ship them anywhere, any time, only please God let there be a nuclear war first so this was worth all the money.

It would be worth it today.

The call had been a weird one from the first ding. Technically, Trini and Roberto were with DNA, the Defense Nuclear Agency. Later it would become part of DTRA, but that particular government mishmash wouldn't be cobbled together until the Defense Department's official reorganization in 1997. Ten years earlier they were still DNA, and their brief was simple and clear: stop everybody else from getting what we have. If you smell a nuclear program, find it and wreck it. If you get a lead on some nightmarish bioweapon, make it go away forever. Expense will not be spared; questions will not be asked. Two-person teams were preferred, to keep things compartmentalized, but there was always backup if you needed it. Trini and Roberto rarely needed it. They'd been to sixteen different hotspots in seven years and had sixteen liquid kills to their names. Kills were not literal; it was agency-speak for a weapons program that had been neutralized. But there had been casualties along the way. Questions were not asked.

Sixteen missions, but none remotely like this one.

THE USAF TRANSPORT HAD ALREADY BEEN WARM-ing up at the base when they bounded up the stairs and came on board. There was only one other passenger, and Trini took the seat directly opposite her. Roberto sat across the aisle, in a backward seat also facing the bright-eyed young woman in well-worn safari gear.

Trini held a hand out to her and the young woman took it. "Lieutenant Colonel Trini Romano."

"Dr. Hero Martins."

Trini just looked at her, nodding and popping in a piece of Nicorette, taking Hero's measure, unafraid to hold silent eye contact while she sized her up. It was disconcerting. Roberto just gave Hero a half salute; he never enjoyed playing the whole I-see-right-through-you game.

"Major Roberto Diaz."

"Nice to meet you, Major," Hero said.

"What kind of doctor are you?" Roberto asked.

"Microbiologist. University of Chicago. I specialize in epidemiological surveillance."

Trini was still looking at her. "That your real name? Hero?"

Hero hid her sigh. It was a question with which she was not unfamiliar after thirty-four years. "Yes, that's my real name."

"Hero like Superman or Hero like in Greek mythology?" Roberto asked.

She turned her gaze to Roberto. That was a question she didn't hear nearly as much.

"The latter. My mother was a classics professor. You know the story?"

Roberto looked up, squinting his left eye and staring into the space just above and to the right of his head, the way he did when he was trying to pull an obscure fact out of his brain's nether regions. He found the nugget of information and dragged it up out of the swamp.

"She lived in a tower on a river?"

Hero nodded. "The Hellespont."

"Somebody was in love with her."

"Leander. Every night he'd swim the river to

the tower and make love to her. Hero would light a lamp in the tower so he could see his way to the shore."

"But he drowned anyway, right?"

Trini turned and stared at Roberto, her displeasure plain. Roberto was good-looking to an irritating degree. The son of a Mexican father and a California blonde mother, he radiated good health and had a head of hair that would last forever. He also had a smart and funny wife named Annie, whom Trini actually found tolerable, which was saying something. Yet he'd been on this plane all of thirty seconds and was clearly trying to charm this woman. Trini had never picked her partner for a jerk before and hoped he wouldn't turn out to be one now. She watched him, chewing her gum like she was mad at it.

But Hero was engaged. She kept on talking to Roberto, ignoring Trini.

"Aphrodite became jealous of their love. One night she blew out Hero's light, and Leander was lost. When she saw he had drowned, Hero threw herself out of the tower to her death."

Roberto took a moment and thought about that. "What exactly is the moral there? Try to meet somebody on your side of the river?"

Hero smiled and shrugged. "Don't piss off the gods, I guess."

Trini, weary of their banter, glanced back at the pilots and spun a finger in the air. The engines immediately whined, and the plane started to move down the runway with a jerk. Subject changed.

Hero looked around, concerned. "Wait, we're going? Where is the rest of your team?"

"You're looking at us," Trini said.

"Are you—I mean, are you sure? This might not be something we can handle on our own."

Roberto conveyed Trini's confidence, but without the edge. "Why don't you tell us what it is," he said to Hero, "and we'll let you know if we think we can handle it."

"They told you nothing?" she asked.

"They told us we're going to Australia," Trini said, "and that you'd know the rest."

Hero turned and looked out the window, watching as the plane left the earth. No turning back now. She shook her head. "I will never understand the army."

"Me neither," Roberto said. "We're in the air force. Seconded to the Defense Nuclear Agency."

"This isn't nuclear."

Trini frowned. "They sent you, so I assume they suspect a bioweapon?"

"No."

"Then what is it?"

Hero thought about that for a second. "Good question." She opened the file on the table in front of her and started talking.

Six hours later, she stopped.

WHAT ROBERTO KNEW ABOUT WESTERN AUSTRALIA could fit into a very small book. More of a flyer, really: one page and with large type. Hero told them they were going to a remote township called Kiwirrkurra Community, in the middle of the Gibson Desert, about 1,200 kilometers east of Port Hedland. It had been established a decade earlier as a Pintupi outstation, part of the Australian government's ongoing attempts to allow and encourage Aboriginal groups to move back to their traditional ancestral lands. They'd been mistreated and cleared out of those same territories for decades, most recently in the 1960s as a result of the Blue Streak missile tests. You can't very well be living on land that we want to blow up. It's unhealthy.

But by the midseventies the tests were over, political sensitivities were on the rise, and so the last of the Pintupi had been trucked back to Kiwirrkurra, which wasn't even the middle of nowhere, but more like a few hundred miles outside the very outer rim of nowhere. But there they lived, all twenty-six Pintupi, as peaceful and happy as human beings can be in a stifling desert without power, telephone lines, or any connection to modern society. They rather liked being cut off, in fact, and the elders in particular were pleased with their return to their ancestral lands.

And then the sky fell.

Not all of it, Hero explained. Just a chunk.

"What was it?" Roberto asked. He'd been holding eye contact with her throughout the brief history so far, and don't think for a second Trini didn't notice. In fact, she was glaring at Roberto, as if psychically willing him to stop.

"Skylab."

Now Trini turned her head and looked at Hero. "This was in '79?"

"Yes."

"I thought that fell into the Indian Ocean."

Hero nodded. "Most of it did. The few pieces that hit land fell just outside a town called Esperance, also in Western Australia."

"Close to Kiwirrkurra?" Roberto asked.

"Nothing is close to Kiwirrkurra. Esperance is about two thousand kilometers away and has ten thousand residents. It's a metropolis by comparison."

"What happened to the pieces that fell in Esperance?"

Hero turned to the next section of her notes. The pieces that fell in Esperance had been, rather enterprisingly, scooped up by the locals and put in the town's museum—formerly a dance hall, but quickly converted to the Esperance Municipal Museum & Skylab Observatorium. Admission was four dollars, and for that you could see the largest oxygen tank from the orbiter, the space station's storage freezer for food and other items, some nitrogen spheres used by its attitude control thrusters, and a piece of the hatch the astronauts would have crawled through during their visits. A number of other chunks of unrecognizable debris were also put on view, including a piece of sheet metal that rather suspiciously had the word SKYLAB neatly lettered in undamaged bright red paint across its middle.

"For years NASA assumed that was all that would ever be found, as the rest of it either burned up on re-entry or is at the bottom of the Indian Ocean," Hero continued. "After five or six years, they figured anything else on land would have turned up by then or was somewhere uninhabitable."

"Like Kiwirrkurra," Roberto offered.

She nodded and turned another page.

"Three days ago, I got a call from the NASA Space Biosciences Research Branch. They'd gotten a message, relayed through about six different government agencies, that someone was calling from Western Australia because 'something had come out of the tank.'"

"What tank?"

"The extra oxygen tank. The one that fell on Kiwirrkurra."

Trini sat forward. "Who called from Western Australia?"

Hero looked down at her notes. "He identified himself as Enos Namatjira. He said he lived in Kiwirrkurra and his uncle had found the tank in the dirt five or six years earlier. Uncle had heard about the spaceship that crashed, so he moved it in front of his house and kept it there as a souvenir. But now there was something wrong with it, and he was getting sick. Quickly."

Roberto frowned, trying to piece it together. "How did this guy know what number to call?"

"He didn't. He started with the White House."

"And it got through to NASA?" Trini was incredulous. Such efficiency was unheard of.

"It took him seventeen calls, and he had to drive thirty miles to get to the phone every time, but yes, he finally got through to NASA."

"He was determined," Roberto said.

"He was, because by that time, people were dying. They finally put him in touch with me about a day and a half ago. I do work for NASA sometimes, inspecting their re-entry vehicles to make sure they're clear of any foreign bioforms, which they always are."

"But you think this time something came back?" Trini asked.

"Not quite. This is where it gets interesting."

Roberto leaned forward. "I think it's pretty interesting already."

Hero smiled at him. Trini tried not to roll her eyes.

Hero continued. "The tank was sealed, and I highly doubt that it could bring anything back from space that it wasn't sent up with. I went through all the Skylab files, and on the last re-supply it seems this particular oxygen tank had been sent up not for O_2 circulation, but solely for attachment to one of the outer pod arms. There was a fungal organism inside the tank, a sort of cousin of *Ophiocordyceps unilateralis*. It's a cool little parasitic fungus that can adapt from one species to another. Known to survive extreme conditions, a bit like *Clostridium difficile* spores. You know those?"

They looked at her blankly. Knowledge of *Clostridium difficile* was not a requirement in their line of work.

"Well, they're pernicious. They can survive anywhere—inside a volcano, bottom of the sea, outer space."

They just looked at her, taking her word for it.

She went on. "Anyway. The sample in the tank was part of a research project. The fungus had some peculiar growth properties and they wanted to see how it was affected by conditions in space. Remember, it was the seventies, orbital space stations were going to be the next big thing, so they needed to develop effective antifungal medications for the millions of people who were going to go live up there. But they never got the chance."

"Because Skylab crashed."

"Right. So, after five or six years sitting outside in front of Enos Namatjira's uncle's house, the tank started to rust. Uncle wanted to spruce it up a little bit, make it shiny and new again, maybe people would pay to come see it. He tried to remove the rust, but it was resistant. According to Enos, his uncle tried a number of different cleaners, finally using a folkloric solution: cutting a potato in half, pouring dish soap on it, and rubbing it on the surface of the tank."

"Did it work?"

"Yep. The rust came off easily, and the thing shined up. A few days later, Uncle got sick. He started to behave erratically, not making a great deal of sense. He climbed onto the roof of his house and refused to come down, and then his body started to swell uncontrollably."

"What the hell happened?" Trini asked.

"From this point forward, everything I say is hypothesis."

She paused. They waited. Whether Dr. Martins was aware of it or not, she knew how to tell a story. They were transfixed.

"I believe the chemical combination that Uncle used dripped through microfissures in the tank's exterior and landed inside, where the dormant *Cordyceps* fungus was rehydrated."

"With the potato stuff?" Roberto wondered. Didn't sound very hydrating.

She nodded. "The average potato is seventy-eight percent water. But the fungus wasn't just rehydrated; it was given pectin, cellulose, protein, and fat. And a nice place to grow. The average temperature in the Western Australian desert at this time of year is well over a hundred degrees Fahrenheit. Inside the tank, it's probably closer to a hundred thirty. Deadly for us, but perfect for a fungus."

Trini wanted to get to the point. "So, you're saying the thing came back to life?"

"Not exactly. Again, I'm speculating, but I think it's possible the polysaccharide in the potato combined with the sodium palmitate in the dish soap to produce a pro-growth environment. Normally, they're both large, boring, inert molecules, but you put them together, you might have some good unpredictable fun. Don't blame Uncle; I mean, the guy was *trying* to produce a chemical reaction."

She was getting warmed up now—her eyes shone with the intellectual exercise of it all—and Roberto couldn't help it, he couldn't tear his eyes away from hers.

"And he did?"

"He sure the fuck did!"

Lord, she swore too. Roberto smiled.

"But I don't think either the polysaccharide or the sodium palmitate was the underlying change agent."

She leaned forward, as if telling the punch line to a joke that everyone was absolutely going to love.

"It was the rust. $Fe_2O_3.nH_2O$."

Trini spit her gum into a tissue and popped in a fresh piece. "Do you think, Dr. Martins, that somewhere inside you lurks the capacity to summarize?"

Hero turned to Trini, her demeanor matter-of-fact again.

"Sure. We sent up a hyperaggressive extremophile that is resistant to intense heat and the vacuum of space, but sensitive to cold. The environment sent the organism into a dormant state, but it remained hyper-receptive. At that point, it must have picked up a hitchhiker. Maybe it was exposed to solar radiation. Maybe a spore penetrated the microfissures in the tank on re-entry. Either way, when the fungus returned to Earth it was reawakened and found itself in a hot, safe, protein-rich, pro-growth environment. And *something* caused its higher-level genetic structure to change."

"Into what?" Roberto asked.

She looked from one to the other of them, the way a teacher looks at a pair of slightly dim students who refuse to grasp the obvious. She spelled it out for them.

"I think we created a new species."

There was silence for a moment. Since it

was Hero's theory, she claimed naming rights. *"Cordyceps novus."*

Trini just looked at her. "What did you tell Mr. Namatjira?"

"That I needed to check some things and he should call me back in six hours. He never did."

"What did you do then?"

"Called the Defense Department."

"And what did they do?" Roberto asked.

She gestured. "Sent you guys."

TWO

The next six hours of the flight passed in relative silence. As they flew over the western coast of Africa and night fell, Trini did what she always did on the way to a mission, which was to take sleep when it was available. She also never passed an available bathroom without using it. It was the little things. Limit your needs. Hero got tired of looking at Trini's boots on the seat next to her, so when the plane was mostly dark, she got up, climbed over her, and crossed the aisle to Roberto's side.

"Do you mind?" she whispered, gesturing to the empty seat next to him. He did not mind. Not in the slightest. He shifted his legs, giving her room to squeeze through, and she made herself as comfortable as possible, settling into the seat next to him. The ostensible reason for the move was that this new seat would give her a place to put her own legs up, but she could have done that in the other seat, Roberto figured. Maybe the real reason had something to do with the slightly furtive eye contact they'd been making since she'd finished the briefing, but it worked better for him, psychologically anyway, if he assumed the obvious was the case, while knowing full well it was not.

The things you tell yourself.

The absolute truth was that Roberto was much less than innocent in this situation. He'd felt an immediate attraction to Dr. Hero Martins, and though it was the last thing in the world he would ever act on, he needed to know that the old charm was still there when he needed it. He and Annie had been married for just about three years, and it had been a rough start. Work was overwhelming for both of them in the first year, Annie had gotten pregnant much sooner than they intended, and the pregnancy was a difficult one, forcing her to stay in bed for the last four or five months of it. That's hard enough for anybody, but Annie had been a perpetual motion machine; she was a journalist and accustomed to life on the road. Home confinement felt like a punishment. Then the baby came, and it was, you know, a baby.

That was pretty much it for their easy years. Where were the just-us years, where was the blissful early marriage time when we enjoyed our youth and beauty and freedom and each other, and where, as long as we're talking, was the sex, for God's sake? Roberto hated being this particular cliché, the married dude who laments the post-baby sex life wipeout, but *still*. He was a human male in the prime of his life. It was difficult, at this point, for him to picture himself and Annie making it to their emeritus years together. Not at this rate.

But he loved her. And he didn't want to cheat.

So he flirted. He'd never really been good at it when it counted, but something about not wanting it to lead anywhere made it easier. Roberto surprised himself with the ease with which he could talk to attractive women at this point in life and how positively they responded to him. A stable and unattainable man with a job in his midthirties was a lot different from a twenty-four-year-old grunt with a hard-on and a tongue tied in knots.

It played neatly into Hero's own predilections and preference. Since the end of her overlong, overly tortured post-college relationship with Max, a man-child doctoral student more or less her own age, she'd had a thing about married men. Not a thing *for* married men—that would suggest a certain amoral craving, doing a thing because it was bad, not doing it in spite of it being bad. No, Hero had a thing *about* married men, i.e., a personal rule or guideline, based on all the obvious advantages, which she had laid out in a notebook one day during an exceptionally dull class on laser micromachining. The advantages were, in order of importance:

1. They tended toward the adult in demeanor, having embraced life's changes by showing a willingness to marry and some concept of shared existence, which by definition involved compromise and other-directed thinking.

2. They were usually better in bed, not just from volume of experience, but from repeated experience with the *same* woman, which couldn't help but lead to a sense of how to give pleasure as well as receive, unless they were complete narcissists, which was usually unlikely, given reason 1.

3. They were polite and grateful and didn't leave a lot of shit on the floor, having been housebroken for at least a few years by an adult woman not their mother.

4. They had somewhere to go, usually within a reasonable time frame after sex, which freed up her evenings for work.

5. They were, by definition, unable to pursue an exclusive relationship, which left her free to do as she liked, on the off chance something better came along.

Hero knew perfectly well that there were many, many reasons that did not work in their favor, that did not speak to the good character of the married lover, which she neatly summed up in a single item on the facing page of her journal:

1. They're cheaters.

And so was she, and she knew it. She didn't cheat on them; she never had multiple lovers—one romantic complication at a time was more than enough in her life. And she wasn't cheating their unlucky spouses, by her estimation, because she didn't know them and had never promised them anything. The only person she was cheating was herself, by hanging out with a succession of people who it seemed, by the very nature of their relationship, did not know how to love.

Still, here she was, and here Roberto was, and here they were, possibly headed to their own doom (rationalize much?), and there surely could be no harm in making a little pleasant, life-affirming conversation with a handsome soldier in his midthirties who clearly had a thing for her. The fact that he wore a wedding ring was a total coincidence.

While Trini slept, Roberto and Hero stretched their legs out on the seats in front of them, reclined as far as they could, and whispered to each other. They weren't tired—the frisson in the air between them was too invigorating—so they talked about his life, with the exception of his wife and kid, and they talked about hers, with the exception of her romantic history with Guys Like Him. They talked about her work, and about his, and the dangers he'd faced, and the exotic and frightening places she'd been in search of new microorganisms. And as they talked, they slid lower and lower in the seats, and their heads inclined ever so slightly closer together, and when the cabin took on a bit of a chill somewhere over Kenya, Roberto got up, found a couple of harsh wool blankets in the storage cabinet nearby, and they snuggled underneath them.

Then she scratched her nose.

And when she put her hand back down, it was on the seat between them, her little finger brushing against the outside of his right thigh. He felt it, and she left it there. Another twenty minutes went by, another twenty minutes of effortless, breathy talk, none of it with even the whisper of impropriety to it, and the next move was his, which he made by shifting in his seat, theoretically to stretch his stiff legs, but when he put them back up on the seat in front of him, his leg was now fully pressed against hers, and she returned the pressure almost immediately. Neither of them spoke of it; neither of them acknowledged it in any way. If you listened to their conversation, you could assume they were two colleagues from slightly different fields who had met at a professional conclave and were having the most innocent, upstanding, and rather boring conversation in the world.

But she never moved her hand, and neither released the pressure in their legs. They knew. They just weren't saying.

After a while, Hero stretched and stood up. "Bathroom."

He pointed toward the back. She smiled thanks, squeezed out of the row, and walked off toward the rear of the plane.

Roberto watched her walk away. Inside, he was panicked, and had been for several hours. He couldn't quite believe what was happening. None of his relatively innocent flirtations had ever gone nearly so far, and it was like sliding into a mud-slicked hole that he couldn't climb out of. Every movement he made only pulled him deeper in, and when he didn't move it was worse, gravity took over and pulled him down.

And he liked it. He was angry, not getting what he wanted or deserved at home, and why *not* this woman, this brilliant, beautiful creature who asked so little of him and found him so fascinating and was clearly, genuinely interested in him? Why not, other than the fact that it was completely wrong? Or maybe it wasn't even happening. Maybe the pressure of her hand and leg had easily explainable and innocent reasons behind them—she probably hadn't even *noticed*, for Christ's sake—and he was letting his overactive sex drive run away with his rational mind, as usual.

Or maybe it was happening, and maybe he wanted it to. Maybe he would get up, wander to the back of the plane, talk to her some more there, and if her eyes happened to linger on his for a few seconds longer than they ought to, he'd kiss her. Maybe that's exactly what he'd do. Maybe that's what he'd get up and do *right now*.

Roberto summoned every bit of resentment he could find, every ounce of righteous indignation he'd acquired over three frustrating years of marriage, and he stood up.

That's when he felt the hand on his arm.

He turned. Trini was awake, staring up at him, the fingers of her strong right hand clamped around Roberto's left forearm.

Roberto looked down at her, his face turning

into a poorly rendered mask of utter innocence. Trini just looked at him, her penetrating gaze bright even in the dim cabin light.

"Sit down, Roberto."

Roberto's mouth opened, but no words came out. He wasn't a very good liar, even worse at wholesale invention, and rather than stammer out something stupid, he just closed his mouth again and shrugged an *I don't know what you're talking about* shrug.

"Sit down."

Roberto did. Trini leaned over and put a hand on the back of his neck.

"That ain't you, kid."

Roberto felt a hot flush rise in his cheeks—anger, embarrassment, and thwarted desire sending any spare blood to his face on the double. "Stay out of it."

"My advice exactly." Trini kept staring.

Roberto looked away. He felt humiliated and wanted to make her feel the same. He turned back to Trini. "Jealous?"

He'd wanted to lash out, and he did; he'd wanted to hurt, and he hit the target. Trini's face fell, ever so slightly, less in wounded pride than in disappointment.

Trini had been on the other side of her first and only marriage for ten years already, and the fact that she'd ever married in the first place was remarkable in itself. The marriage fell apart not because of the travel and secrecy required in her line of work, but because of her innate distaste for other human beings. People were okay; she just didn't like looking at or listening to them. She'd been alone for a decade now and liked it.

In her mind, she'd always thought of her occasional attraction to Roberto as a purely chemical response to his rather overstated good looks. She liked him fine, she enjoyed working with him, she deeply admired his professionalism and the fact that he felt no compulsion toward small talk, but she'd never had any romantic interest in him whatsoever. He was her co-worker. Her incredibly good-looking co-worker. Sometimes even people who don't like sweets admire a piece of chocolate cake. That's what it's designed to do: it's *supposed* to look good. So was he. And he did, usually. No big deal. Trini kept it to herself.

But in '83 she had been in a jeep accident and had broken two bones in her lower back, an exceptionally painful injury that resulted in her subsequent addiction to the painkillers the base physician had liberally prescribed to her. It was at bedtime that Trini liked them best; she'd take one an hour before bed and then nod off into drifty opiate sleep, feeling like nothing hurt, and not only that, even more than that, nothing ever would hurt, then or ever again. And where else in life can you get that assurance?

The addiction dug in and grew. It went on for nearly six months, undetected by everyone except Roberto. He confronted his friend about it and then gave enormous amounts of time, energy, and emotional support to help Trini get clean. Trini insisted on doing it without any other outside help whatsoever, and Roberto agreed to try.

Early on, during one of Trini's worst shaking, sweating, sleepless nights, she'd started to panic, and Roberto had climbed in bed with her and held her, just trying to get her through it all. Trini had looked up at him at one point, told Roberto she was in love with him and always had been, and moved to kiss him. Roberto deflected, told his friend to shut up and go to sleep, and Trini did.

They slept that way all night, and nothing happened. Roberto never told Annie about it, and in fact he and Trini had never spoken of it again themselves.

Until now, when Roberto wanted to hurt her.

Which he had.

From the other end of the plane, the bathroom door closed with a soft *click*. Hero came out and headed back to her seat.

Trini turned the other way and slouched down to go back to sleep.

Roberto moved to the window, shoved a pillow up against it, pulled the blanket up to his chin, and pretended to be out like a light when Hero got back.

In this way, the three of them flew on to Australia carrying considerably more baggage than they'd left with.

THREE

The biohazard suits were uncomfortable as hell, and the worst part, in Trini's opinion, was that there was nowhere to put a gun. She waved her Sig Sauer P320 around in the air near her hip, flapping her lips inaudibly behind the glass of her face piece.

Hero just looked at her, still puzzled by these soldiers and their inexperience with the very sort of event they'd been sent to investigate. She tapped the buttons on the side of the helmet, and her voice crackled in Trini's headset.

"Use the radio, please."

Trini fumbled on the side of her head until she found the right button and pressed it.

"Doesn't this goddamn thing have a pocket?"

Outside Kiwirrkurra, they had changed into level A hazmat suits, which were fully encapsulating chemical entry suits with self-contained breathing apparatuses. They also wore steel-toed boots with shafts on the outside of the suit and specially selected chemical-resistant gloves. And no, there were no pockets, which would sort of defeat the purpose of the whole thing, providing both a nook and a cranny for God knows what to ride home with you.

Hero decided a simple "No" would suffice to answer Trini's grumpy question. Trini had sucked down three cigarettes in quick succession after they'd landed—she'd been on Nicorette *and* the new nicotine patch for the entire flight—and she was wound tighter than the inside of a golf ball. Best to keep one's distance, Hero decided.

Roberto turned and looked behind them, at the vast expanse of desert they had just crossed. Their jeep had kicked up a massive fantail of dust and the prevailing winds were blowing their way, which meant a few hundred kilometers' worth of sediment was airborne and swirling toward them.

"Better get started while we can still see," he said.

They turned and started the walk into town. They'd parked half a mile away and the going was slow in the suits, but they could see the structures that dotted the horizon from here. Kiwirrkurra was a collection of one-story buildings, a dozen at the most, unpainted, a patchwork of colors coming from the cast-off wood and scrap particle board that had been given to the residents by the resettlement commission. As far as planned communities went, it didn't show much planning—just a main street, structures on either side of it, and a few outbuildings that had been thrown up later, possibly by latecomers who preferred a bit of space between themselves and their neighbors.

The first odd thing they saw, about fifty yards outside of town, was a suitcase. It sat in the middle of the road, packed and closed and waiting patiently, as if expecting a ride to the airport. There was no one and nothing else around it.

They looked at one another, then went to it. They stood around the suitcase, staring at it as if expecting it to reveal its history and intentions. It did not.

Trini moved on, holding the gun in front of her.

They reached the first building, and as they came around the front of it, they saw this one had only three walls, not four, built that way on purpose for maximum airflow in the intensely arid environment. They paused and looked inside, the way you'd look into a dollhouse. There were cutaway areas: a kitchen, a bedroom, a bathroom (that room had a door), and another tiny bedroom at the far end of the structure. In the kitchen, there was food on the table, buzzing with flies. But there were no people.

Roberto looked around. "Where is everybody?"

That was the question.

Trini backed away, into the street again, turning in cautious semicircles, scanning the place.

"Cars are still here."

They followed her gaze. There were cars, all right, just about one per driveway, a jeep or motorcycle or pickup or old sedan. However the residents had managed to get where they were going, they hadn't driven.

They continued on, past what might have been a playground, more or less in the center of town. An old metal swing creaked on its chain, blowing in the wind that now swept the desert sand and dust into town ahead of it. Roberto turned and squinted into the coming clouds. The sand ticked against the glass of his faceplate, and it was hard not to blink, though of course he didn't need to.

Another thirty yards and they reached the other side of town. The front door to the biggest house was ajar, and Trini pushed it open the rest of the way, using the barrel of the Sig Sauer. Roberto gestured to Hero to wait on the porch, and he and Trini stepped inside, one after the other, in a practiced maneuver.

Hero waited in front, watching their movements through the open door and the dirty front window. They searched the place, room by room, Trini always in the lead, gun in hand. Roberto was the more thorough and perhaps the more cautious of the two, moving carefully and steadily and never facing in the same direction for too long. Hero admired the grace and ease with which he moved, even in the cumbersome suit. But she also knew there was nothing to fear in there. Everything about Kiwirrkurra so far suggested a ghost town—she was sure of their result before Trini came out a few minutes later and announced it.

"Fourteen houses, twelve vehicles, zero residents."

Roberto put his hands on his hips, relaxing his guard a bit. "What the actual fuck?"

That was when Hero saw what they'd come for. There, at the far end of town, in front of one of the best kept of the very modest houses, was a silver metal tank, its finish recently polished to a bright and reflective shine.

"I don't think that's from here."

They walked toward the tank, wary. The wind swirled harder, and the dust in the air billowed around the houses, rearing up in columns in front of them before dust-deviling back to the ground in a corkscrew and moving on. It was getting hard to see.

"Stop here." Hero held a hand out when they were still ten feet from the tank. She scanned the ground around them as best she could in the billowing sand, then continued on, searching the ground carefully before she placed each step.

"Walk in my footsteps."

They did, following her in single file, careful to place their feet directly onto her boot prints as they went.

Hero reached the tank and squatted down. She saw the fungal covering immediately, but only because of her practiced eye. An untrained observer wouldn't have perceived anything more than a greenish patch on the rounded surface of the tank, a bit like oxidized copper. The tank wasn't in pristine condition anyway; it had made an uncontrolled re-entry into Earth's atmosphere, after all, that's going to put a few dents in anything. But to Hero, the unremarkable green-ish patch read like a semaphore.

Trini looked around them, still with her gun at the ready, just in case. She took a few steps toward the house, watching where she walked. She stopped, studying the building, which wasn't very different from the other ones. But there was one thing she noticed—the car. An old Dodge Dart, it was parked at an odd angle to the house, its hood pushed almost right up against a porch pillar. The porch had a low-slung, corrugated roof that bent down at an angle, and from where the car was parked it wasn't a very big step up from the hood to the roof. Trini looked up, thinking.

Back at the silver tank, Hero bent down, pulling her sample case around in front of her. She clicked it open, snapped out a 20x magnifying lens, and squeezed it to activate the LED lights around the edge of the beveled glass. Through the lens, she got a closer look at the fungus. It was alive, all right, and florid, visibly seething even at this magnification. She leaned as close as she dared, looking for active fragmentation. There was movement there, and she wished like hell she had a more powerful magnifier, but twenty power was the most the field kit carried, which meant she had to get closer still.

She looked back, over her shoulder, at Roberto.

"Slide your hand through the loop in the suit between my shoulder blades."

Roberto looked down. There was a tight vertical flap of fabric sewn into the back of the suit, a handle of sorts, with just enough space to get his fingers through. He did as she asked.

"Now hold on tight," she said. "I'll pull against you, but don't let me go. If I start to fall, give me a hard pull back. Don't be shy about it. Don't let me touch it."

"You got it."

He held on tight. Hero braced her feet just short of the tank, about a foot away from it, and leaned forward, putting the magnifying glass and her mask as close to the surface of the middle of the tank as she possibly could. Roberto hadn't expected her to have quite as much confidence in him as she apparently did, and he swayed a little as she let her weight fall forward. But he was strong and recovered quickly, resetting his feet and holding her steady.

The faceplate of Hero's helmet moved to within three inches of the surface of the tank, she switched the lens to max magnification and close focus and flicked the LEDs to their brightest setting.

She gasped. Through the lens, even at this minimal magnification, she could clearly see fruiting bodies sprouting off the mycelium, stalks with a capsule at the top, swelling at their seams with ready-to-spread spores. The mycelium's growth was so fast it was visible.

"Jesus *Christ*."

Roberto couldn't see around her bulky suit, and the curiosity was killing him. "What is it?"

Hero couldn't tear her eyes away.

"I don't know, but it's huge, and it's *fast*. And heterotrophic; it's got to be pulling carbon and energy out of everything it touches, otherwise there's no way it . . ." She trailed off, staring at something intently.

"No way what?"

Hero didn't answer. She was fascinated by one of the fruiting bodies. Its capsule was bloating beneath the lens, ballooning up off the surface of the tank.

"This is the most aggressive sporing rate I've ever—"

With a sharp pop, the entire fruiting body burst, and the lens of the magnifying glass was flecked with microscopic bits of goo. Hero shouted and involuntarily lurched backward, away from the tank. She was more startled than frightened but lost her balance for a moment and threw her right foot out to the side to steady herself. Her boot squished through something soft before finding solid ground next to the tank, but it was too little too late; she was past the tipping point and on her way down, right into whatever she'd just stepped in. She watched as the ground moved up toward her in slow motion.

And then she was moving upward again. With one strong, controlled tug on the loop at the back of her suit, Roberto pulled her onto her feet next to him.

She looked up at him, grateful.

He smiled. "Careful."

A voice called from nearby. "Hey."

They turned. Trini was standing on the roof

of the house, about ten feet above them. "I found Uncle."

It wasn't much of a climb, even in the suits. First onto the hood of the car, then one big step up onto the porch roof, then a sort of jump with a shoulder roll, and they were all the way up. Roberto went last, so he could give Hero a shove up onto the roof if needed, and he was so preoccupied with making sure she didn't fall that he failed to notice the sole of her boot, even when it passed within a foot of his face. He would have had to be pretty eagle-eyed to see it anyway, because there wasn't much of the stuff, but it was there.

Near the heel, between the fourth and fifth hard rubber corrugated ridges of her right boot, there was a smear of green fungus she'd picked up when she lost her balance back at the tank.

Hero scrambled the rest of the way over the edge of the roof, Roberto flipped himself up to join her, and they walked the few paces over to where Trini stood looking down at something. The wind and dust had picked up substantially, so her view was partially obscured, but Trini knew a human corpse when she saw one. This one was in rough shape. Uncle couldn't have been dead for all that long, but the damage to his corpse was extensive, and it wasn't postmortem. The flesh wasn't mangled from the outside, by scavengers or weather.

"He exploded," Hero said.

Boy, did he ever. What used to be Uncle was now a husk that had been turned inside out, everything internal made external. His rib cage was wrenched open cleanly and violently at his sternum, parted like a suit coat lying on the floor with nobody in it. His arms and legs were denuded of flesh, their bones pockmarked with what looked like more tiny explosions from within, and the plates of his skull had been split apart along their eight seams, as if the glue that held him together suddenly failed all at once.

Roberto, who had seen a lot of ugly things, had never seen anything like this. He turned away, and as he did so the wind let up, the dust cleared for a moment, and all at once he had an unimpeded view looking back the way they'd come. Every building in town was more or less the same height, and from up here on top of Uncle's house, he could see onto all the other rooftops.

"Oh my God."

The others turned and saw what he saw.

The rooftops were covered with dead bodies, every single one of them burst open in the same way as Uncle's.

Roberto didn't need to count to know there would be twenty-six.

AT THE MOMENT THEY STOOD ON THE ROOF, PIECING together what had happened to the residents of the doomed village, the fungus was busily at work between the corrugated rubber ridges of Dr. Hero Martins's right boot. *Cordyceps novus* had reached a barrier, the hard rubber sole between the boot and her foot, and if there was one thing it hated, it was a barrier. But every good villain has a henchman.

In its mutated state, the fungus housed an endosymbiont, an organism that lived within its body in a mutualistic relationship. What the fungus couldn't do, the endosymbiont could—in this case, catalyze the synthesis of random chemicals in a special new structure in order to break through barriers. It was like having your own chemistry set.

The endosymbiont, which lived on the surface of the fungus in the form of a light sheen, was exposed to the atmosphere every time Hero took a step. It absorbed as much oxygen as it could, combined it with carbon drawn from the dust and dirt particles that had stuck to the goo, and formed a tight network of carbon-oxygen double bonds. These carbonyl groups, now active ketones, pushed their way upward, toward the sole itself, until stopped there by the hard, unyielding mass.

So it hybridized again. The new ketone sampled available elements from the rubber and dirt and dust and cycled quickly through a variety of carbon skeletons. It mutated into oxaloacetate, which is great if you want to metabolize sugar but no use getting through the sole of a boot. Undaunted, it mutated again, into cyclohexanone, which would have been good for making nylons, and then into tetracycline, superb if you're fighting pneumonia, and then, finally and most damagingly, it recomposed itself as H_2FSbF_6—fluoroantimonic acid.

The powerful industrial corrosive began eating its way through the rubber bottom of Hero's boot.

The mutation process so far had taken just under ninety seconds.

Hero, of course, was unaware of what was happening. As they climbed down from the roof and hurried back to the tank, she was distracted, trying to explain what they had just seen. The fungus, she speculated, was mimicking the reproductive pattern of *Ophiocordyceps*, a genus that consisted of about 140 different species, each one of which reproduced by colonizing a different insect.

"How's it do that?" Trini had her gun out again and her head was on a swivel as they climbed down onto the roof of the car.

Hero explained: "Let's say its target species is an ant. The ant walks along the forest floor, and it passes over a tiny spore of the fungus. The spore adheres to the ant, digs through its outer shell, and nests inside it. It moves through the body as quickly as it can, making its way to the ant's brain, where the rich nutrients send it into an exponential growth phase, helping it reproduce up to ten times as fast as it would in any other part of the body. It spreads into every portion of the brain until it controls movement, reflex, impulse, and, to the extent that an ant can think, thoughts. Even though the ant is still technically alive, it's been hijacked by the invader to serve its needs." She jumped to the ground. "And the only thing a fungus needs is to make more fungus."

Roberto looked around, understanding the town better now. Or the people, anyway. Jesus, the people, *all of them.*

Hero walked quickly to the tank and knelt down beside it, flipping open her sample case again. "The ant stops acting for itself. All it knows is it has to move. *Up.* It climbs the nearest stalk of grass, clamps its jaws down as hard as it can, and waits."

"For what?" Trini asked.

"Until the fungus overfills the body cavity and it explodes."

Roberto looked up at the roofs of the houses and shivered. "That's why they climbed. To spread the fungus as far as they could."

Hero nodded. "It's a treeless wasteland. The roof was the highest spot they could find. You work with what you've got." Her gloved hands picked carefully through the sharp metal tools in the case. She picked a flat-bladed instrument with a ring grip, slipped it over her right index finger, and flipped open a sample tube with her left hand. Carefully, she scraped as much of the fungus into the tube as she could. "It's an extremely active parasitic growth, but that's about all we'll know until I can isolate the proteins with liquid chromatography and sequence its DNA."

Roberto stared as she flipped the tube shut with a practiced gesture.

"You're bringing it *back*?"

She looked up at him, not understanding. "What else am I supposed to do?"

"Leave it. We've got to burn this place."

"Go right ahead," she said. "But we need to take a sample with us."

Trini looked at Roberto. "She's right. You know she's right. What's the matter with you?"

Roberto didn't get scared very often, but suddenly he was thinking about his little boy and about the possibility that he might never see him again. He'd heard having a kid could do that to you, make you tentative, aware that you served some purpose larger than yourself. *To hell with the rest of the world, I make my own people now, and I have to protect them.* Nothing else mattered.

And then there was Annie. *I have a wife, a woman I love completely whom I was this close to betraying, and I would like very much to get back and get a head start on making that up to her, for the rest of our lives.* That's what was the matter with him, that's what he was thinking, but he said none of it.

Instead, he said, "For Christ's sake, Trini, it has an R1 rate of 1:1. Everyone who came in contact with it is dead, *every single person*. The secondary attack rate is a hundred percent, the generation time is immediate, and the incubation rate is . . . we don't know, but less than twenty-four hours, that's for goddamn sure. You want to bring *that* back into civilization? We've never seen a bioweapon with anything remotely close to this kind of lethality."

"Which is exactly why it has to be tanked and studied. C'mon, man, you know that. This place won't stay a secret, and if we don't bring it back, somebody else'll come get it. Maybe somebody who works for the other side."

It was a valid debate, and while they carried on with it, the corrosive inside Hero's boot heel continued to work with single-minded purpose. The fluoroantimonic acid had proven to be just the thing for eating through hard-soled rubber, but it wasn't so much digging a hole as changing the chemical composition of the boot itself as it went along. Minor mutations occurred almost in a spirit of experimentation as the strength of the boot's chemical bonds varied. The substance was a nifty adapter, zipping through most of the benzene group till it found the exact compound it was looking for. Finally, it reached the other side of the sole, evolving out onto the surface of the inner boot, just beneath the arch of Hero's right foot. *Benzene-X*—it had hybridized so many times at this point that it defied classification according to current known chemical compounds—had opened a door for the fungus, which was so much larger in molecular size, to pass through to the interior of Hero's suit.

Which is where *Cordyceps novus* found nirvana. The boot, like the rest of the hazmat suit, was loose-fitting, designed to encourage air circulation to prevent the wearer from overheating. The breathing apparatus contained a small fan for oxygen recirculation, which meant a fresh supply of O_2 was continually moving through the inside of the suit. Strands of grateful fungus spun off into whispery tendrils and went airborne, drifting upward on a rising column of warm CO_2, until they landed lightly on the bare skin of Hero's right leg.

Still unaware of the enemy invasion going on inside her suit, Hero screwed the top onto the sample tube, broke a seal on its side, and the tube hissed, a tiny pellet of nitrogen flash-freezing it until it could be reopened in a lab and stored permanently in liquid nitrogen. She dropped the tube back into the foam-padded slot in the case, clicked it shut, and stood up. "Done."

The debate over what to do next had been resolved the way it always was, which is to say that Trini prevailed. She heard Roberto's arguments, let them go a little bit past the point she felt was necessary, given the difference in their ranks, then looked directly at her friend, lowered her voice a tone or two, and said just one word.

"Major."

The conversation was over. Trini was the officer in charge, and the advice of the scientific escort was on her side. The outcome had never been in doubt, but Roberto had felt a humanitarian urge to object anyway. What if, just this once, they did what was obvious and right, *even if* it was directly contrary to procedure? What if?

But they'd never find out, and in the end, Roberto settled on a secondary assurance: they would take one sample, *one*, carefully sealed in the biohazard tube, and would not leave Western Australia until the two respective governments had agreed to drop an overkill load of oil-based incendiary bombs on the place. Anything would suffice, even old M69s or M47s loaded with white phosphorous would do the job. There was nothing left to save here anyway.

They left town and walked back toward the jeep.

FOUR

Inside Hero's suit, *Cordyceps novus* found what it had been looking for: a tiny scratch in the surface of Hero's calf. Even an overwide pore opening would have been big enough for it to gain entry into her bloodstream, but the open scratch, which cut through two layers of her skin, fairly yawned with possibility.

Hero didn't even know she had an open wound. It had been an absent-minded scratch; she was reacting to an itch produced by a changed cleaning product—the hotel that washed her jeans last week had used a cheap optical brightener with a higher concentration of bleach than she was used to. So it itched. And she scratched. And the fungus entered her bloodstream.

"What's that smell?" Hero asked. They were fifty yards from the jeep.

Roberto looked at her. "What smell?"

She sniffed again. "Burnt toast."

Trini shrugged. "Can't smell anything." She looked back, glad to leave the town behind. "This whole place is gonna smell like burnt toast by the end of the day."

But Roberto was confused, still looking at Hero. "In your suit?"

Hero held up an arm and regarded it, as if reminding herself she was wearing a sealed biohazard suit. "That doesn't make sense, does it?"

In fact, it made perfect sense. *Cordyceps novus* was really warming up and had superheated the starches and proteins just inside Hero's epidermis. As a by-product of the reaction, they outgassed acrylamide, producing the same smell as burnt toast. It was generating heat as well, and the sudden rise in temperature on Hero's skin would surely bother her soon. But the fungus was attentive to that possibility and was moving fast through her bloodstream, racing to get to her brain, where it would intercept the messages from her pain receptors. This in itself was no great trick—a tick does the same thing, releasing a surface anesthetic as soon as it burrows into its victim's skin so its bloodsucking can go unnoticed for as long as possible. But the fungus had a long way to travel and a lot of receptors to block. Hero's heartbeat accelerated, which circulated her blood faster, inadvertently helping her would-be killer.

She stopped walking. "There can't be a smell in my suit, it's sealed and overpressured. There's nothing in here but oxygen and clean CO_2. Why is there a smell in my suit?"

She was starting to panic. Trini tried to defuse it. "There are probably a lot of jokes I could make here—"

"It's not fucking funny," Hero snapped.

"It's not, Trini, shut the hell up. Something penetrated her suit."

"That's not possible," Hero said, to convince herself as much as anyone else.

"Just keep moving," Trini advised. "We'll lose the suits at the jeep. We can't take them out of here anyway, they need to burn. We'll check yours for breaches." She looked at Hero, her manner serious. "Do you feel anything?"

Hero thought. "No."

Roberto persisted. "Take a minute. Focus on each part of your body. Anything different at all?"

Hero's breathing steadied. She considered the question, going through her anatomy from the bottoms of her feet to the top of her head. "No. Nothing different."

Inside her body, it was a different story. The fungus had penetrated Hero's brain and was reproducing at nightmare speed, seeking out and blocking her nociceptors the way an invading army shuts down the internet and television stations. There was a red alert blaring in Hero's brain, flags were waving, alarm bells ringing, but the ends of her sensory neurons' axons had been taken over and blocked from responding to damaging stimuli. They could no longer send potential threat messages to her thalamus and subcortical areas. They were screaming into a void.

Hero Martins was dying, but the neural message she got from her brain was that everything was fine, just fine, don't worry about a thing.

"I'm okay."

"You're sure?" Roberto asked.

She nodded. "Let's just get out of here."

They started walking again, now forty yards from the jeep. Hero's brain thought through possible reasons a foreign smell should have presented itself inside her suit. Nothing believable came to mind. She decided she would not destroy this suit; she was going to tank and return it, she wanted to have a chance to take it apart and look at every inch of it in case there was a tear or foreign substance inside, in which case somebody in PPE was going to get an earful about procedure.

The jeep was now thirty yards away. Hero felt light-headed and realized she hadn't eaten since nine or ten hours ago. Then again, looking at Uncle's mutilated corpse wouldn't exactly stimulate anyone's appetite, so there was no reason to think anything unusual about that. She ran through her physical inventory once again, but other than an elevated heart rate and some quickened breathing, there wasn't anything physically different about her that she could detect. She squinted up at the sun, and as she did a thought floated through her mind.

except there's no telephone service out here

Well, no, there wasn't. What did that matter? She looked down at the case in her hand, thinking about what she had inside the tube. People were going to lose their minds over this one. She wondered if the CDC would even accept it.

so there's no telephone poles

She shook her head to clear it and resumed her train of thought. There were only a handful of labs in the Western Hemisphere that were set up to store biosafety level 4 pathogens, and Atlanta and Galveston would reject it outright, improperly classifying it as extraterrestrial because of its trip outside Earth's atmosphere.

maybe an electrical tower

The U.S. Army would fight for it, no question about that, but Fort Detrick had suffered a breach eighteen months ago and no one was eager to—

they've gotta have power right don't they have power?

She snapped her head to the side, *Come on, focus.* They were ten yards from the jeep. Her image of it suddenly shuddered and divided into sixteen identical rectangular boxes, sixteen images of the jeep, neatly separated and replicated. Hero felt her skin go cold because that wasn't something you could easily ignore or pass off to hunger or exhaustion, but *then again*, she thought, *I used to faint when I was a kid, in school assemblies sometimes, and didn't it feel like this?*, wasn't there a prickling in her scalp and then her vision would go weird and she'd see double right before she keeled over sure that was probably it low blood sugar or

a radio tower, fifty kilometers back, didn't I see something, wasn't it a radio tower?

The image swam through her mind, crisp and clear: they had driven past a radio tower in the middle of the desert, just alongside the road, about a hundred meters high, with a small black utility box at the base of it.

"That's exactly what it was."

She'd said that last bit out loud, and Roberto and Trini turned and looked at her.

"What?" Roberto asked.

She looked at him. "Huh?"

"That's exactly what what was?"

Hero had no idea what he was talking about. Was it possible that Roberto had somehow become infected by the fungus, that it was *his* suit that had malfunctioned, and that he was starting to lose his mind? She certainly hoped not, he was a nice enough guy, even if he was a total flirt, she really had to lay off the married men, never again, she vowed, right there and then, from now on either find someone appropriate or be content with

It can't be that hard to climb.

Oh, shit. She had to think this through.

To climb. The radio tower. It had lateral struts about four or five feet apart, but there's probably a service ladder inside the structure, how else would they repair anything that broke near the top of the thing? I could climb that.

For the last time, the weight and pressure of the healthy, functioning neurons in Hero's brain outweighed those that had been consumed, destroyed, or shut down by *Cordyceps novus*. Her prefrontal cortex, which handled reasoning and sophisticated interpersonal thinking skills, reasserted itself in a burst of clarity and control, and told her quite clearly that based on:

A. her disordered thought processes;

B. the smell of burnt toast inside her suit that indicated a foreign contaminant;

c. the expressions on the faces of Trini and Roberto, who clearly thought something was wrong with her; and

d. her sudden and irrational fixation on the feasibility of *climbing a fucking radio tower*, for Christ's sake, she had likely been infected by the fungus and was moments away from coming under the control of a rapidly replicating fungus that constituted an extinction-level threat to the human race.

Still walking, she glanced to her right and saw Trini was carrying her handgun loosely at her side as she and Roberto looked back and forth from her to each other, trying to communicate their concern wordlessly rather than over the radio system, which she would be able to hear.

Take the jeep and drive to the tower.

Hero walked faster, headed for the jeep. They let her, happy to fall behind so they could keep an eye on her.

Climb the tower.

As Hero neared the jeep, she saw the keys, the sunlight shining off them in the ignition. She felt pulled toward them.

Climb the tower.

Hero's frontal lobe was in a doomed fight for control. It made up a third of the total volume of her brain, but was now overrun with a florid, healthy colony of *Cordyceps novus*. Her flag of intellectual independence fell. Still, her conscious thought didn't give up; it merely darted away, blew through the wasteland of her already conquered temporal lobe, and turned in desperation to the last part of her mental apparatus that was still free—her parietal lobe. There, her thought stream was precariously her own, but severely limited.

just math now, math and analytics, where X = regeneration of healthy brain tissue probability is zero-X, try recovery rate, recovery rate in event of default

She was pulling up a freshman economics class now, but it was the only scrap of useful knowledge left kicking around unfettered in her head, the only avenue of reasoning left open to her, and it was going to have to do. So, let's try a calculation, shall we? The equation to be formed would need to answer only one question: Could she survive this?

recovery probability versus loss given default (RP < or > LGD) dependent on instrument type (where IT = hypereffective mutating fungus), corporate issues (where CI = major default of more than 50 percent of healthy brain tissue), and prevailing macroeconomic conditions (where PMCs = every single other person who ever encountered this thing is dead), so RP = IT/CI × PMC = there is no fucking chance whatsoever.

The answer was no. She could not recover. She was going to die. The only question was how many people she was going to take with her when she did.

CLIMB THE TOWER, her brain told her.

And with the tiny bit of volition Dr. Hero Martins still had left, she replied.

NO, she said.

She turned around, fast. Trini didn't have time to react, in part because she was too stunned by the sight of Hero's swollen, heaving face, which was distended and discolored, the skin stretched so tight it was cracking. Hero was on her before Trini knew what was happening. She wrenched the gun from Trini's hand—

"*Gun out!*" Trini shouted, but Roberto had already seen it. He yelled at Hero to stop, but she was backing away from them already, backing away and turning the gun around on herself. She reached up with her left hand and ripped her suit's Velcro flap over the zippered O_2 access port, tore that open, shoved the gun inside the suit, sealed the Velcro flap around the barrel, pressed the barrel of the gun up against her chest—

"*Don't!*" Roberto yelled, knowing it was too late even as he said it.

Hero pulled the trigger.

The bullet broke her skin and crashed through her breastbone, tearing open a hole in her chest the size of a quarter. Like a balloon popped by a pin, the rest of her went all at once, bursting at the sudden release of pressure. All Trini and Roberto saw was her head, which in one moment was a disfigured, although recognizable, human head, and the next moment was a wash of green gunk that completely covered the inside of her faceplate.

Hero fell, dead.

But she'd kept her suit intact.

LESS THAN SEVENTY-TWO HOURS LATER, TRINI AND
Roberto were in the car, just over three miles
away from the Atchison mines, their eyes glued
to the box in the back of the truck just ahead
of them. Hero's field case had been packed, un-
opened, into a larger sealed crate filled with
dry ice.

So far things had gone smoothly. Gordon
Gray, the head of the DNA, had taken Trini
and Roberto exactly at their word, because they
were the best, and he ordered their explicit instructions be followed to the letter. When Gordon Gray gave an order, people *followed* it, and
since all the residents of the town were dead
and the land itself held no value, there was no
one and no reason to object. The firebombing
of Kiwirrkurra was agreed to without debate by
the respective governments. The unlucky place
burned, and with it every molecule of *Cordyceps
novus*, except for the sample in Hero's biotube.

The question of what to do with the tube was
tougher to answer. As Hero had speculated, the
CDC wanted no part of storing something that
had been born, or at any rate partially bred, in
outer space. Though the Defense Department
was willing, its only suitable facility was Fort
Detrick, which was out of the question. The
breach there eighteen months earlier had triggered a top-down review that was only now en-

tering its second stage, and the idea of cutting short a safety analysis in order to store an unknown growth of unprecedented lethality was not met with enthusiasm.

Atchison was Trini's idea. She'd worked with the National Nuclear Safety Administration in the early '80s on weapons dismantlement and disposition readiness, as the idea of nuclear disarmament became politically palatable under the Reagan administration's INF Treaty initiative. Sub-level 4 of the Atchison mine facility had been conceived and dug out as an alternative to the Pantex Plant and the Y-12 National Security Complex, disposal centers that were at capacity already, dealing with outmoded fission devices from the late '40s and early '50s. But as INF negotiations dragged on it became clear that Reagan's strategy was really to get the *other* guy to disarm, and Atchison's lowest sub-level sat empty and secure, never to be used.

The location was ideal for their needs. Because the mines were uniquely situated over a second-magnitude underground cold spring that pushed near-freezing water up from the bedrock at 2,800 liters per second, the lowest subterranean level at Atchison never rose above 38 degrees Fahrenheit. Even in the unlikely event of an extended power outage, the temperature at which the fungus would be stored was guaranteed to remain stable, keeping it in a perpetual low- or no-growth environment, *even if* it somehow broke free of its containment tube. It was a perfect plan. *Cordyceps novus* was thus given a home, sealed inside a biotube three hundred feet underground in a sub-basement that didn't officially exist.

AS TIME WENT BY, FEWER AND FEWER PEOPLE AT DTRA came to share Trini and Roberto's alarmist view of the destructive capabilities of *Cordyceps novus*. How could they? They hadn't seen it. There were no photographic records. The remote town had been incinerated, and the only remaining sample of the fungus was locked away, out of sight and out of mind. People forgot. People moved on.

Sixteen years later, in 2003, the DTRA decided the mine complex was a Cold War relic that could be dispensed with. The place was cleared out, cleaned up, given a coat of paint, and sold to Smart Warehousing for private use. The self-storage giant threw up some drywall, bought 650 locking overhead garage doors from Hörmann, and opened it up to the public. Fifteen thousand boxes of useless crap were thus given a clean, dry, and permanent underground home. That thirty-year-old drum kit that you never played could now survive a nuclear war.

The storage plan for *Cordyceps novus* was a perfect one.

Unless, that is, Gordon Gray took early retirement.

And his successor decided sub-level 4 was better off sealed up and forgotten.

And the temperature of the planet rose.

But how likely was any of that?

MARCH 2019

FIVE

Your Honor, I get it. I mean, you are look-ing at a man who *gets it*."

Teacake hadn't prepared anything, but for him words came whether he wanted them to or not, so even though he knew he wasn't the best person to speak in his own defense at his sentencing hearing, he figured he was the most qualified to wing it.

"Okay, so the last time we met, here in Your Honor's courtroom, a few years ago, you made a great suggestion. 'Hey,' you said, 'what if instead of me sending you to Ellsworth, you join the military instead?' That was a great idea, thank you for that, and I totally took Your Honor up on that one. Two years in the navy, submarine corps, and let me tell you, that pressure testing is no picnic. Great experience for me, though. Honorable discharge."

The judge looked down at the sentencing report on the bench in front of him. "Says here 'General Discharge, Honorable Conditions.'"

"Right, yeah. Exactly. So, similar thing there."

The public defender assigned to Teacake gave him a look that said, *You are not helping*.

But Teacake pressed on. "Point is, I got it then, and I get it now. Victim of being in the wrong place at the wrong time, I mean, I know that's not gonna cut it with you, but there are, like, super-mitigating circumstances here. I get talked into stuff, that's my problem, but my personal feeling is I should never have to do time for this. Not for basically sitting in a car, basically. I mean, it's no way to treat a veteran, for starters. But you probably took one look at me and were like, 'You again,' and I get that, I do."

"Are you finished?"

"Yeah, I'm gonna wrap up. Long story short, if you have a buddy who goes by Hazy Davy and he ever asks you to stay with the car while he runs in to do this one quick thing super quick and you already know your name is sorta mud in Pottawatomie County, Kansas, you should for sure remember a previous commitment. That's all I'm saying."

He started to sit down, then stood up again.

"Sorry, one more thing, real quick. I also been sick with the modern disease known as white privilege, for which I am very sorry. Although, that one's kinda not on me, I gotta say, I can't help I'm white. Anyway, uh, thank you."

Teacake sat down abruptly and didn't dare glance at his lawyer. He could read a room. The judge put on his glasses, picked up the sentencing report, and said six words.

"Thank you, Mr. Meacham. Nineteen months."

By the time he got out of prison, Teacake's post–high school résumé had exactly two things on it: a mediocre service record and his stint in Ellsworth Correctional. So the job at Atchison Storage was the best thing that could have possibly happened to him, even at $8.35 an hour. Corporate didn't like a lot of employees to chase around and look after, so everybody did twelve-hour shifts, six to six, four days a week. Teacake was the new man and got nights, Thursday through Sunday. Truth is, he didn't much like the few friends he still had around here, and he wasn't looking to make any new ones unless maybe one of them was Her, so saying he'd take the social graveyard shift was no big deal. It might have been the reason he got the job. That, and the fact that he had all his teeth, which meant he was reasonably clean. Around here a full toothy smile was the only character reference you needed to sit at a reception desk and look after 650 locked underground storage units in the middle of the night. It was not, as they say, the science of rocketry.

Teacake always tried to get to work early on Thursdays because he knew Griffin liked to get a jump on his weekend buzz and would beat ass out of there a few minutes before his shift was over. Griffin knew he could bail early because he could count on how badly Teacake needed the job and for nothing to go wrong. Sure enough, as Teacake came around the long curve at the base of the bluffs, he could see Griffin's sweaty bald head glowing in the setting sun as the thickneck popped open a Pabst Blue Ribbon tall boy, two or three of which were kept in his Harley Fat Boy's saddlebags for—well, they were kept in the saddlebags at all times.

Griffin drained the beer, tossed aside the empty can, kicked the bike to life, and raised a middle finger to Teacake as he blew gravel out of there.

The thing about Griffin, and everyone would agree on this, was that he was an asshole. Teacake flipped the bird back at him, a more or less friendly gesture at this point, and it was what passed for human contact in his day. As Teacake's Honda Civic passed the motorcycle, he breathed a sigh of relief that his boss had given him a miss, that he wouldn't have to have that same goddamn conversation with him again.

But no such luck. He could see in the rearview. Griffin was looping back, bringing the Fat Boy around the hood of the Civic. He pulled up next to the driver's door, idling as Teacake got out.

"Well?" Griffin asked.

So, it *would* be that conversation again. "Told you, I can't help you."

"Knew you were stupid didn't think you were that stupid." Griffin spoke in staccato bursts, some words so fast they slammed together, others with odd pauses in between them, as if punctuation hadn't been invented yet.

"I'm not stupid," Teacake said. "Like at all. Okay? I would love to help you if I could, but it's fucked up for me vis-à-vis my, you know, personal situation, and I'm just not gonna do it."

"Okay so you'll think about it."

"No! I wish I didn't even know about it."

The truth was he knew only a part of it, the part about the two dozen fifty-five-inch Samsung flat screens that Griffin was selling off one by one, but Teacake guessed that where there was hot-stolen-consumer-goods smoke, there was hot-stolen-consumer-goods fire, and it was the last thing he needed in his life.

Griffin wasn't giving up. "I'm asking you to buzz the gate for a few friends of mine every once in a while and use your master key what's the big fuckin' deal."

"They don't have accounts with us. I can't let in anybody who doesn't have an account."

"Who's gonna know?"

"I have heard these words before," Teacake said. "You do it."

"I can't." Griffin shrugged.

"Why not?"

"Nobody's gonna fuckin' come in the daytime and I don't work nights." Case closed. "Just do it, so you and me don't have a problem."

"Why do we gotta have a problem?" Teacake asked.

"'Cause you know stuff and you're not in and if you're not in and you know then there's a problem. You know that."

There was no getting rid of him and he was never going to drop it, so Teacake did what he'd been doing for the past six weeks, which was to slow play it and hope it would go away. Was it a strategy that had shown even the slightest signs of working? No, but that was no reason to give up on it. "Yeah, well, you know, I don't know about this thing, or these things," Teacake said, "or what have you. I mean, just, whatever, right? Okay?"

There was no imaginable way a person could have made it any vaguer than that, not without a law degree and decades of experience testifying before Congress. Teacake hoped it would do. He turned and walked toward the building.

Griffin revved the bike and pulled his goggles down. He shouted something at Teacake as he dropped the bike in gear, just two words, but here's where Griffin's essential nature as an asshole came in again—he'd hooked up a noncompliant straight-pipe exhaust on his bike to make it extra loud and annoying to the rest of the world, so there was really no shot at all that his words would be understood over it. To Teacake it sounded like he yelled "Monday's bleeding," but in fact what his boss had shouted was "Something's beeping."

Teacake would find that out for himself soon enough.

THE FACT THAT GRIFFIN WAS PUT IN CHARGE OF anything was a joke, because not only was he dumb, racist, and violent, but he was a raging alcoholic to boot. Still, there are alcoholics and there are functioning alcoholics, and Griffin managed to be the latter by establishing a strict drinking regimen and sticking to it with the discipline of an Olympic athlete. He was dead sober for three and a half days of the week, Monday through Wednesday, when he worked the first three of his four twelve-hour shifts, and he didn't start drinking until just before six P.M. on Thursday. That, however, was a drunk that he would build and maintain with fussy dedication, starting right now and continuing through his long weekend until he passed out on Sunday night. Really, the Monday hangover was the only hard part, but Griffin had been feeling them for so long now they just seemed like part of a normal Monday morning. Toast, coffee, bleeding from the eyeballs—must be a new workweek.

Griffin was born over in Council Bluffs and spent six years working in a McDonald's in Salina, where he'd risen to the rank of swing manager. It was a tight little job, not least because of the tight little high school trim that he had the power to hire and fire and get high with in the parking lot after work. Griffin was an unattractive man—that was just an objective reality. He was thick as a fireplug, and his entire body, with the notable exception of his head, was covered with patchy, multicolored clumps of hair that made his back look like the floor of a barbershop at the end of a long day. But the power to grant somebody their first actual paying job and to provide the occasional joint got him far in life, at least with sixteen-year-olds, and when he was still in his not-quite-midtwenties. Soon enough the sixteen-year-olds would wise up and the last of his hair would go and his "solid build" would give way to what could only be called a "fat gut," but for those few years, in that one place, Griffin was a king, pulling down $24,400 a year, headed for a sure spot at Hamburger U, the McDonald's upper management training program. And nailing underage hotties at least every other week.

Then those little fuckers, those little wise-ass shitheads who didn't really *need* the job, who just got the job because their parents wanted them to learn the Value of Work, those little *douchebags* from over in the flats—they ruined everything. They were working drive-through during a rush when it happened. Why Griffin had ever scheduled them in there together is beyond him to this day; he must have been nursing a wicked hangover to let those two clowns work within fifty feet of each other, but they started their smart-ass shit on the intercom. They'd take orders in made-up Spanish, pretend the speaker was cutting in and out, declare today "Lottery Day" and give away free meals—all that shit that's so hilarious because real people's jobs don't mean anything, not when you're going to Kansas State in the fall with every single expense paid by Mommy and Daddy, and the only reason this job will ever turn up on your résumé is to show what a hardworking man of the people you were in high school. There they are, your fast-food work dues, fully paid, just like your $10,000 community service trip to Guatemala, where you slowed down the building of a school by taking a thousand pictures of yourself to post on Instagram.

On that particular day there was a McDonald's observer from regional in the parking lot, a guy taking times on the drive-through and copious notes on the unfunny shenanigans going on in there. The good-looking creep—the smarmy one, not the half-decent redheaded kid who just went along with the bullshit, but the handsome fucker, the one who was sleeping with the window girl in the docksiders whom Griffin himself could never get to even look at him—*that* kid knew the guy was out there. And he sat on that nugget of information for a good half hour, until he finally smirked past the office and said, "Oh, hey, there's a McDonald's secret agent man parked out by the dumpster."

Griffin was demoted to grill the next day, and he quit before he ended up at the fry station. He had the job at Atchison Storage three weeks later, and when the current manager there moved to Leawood to get married, Griffin inherited the fourteen-dollar-an-hour job, which, if he never, ever took a week off, meant $34,000 a year and three free days a week to get wasted. He also figured he could pull in another $10K in cash for housing the Samsungs and other items of an inconvenient nature that showed up needing a temporary home from time to time. The previous manager had clued him in about the side gig, which Griffin understood was a common perk of the self-storage management community. Hang on to this stuff, let people pick it up, take a cut of whatever it sells for. Zero risk. All in all, it was a decent setup, but not half as good as what could have been. He could have had a career in management, *real* management. Sitting at a desk all day so you can help a parade of freaks and hillbillies get access to their useless shit is a hell of a lot different from presiding over a constant parade of job-seeking teenage sluts. But you takes what you can takes. Atchison, Kansas, was not a buffet of career opportunity.

Despite everything that happened, Griffin's only regret in life so far was that he could never get anyone to agree to call him Griff. Or G-Dog. Or by his goddamn first name. All the man wanted was a nickname, but he was just Griffin.

TEACAKE PUNCHED IN BEHIND THE FRONT DESK. HE heard the beep, but he didn't hear the beep; it was one of those things. Whatever the part of your brain is that registers an extremely low-volume, high-pitched tone that comes once every ninety seconds, it was keeping the news to itself for the first half hour he was at the desk. The faint beep would come, it would register somewhere in the back of his mind, but then it would be crowded out by other, more pressing matters.

First, he had to check the monitors, of which there were a dozen, to make sure the place was clean and empty and as barren and depressing as always. Check. Then a quick glance over at the east entrance to see if She had shown up for work yet (she had) and to think for a second whether there was any plausible reason to orchestrate running into her (there wasn't). There was also the stink. Griffin was never a big one for tidying up, and the trash can was half full of Subway wrappers, including a former twelve-inch tuna on wheat, from the smell of it, and the reception area reeked of old lunch. Somebody would have to do something about that—twelve hours with tuna stench would be a long-ass shift. And finally, there was a customer, Mrs. Rooney, coming through the glass front doors, all frazzled and testy and all of a sudden.

"Hey, Mrs. Rooney, what up, you staying cool?"

"I need to get into SB-211."

Teacake was not so easily deterred. "It's hot out, right? Like Africa hot. Weird for March, but I guess we gotta stop saying that, huh?"

"I need to get in there right quick."

In unit SB-211 Mary Rooney had twenty-seven banker's boxes filled with her children's and grandchildren's school reports, birthday cards, Mother's Day cards, Father's Day cards, Christmas cards, and all their random notes expressing overwhelming love and/or blinding rage, depending on their proximity to adolescence at the time of writing. She also had forty-two ceramic coffee mugs and pencil jars made at Pottery 4 Fun between 1995 and 2008, when her arthritis got bad and she couldn't go anymore. That was in addition to seven nylon duffel bags stuffed with newspapers from major events in world history, such as coverage of the opening ceremonies of the 1984 Olympics in Los Angeles, and a vinyl *Baywatch* pencil case that was stuffed with $6,500 in cash she was saving for the day the banks crashed For Real. There were also four sealed moving boxes (contents long forgotten), so much old clothing that it was best measured by weight (311 pounds), and an electric metal coffeepot from 1979 that sat on top of the mountain of other crap like a crown.

At this moment Mrs. Rooney had two shoeboxes under her arm and that look on her face, so Teacake buzzed the gate that led to the storage units with no further attempt at pleasantries. Let the record show, though, that the heat that day was most certainly worthy of comment: it had been 86 degrees in the center of town at one point. But whatever, Mary Rooney needed to get into her unit right quick, and between her stuff and Mary Rooney you had best not get.

Teacake watched her on the monitors, first as she passed through the gate, then into the upper west hallway, her gray perm floating down the endless corridor lined with cream-colored garage doors, all the way to the far end, where she pushed the elevator button and waited, looking back over her shoulder twice—*Yeah, like somebody's gonna follow you and steal your shoeboxes filled with old socks, Mary*—and he kept watching as she got into the elevator, rode down two levels to the sub-basement, stepped off, walked halfway down the subterranean hallway in that weird, shuffling, sideways-like-a-coyote stride of hers, and slung open the door on unit SB-211. She stepped inside, clicked on a light, and slammed the door shut behind her. She would be in there for hours.

When you find yourself staring glassy-eyed at a bank of video monitors, watching as a moderately old lady makes her slow and deliberate way through a drab, all-white underground storage facility so she can get to her completely uninteresting personal pile of shit—when you do this with no hope whatsoever that this lady will do anything even remotely interesting, *that* is the moment you'll know you've bottomed out, entertainment-wise. Teacake was there.

And then everything changed.

His eyes had fallen on the upper right-hand screen, in the corner of the bank of monitors, the one that covered the other guard desk, on the eastern side of the facility.

Naomi was on the move.

The cave complex was enormous and cut right through the heart of the bluffs, so to save the trucks from Kansas City having to drive all the way around Highway 83 to Highway 18 to Highway E, the U.S. Army Corps of Engineers had cut in two entrances, one each on the eastern and western sides of the massive chunk of rock. As a result, Atchison had two reception areas and two people working the place at any given time, although they had different sections to monitor, so running into your co-worker almost never happened.

Unless you made it happen, which Teacake had been trying to do for two weeks now, since the day Naomi started. Her schedule was erratic—he could never put his finger on when she was going to be working and when she wasn't—so he'd tried to just keep an eye on the monitors and engineer a run-in, but it hadn't happened yet. There'd been a few times she was doing rounds when he almost took a shot at it, but when she was on the move he never knew where she was headed, so he hadn't come up with a scenario that would have given him quite the right degree of natural. The place was so big that the only way to make it work would be to check her location and then go into a full-on sprint to get near her while she was still even remotely in the area. It would have been more hunting her down than running into her. There's something about showing up breathless and sweaty for a "coincidental" bump-in with an attractive woman that is bound to come off as scary.

Now, however, opportunity was pounding on his door with both fists, because Naomi was walking down the long eastern main hallway with a full trash can under her arm, and that could mean only one destination: the loading dock, where the dumpsters were.

Teacake grabbed the brimming trash can from next to the reception desk—*Thank you Griffin, you pig, you bet I'll clean up your disgusting lunch*—and he took off for the loading dock.

SIX

Three things Naomi Williams knew about her mother—that she was smart, athletic, and had horrible taste in men. Worse, Naomi knew that she herself was exactly the same in all three respects. The difference was that Naomi had seen her mother's mistakes, she'd watched them play out, one after another, as easily predictable slow-motion car wrecks. She was keenly aware of where each and every twist of the wheel and stomp of the brake had caused the careening momentum of her mother's life to go into an unrecoverable spin. She knew from careful observation how to drive a life in order to crash it, and she was not about to make the same desperate moves with her own. She kept up her grades, she had decent extracurriculars, and she knew what she wanted. She had planned and rehearsed her post–high school escape route so many times she could drive it in her sleep.

But then the night of graduation she got pregnant, and all that shit was out the window. Because she had to have the baby. It wasn't her family who were the religious freaks; she and her mom and whoever her current stepfather was went to church on Christmas and for funerals, like most people did around here. But Mike's family—Jesus Christ, no pun intended, the Snyders banged the God drum hard. That wasn't unusual; there were a lot of religious people in this part of the country, ever since the big wave of evangelism that spread around the South and Midwest in the late 1970s. But the Snyders were born-again chest beaters, not the haunted, reliably depressive old kind of Catholic, but the joyful new kind of Catholic. They loved everybody. I mean, they really, actually loved you.

The Snyders had five kids, and though each one of them started out fairly normal and willing to grab the occasional beer or take a hit off a joint, by the time they hit fourteen or fifteen their parents had roped them into the family spiritual racket. It wasn't like it was a scam or anything—they really meant it. Naomi thought it was cool at first; it was a lot of love and attention, way more than she got at home, and when she and Tara Snyder became best friends in eighth grade, Naomi started sleeping at their house two or three nights a week. Her own mother, distracted by her decaying third marriage, seemed grateful that Naomi had a place to go.

As the God love spread throughout the Snyder family over the next couple of years, Naomi and Tara managed to skate around it. Everybody's got their familial role to play, and Tara was happy to be the wild child. She and Naomi drank too much, partied too much, and hung out with the wrong kinds of guys. But it was all working. Admittedly, it worked better for Naomi than for Tara. Naomi got mostly A's in school without trying very hard, she could still score in the teens at a basketball game even if she'd been up most of the night drinking, and she'd already gotten into Tennessee-Knoxville with a kickass grant-and-aid package. Yes, she would finish with sixty grand in debt, but UT had a great veterinary program, and she'd be done and licensed and making at least that much per year in five and a half. If anybody had a right to party and sleep around a little, it was Naomi Williams. The God-loving stuff was something she was happy to fake, or even mean it a little sometimes, in exchange for the Snyder embrace, which was warm and undeniable, even in its sappiest and most suffocating forms.

God wasn't the problem.

Mike Snyder was the problem.

He was two years older than Naomi and started hitting on her when she was about fifteen. Mike was something of a mythical figure around town. He had a reputation so thoroughly unearned that it defied reason, but there is almost no limit to what a person can achieve early in life when he has the total and unwavering support of a large and uncritical family. It's later that it all turns back on you. But in his early years and in the Snyder view, Mike was an artist and interpretive dancer and brilliant musician. He was an immensely gifted child of God who must be given space and respect and freedom and money.

Plus blow jobs, in Mike's opinion. Naomi held off for a while, but he was so earnest, so tortured and pleading and clearly screwed up beyond his family's ability to see, that she took pity on him. She knew it wasn't right, it wasn't how things were supposed to be, and looking back, she can't believe she was ever so passive. Why did she feel this weird obligation to him that she didn't feel to herself?

But she did. They'd go through periods where things would heat up and cool down; there were times she thought she loved him, times she was pretty sure she hated him, but most times she just felt vaguely bad for him. The kid knew he was an imposter even if he couldn't come out and say it, and she wanted to make him calm down and leave her alone.

Mike never wanted intercourse, even when Naomi did, probably because he was tortured by the holdovers of the family's start in rigid Catholicism. Mike was the oldest, the only one who'd gone to Catholic grade school, and the talons of guilt were sunk into him but good. There was no sexual encounter with Mike that was not wholly shot through with his crippling sense of shame. Naomi, whose own feelings toward physical love were about a billion times less complicated, didn't press the issue. The last thing she needed was a short, unsatisfying coupling on the floor in the Snyder basement, followed by an image of Mike seared onto her eyeballs: Mike, naked, sobbing in the corner of the half-lit, deep-pile-carpeted basement; Mike, curled up over there next to the

Addams Family pinball machine, rocking on his haunches and apologizing to God.

But that's exactly what she got on graduation night.

Mike had been desperate to find some cultural or chronological benchmark by which he could move fucking Naomi into the realm of the Spiritually Acceptable, and he'd seized on her high school graduation with the fervor of a horny zealot. He planned his seduction for months. When the moment finally came, she was half-drunk, he was half-erect, and the result was All-World fumbly, but at least it was quick and now it was done. Naomi stared at him, over there in the corner, just a sad, twisted little kid, really. She still felt sorry for him, but mostly she felt relieved that this, at least, would never come up again.

So of course she got pregnant.

At that point Naomi made three huge mistakes in quick succession that altered the trajectory of her life. First mistake: she told Mike. *Mike*, she told, the Uncritically Loved Artistic Genius who was now twenty years old, still living in his parents' house with no job, no plans for school, and no real artistic talent, a message that the world was in the process of tattooing on his forehead in the unloving and inconsiderate way that the world has with guys like him. But who else was she going to tell?

Strategically, it was hard to see that move for the gigantic tactical error that it was until it played out. Because Mike was overjoyed. Mike loved her. Mike wanted to marry her. And Mike immediately told his parents. That really threw Naomi; she rarely miscalculated when it came to guessing human behavior, but she missed this one by a mile. She'd assumed Mike—sobbing-naked-after-bad-sex Mike—would be overcome by remorse and do anything to keep his filthy secret to himself, but she didn't consider the full impact of the adoration he had received all his short life. That, coupled with a terrifying early exposure to the ecstasy of the Catholic guilt-and-confession wash-and-dry cycle, made him a real loose cannon. The way Mike saw it, he'd been given a rare gift, the chance to do the right thing, and by God he was going to do it. His parents were similarly overjoyed—they had a couple of sinners to forgive, and it was time to get busy forgiving. The fact that Naomi was one of only a few hundred African Americans in Atchison to boot only made it better. It made *them* better.

Plus they'd all have a baby to raise. Everybody wins.

Mistakes two and three for Naomi fell fast after that first one, and they were things she failed to do rather than things she did. She failed to drive immediately to CHC in Overland Park to get an abortion, and she failed to tell Tara Snyder, who would have driven her immediately to CHC in Overland Park to get an abortion. Instead, she allowed the Snyder parents to sit her down and paint a picture of such joyous, multigenerational familial love around the presence of this new young life that it carried her through her first trimester and most of her second in conspiratorial silence. It wasn't until her well-conditioned eighteen-year-old body finally started to show in the fifth month that she knew, for sure and for real, that she had made a massive mistake. But by then it was too late to do anything about it.

Sarah turned four the other day, and Naomi would be the first to tell you that she thanked God she had the kid after all. It was impossible to look at that little face and think otherwise, but that didn't mean Naomi's life was any better because things turned out this way. It was just different. Mike had taken off to join the Peace Corps within a week after the baby was born, and in truth that was a relief; he'd turned into a real pain in the ass once it sank in that Naomi wasn't going to marry him, or sleep with him ever again. He would have made a lousy father anyway.

The Snyders made good on their offers to help raise the kid, but Naomi's hand to God, they were morons, and she ended up living with her sister in a half-decent two-bedroom in a new development called Pine Valley, which had nary a pine tree nor a valley within its borders. But the apartment was clean, and things were okay. Naomi had gotten used to radical changes in her domestic situation with her mom, so what she was most comfortable with was something that was safe, temporary, and had an uncertain future. Boxes checked on all that. She'd started a job and classes at the community college once Sarah was old enough for day care, and if she played it all just right, she could be done with veterinary school in another six and a half years.

The most painful part of all of it was the part she never told anyone. Naomi Williams didn't like her child. Yes, she adored her. Yes, she felt a deep and uncompromising love for her. But in moments when Naomi was honest with herself, she would silently admit that she didn't really *like* her kid. Sarah could be the most loving child you'd ever met in your entire life, and also the most hateful, angry, and debilitating. For two years after Naomi's father died of a sudden heart attack at age fifty-three, Sarah, just picking up on the concept of death, had brought up the sensitive issue to her young, grieving mother with the painful consistency of an abscessed tooth. Someone would mention fathers and the kid would say, "But you can't ever talk to your daddy again, right, Mama?"

Or the subject of parents in general would come up, and Sarah would look at Naomi and say, "You only have one parent now, and your other one won't ever come back, right, Mama?"

Or, shit, people would just mention that they'd called somebody on the goddamn phone, and the kid would say, "Your daddy won't ever call you again, will he?"

Everybody would wince and laugh and say, "She's trying to make sense of death, the poor thing!" but Naomi knew vindictiveness when she saw it. Her own kid didn't like her, and she guessed that was okay, because it cut both ways. Yeah, yeah, she loved her, but . . . she didn't know. Maybe someday. Right now, she just wanted to keep her head down, grab night shifts at the storage place whenever she could, and put a little more money away. Vet school. That was the prize. Both eyes on it at all times.

NAOMI DUMPED THE TRASH IN THE BIG BIN IN THE far corner of the loading dock and was turning to head back inside when she almost physically bumped into Teacake, who'd just burst through the security door from the other side of the complex, feigning a casual demeanor.

"Oh, hey," he said. "You work here?"

Naomi glanced down at her uniform shirt, then back up at him. "Doesn't everybody wear these?"

He laughed. "I'm Teacake."

"Teacake?"

"Nickname."

"Clearly," she said. "You must have loved that book."

"What book?"

"*Their Eyes Were Watching God.*"

"Never heard of it."

"Well, somebody named you after a famous character in it."

"Nah, that's not it," he said.

"How'd you get the name?"

"Long story, fairly annoying."

It wasn't like Naomi didn't have time, so she just looked at him, waiting. Her brown eyes, Jesus, he never knew, you couldn't tell from the video, those brown eyes, they didn't look away, and did she ever blink? Her eyes told him to keep going, so he did.

"I was, like, sixteen or thereabouts, or what have you, me and some of my boys are rolling around. We got the munchies, so we pull into the Kickapoo on 83. Gonna get some Twinkies. I'm last one in, though, they scoop up all the good Hostess stuff and whatnot, all's they got left is Sno Balls, and coconut makes me gag, right?"

"If you say so."

"I do," he said. "For real. Like, it closes off my throat? What's that one dessert? It's got, like, chocolate powder on it, I had it at an Italian restaurant in Wichita, and if you breathe in wrong, you suck up all the powder and it closes up your throat and you choke and you can't breathe?"

"I can't say I've ever had that experience."

"Well, it's weird. Coconut's like that for me, but chunkier. Hang on, where was I? I wander sometimes. Like, verbally."

"All the Hostess was gone."

"Right! So the only thing left is something called an Aunt Sarah's Teacake. I buy it, I eat it, it's pretty good, so, I don't know, is that a crime? I say I want to go back and get another one, my boys, they think this is some kind of hysterical funny shit, 'He wants a teacake, he wants a teacake, hey, Teacake, where's your teacake?'— you know, like, crazy brilliant witty shit like that starts flying around."

"Were there any of those marijuana cigarettes that I've heard about involved in this situation?"

"I have no idea what you're talking about. Anyway, that was it, I was Teacake, and I haven't heard my given name since."

"Your parents call you Teacake?"

"My dad thinks it's a riot."

"Your mom?"

He shrugged. "Even longer story."

She held out her hand. "I'm Naomi."

He took her hand, trying not to look at the way her beautiful brown skin folded gently over her knuckles, not all gross and shit the way some knuckle skin can be, those weird crackly semi-circles that look like an evil knothole in a tree in that one cookie commercial or whatever, but that's how his mind was, it grabbed hold of something and ran off with it, and now he was holding her hand too long, thinking about *knuckles*, for Christ's sake.

She reclaimed her hand with a light tug.

He tried to extend the moment any way he could. "I know you haven't been here long, so if there's anything, you know, I don't know, like, that you don't know, or whatever, just hit me up, okay?"

"Nothing I can think of, but thanks. Guess I gotta go."

"Yeah, me too, super busy. This place, man. Always something, except it's never anything."

She smiled at him. It was hard not to find Teacake moderately charming. She noticed the badly inked snake wrapped around his right biceps, but let it pass without comment. His ink was his business, and she'd seen enough to know where that kind of sloppy tattoo probably came from.

He noticed her noticing, and he saw the slight change in the way she looked at him. A tiny lowering of her shoulders, the minutest tilt of the head away from him. It was always the same. If women were smart enough to know him, they were smart enough to not get to know him any better.

Shit. Why did he bother?

"See you around." She headed for the door to the dock. He started to follow, but she glanced at him and the half-full trash can he was holding.

"Didn't you want to dump that?"

"Oh, right. Yeah. Duh. Right."

She turned back to the door and, busted, Teacake had no choice but to head for the dumpster. He was almost there when she called out, "Oh, there might be one thing."

He turned back.

"Over on your side."

"Yeah?"

"Do you hear a beeping sound?"

He looked at her for a long moment, and the voice in the back of Teacake's brain that had been trying to get ahold of his attention finally broke through. *See?!* the voice said. *I told you there was a beep!*

Teacake looked at Naomi, his eyes lighting up with the realization. "Your side too?"

SEVEN

Teacake and Naomi stood stock-still in the middle of the floor on his side of the complex for a good forty-five seconds before he couldn't take it anymore and had to say something. He usually found it hard not to fill silences, but being around her made it worse.

"I swear it was there before, maybe if we—"

She held up a hand, stopping him. Naomi had patience. Another five seconds went by in silence, then ten, then five more, and then there it was, right down at the bottom of human hearing levels, maybe 0.5 dB, if that, but the numbers didn't matter, what mattered was that it absolutely positively was there.

Beep.

Their faces lit up in smiles, kids who'd just found their Easter baskets.

"Aha!" she shouted.

"I *knew* it!" he said, and they took off in opposite directions, he toward the north wall and she for the south.

"What are you doing?" Naomi asked as they passed each other in the middle of the floor.

"It was over here."

She shook her head vigorously. "It was *definitely* over here," and she planted herself, still again, listening by the far wall.

He called from across the room. "Lady, I heard this thing for half an hour after I got in, it didn't register but it did, you know how sometimes you know something but you don't, like, know it all the way, and then it just sort of pops up and—"

"Will you please be quiet?"

"I'm saying. This wall."

"You are very chatty."

"I know. It's a thing. I—"

"*Shh.*"

He shushed. They stood still again. They waited the full rest of the minute.

Beep.

There it was again, like a starter's signal, and they took off, each to the other's wall, passing in the middle of the floor again, looking at each other with incredulity.

"What are you doing now?" she wanted to know.

"What are *you* doing?"

"It's over here, you were right!"

They reached each other's former positions, grinning. It was kind of fun, or a hell of a lot better than sitting alone and staring at their monitors all night, anyway. They waited again, trying not to giggle, failing a bit, but knowing they had thirty seconds to spare. Their eyes caught, both their faces wide and childlike, and wouldn't it have been nice if the beep never came again and this moment could just last and last and last and—

Beep.

This time nobody moved. Teacake laughed.

"What?"

"I'm afraid to say."

"You think you were right the first time."

He nodded. Naomi looked up at the vaulted cement ceiling above them. It was steepled, like a roof but a shallower angle. The rake of the cement was funneling the noise, scooting it along the surface of the stone before dropping it down on opposite sides of the room.

"We're both right," she said. She crept to the center point of the room, trying not to make any noise, and waited.

Beep.

Her head snapped in the direction from which the sound had come. Now she had a bead on it. She eased over to the reception desk, reached behind the counter, and buzzed herself through the gate. She went to the wall ten feet behind the desk, laid her ear against it, and waited.

BEEP.

The sound was most definitely coming from behind this wall, but the other side was just another corridor, running along the interior of the first row of storage units in the ground-level section. It wasn't till you walked back through the doorway, into the reception area, and stopped to look at the wall in profile, so to speak, that you noticed the extra space. There was about eighteen inches more than there should have been between the wall in the reception area and the wall on the other side.

"Why would anybody do that? Leave empty space like that?" Teacake asked.

"Insulation?"

"Between two interior walls? That's some fucked-up useless insulation."

"What is this, drywall?" she asked.

"Yeah."

"You're sure?"

"I have hung my share of it."

BEEP.

He looked at her. "You want to call Griffin?"

"Under no circumstances do I want to call Griffin."

He caught the extra meaning in it and was disappointed. "He tried that shit already?"

She shrugged. "He's a pig."

"Could have told you that."

BEEP.

She looked at him. "So what do you want to do?"

"Well, what I *want* to do is take that picture down," he said, gesturing to a large framed aerial photograph of the caves, circa 1940s, that hung more or less over the exact spot that the beeping was coming from, "pick up that chair over there"—now he pointed at the uncomfortable-as-hell metal office stool that was parked behind the desk—"smash it through that cheap-ass three-eighths-inch gypsum Sheetrock, and see what the fuck is beeping back there."

"I'm okay with that if you are."

He laughed. "I said that's what I want to do, not what I'm gonna do."

"Oh."

They looked at the wall for a while. It beeped again.

She couldn't take it. "Oh, come on. We can hang the picture back up over the hole to cover it and bring in a piece of Sheetrock tomorrow. I'll help you patch it up. Nobody'll know the difference."

"Why would we do that?" he asked.

"Curiosity. Boredom."

"You get bored, it makes you want to smash through walls?"

"Apparently. Don't you?"

He thought about it. Not particularly, but She was asking. Why did people always come to him with their shit, and why did he usually do it? He was going to get on top of that question real soon, but first he ran some quick numbers in his head.

"Four-by-eight piece of drywall is fifteen bucks," he said. "Plus a roll of joint tape, that's another eight or nine."

"I will give you twelve dollars and we can use a sampler can of paint from the paint store. It's easy."

"All so we can see a smoke alarm with a dead battery."

"Maybe," she said. "Or maybe we see something else."

"Like what?"

"Well, we don't know. That's the thing."

"I need this job."

"You're not gonna lose it."

"No, I *have* to have the job."

"I get it," she said.

He was getting heated. "No, you don't. It's, like, a *condition*."

"I said I get it. I've lived here all my life, I know what a parole condition is, and I know where black-and-gray tattoos with shitty ballpoint ink get done. Ellsworth, right? I mean, I'm hoping it was Ellsworth."

"It was."

"Good. So you're not violent. Now will you please pick up that chair and throw it through the wall for me? Please?"

She fixed her brown eyes on him, and he looked into them.

THE LEGS WERE SPINDLY METAL AND THEY WENT through the drywall easy enough, and the biggest chunk of gypsum came off when he pulled it back out. The real challenge was not to pull too much, so they wouldn't have to replace more than one panel. They didn't need the chair after that first blow; they used their hands, carefully tearing away a few larger pieces until there was a hole big enough for Teacake to get his head and shoulders through.

There was a space back here all right, about sixteen inches of gap between this wall and the far one, and it was dark except for a red flashing light at eye height, three feet to his left.

BEEP.

It was much louder now, and a tiny light strobed white in sync with the sound. Teacake and Naomi looked across the concealed interior wall, checking it out. It was covered with dials and gauges, long out of use and cut off from power. They were set in an industrial-looking corrugated metal framework of some kind, painted in the sickly institutional green used back in the '70s because some study said it was supposed to be soothing. Or maybe the paint was just cheap.

BEEP.

Both their gazes turned back to the flashing light. There was writing etched into a panel underneath it, but they couldn't quite read it from here.

"You got a flashlight on your phone?" he asked Naomi.

She dug her phone out of her pocket, turned on the flashlight feature, and shined the beam through the hole, but they still couldn't read the words underneath the panel.

"Hang on to the thing," Teacake said. He put one foot on the stool, grabbed the edges of the hole, and hoisted himself up and through without waiting for a response. The stool pitched and started to fall. Naomi caught it, but not before it had knocked Teacake off balance and dumped him, upside down, into the space between the walls.

"I said hang on to the thing!"

"Yeah, I didn't say 'okay.' Traditionally, you want to wait for that."

Teacake sneezed six times. When he recovered, he looked up from his semi-inverted position and saw Naomi's hand holding out a Kleenex through the hole in the wall. He looked at it, impressed. Who has a Kleenex in this situation?

"Thank you." He took it and blew his nose. He offered the soiled Kleenex back to her.

"You can go ahead and keep that one," she said. "Can you get up?"

He shimmied himself into an upright position and scooted sideways down the wall through the tight space, moving toward the flashing panel.

"Shine the light over there," he said.

She did, moving the beam onto the panel beneath the blinking light.

He read it. "'NTC Thermistor Breach. Sub-basement Level Four.'"

From the hole, she turned her light on him.

He winced. "Could you get that out of my eyes?"

"Sorry. Thermistor what?"

"'NTC Thermistor Breach.' There's a whole bunch of stuff back here."

She moved the light back onto the board and he looked up and down it, where a number of other monitors and displays were stacked.

"'Airtight Integrity,' 'Resolution' with a plus sign that's, like, underlined—"

"Plus or minus."

"Okay, 'plus or minus 0.1 degree Celsius.'" Naomi kept the light moving and he read the stamped letters under each of the deactivated gauges and displays. "'Cold Chain Synchronicity,' 'Data Logger Validation,' 'Measurement

Drift Ratio,' 'LG Internal,' 'LG Probe,' 'LE1 Probe,' 'LE2 Probe,' 'LD Internal,' Jesus, there's, like, twenty of 'em." He turned back to the gauge right in front of him as it beeped and flashed again. "But this is the only one that's flashing."

"NTC Thermistor Breach."

"Yeah. You know what that means?"

She thought a moment. "A thermistor is part of an electrical circuit. There's two kinds, the positive kind, their resistance rises with temperature, and the negative kind, their resistance falls if the temperature goes up."

"So it's a thermometer?"

"No. It's a circuit that's reactive to temperature."

"Like a thermometer."

"It is not a thermometer."

He turned and looked at her. "What are you, all science-y and shit?"

"I wouldn't say 'and shit,' but I take a lot of science. Prerequisites for vet school."

The alarm beeped again, and Teacake turned back to it. "This is thirty or forty years old. How come it's still on?"

She shrugged. "Guess they wanted to keep an eye on temperature."

BEEP.

"Why?" he asked.

"Good question. And what the hell is sub-basement four?" She shined her light in his eyes again. "I thought there was only one."

EIGHT

Mooney had been driving around with the bodies in the trunk for two days and they were starting to reek. At first, he'd been able to pretend the smell wasn't there, or that it was the brewery on the other side of the river, or maybe it was that weird syrupy smell that had been blowing in and out of the river valley for the past couple of years, or even that it was he himself, just smelling like a man during a heat wave, as one does in these complicated climatic times we live in. But he knew it wasn't any of that.

Mooney never did well in the heat, which was what had made Uganda such an odd choice, but hey, you don't always choose your path in life; sometimes it chooses you. Right now, life had selected him to be the custodian of the mortal remains of the two unlucky bastards in the trunk of his car, and so far, he was doing a shitty job of it. A final goddamn resting spot was harder to find than you'd think, once you ruled out all official channels (for obvious reasons), garbage dumps (out of respect for the dead), and anyplace that smacked of future housing or commercial development (for fear of eventual disinterment). That didn't leave a hell of a lot of Pottawatomie County open to surreptitious burial, and Mooney was starting to wonder if the whole car wasn't going to have to end up in the river when he saw the ad for the self-storage place on TV.

The first and most obvious thought that crossed his mind was that he'd buy some kind of airtight vault, seal them both up inside it, wheel the thing into the smallest possible unit they had, lock the door, toss the key, and never think about it again. But on his first scouting mission out to Atchison Storage, earlier this afternoon, the smell had really started to settle itself into the metal and fabric and fiber of the car, and he just didn't see anything made by God or man that would hold that stench in forever and ever. Except for Mother Earth herself.

Plus there were the storage bills: $49.50 a month? To hell with that. He'd buy a couple gallons of gas and torch them in his parents' backyard first.

He'd turned around in the driveway and was on his way out of the eastern side of the storage place when he saw the wooded glade, up on the hillside near the crest of the bluff. Immediately, he knew the two rotting corpses in the trunk had just found their personal Valhalla. He hiked up onto the bluff, took a look around at the trees and the view and the peacefulness under the whispering pines, and he hugged himself. It was something he did sometimes; he'd wrap both arms around himself and squeeze, sometimes making a little cooing noise, just something to let him know he was alive and he was loved, even if only by himself at times. But from tiny acorns great oak trees of love do grow, right?

This was the spot. He'd treat those poor dead souls properly, dig them a hole down under the frost line right here on this glorious, unbuildable bluff that overlooked the river on one side and a mountain of rock on the other. Those were two natural wonders that he could count on to stay exactly where they were, unchanged, for a good forty or fifty thousand years. The corpses would be undisturbed.

Yes. This place would do nicely.

So now he was back, under cover of darkness and with a shovel. He pulled off the driveway fifty yards short of the eastern entrance and killed the lights around ten P.M. There was just one car down below in the parking lot, probably the guard's, and it looked kind of familiar. But nobody guards an unlit bluff on the wrong side of the Missouri River, so Mooney figured he was safe over here.

He got out of the car, went around to the trunk, and winced at the foul smell that was seeping out of the cracks along the edges of the metal. He turned his head away, took an enormous gulp of fresh air, turned back, opened the trunk in one swift motion, and got smacked in the face with the most assaultive stench he'd ever smelled in his entire life. It wasn't just that it smelled *bad*—you couldn't just say *bad*, that didn't come anywhere close to covering it. It's that the smell *hurt*, it was so powerful. It had a thickness to it, a body and form; the smell was all hands and they were all over him, grabbing him by the face and throat and nostrils and lungs and forcing their thick fingers into him.

Mooney snapped his head away as fast as he could, barely getting a glimpse of the rapidly decaying contents of the trunk. He fumbled around for the shovel. It should have been right on top, that was where he'd left it, how could it have moved, Jesus Christ, where was the goddamn shovel? Face still averted, he slapped his hand around the trunk a few times, an angry dad swatting at the kids in the back seat while trying to keep his eyes on the road, but every place his hand landed was worse than the place before—that part was wet, and this part was hot (not just warm, mind you, but *hot*)—but wait, here it was, hard and wooden and *shovel*! His fingers closed around the handle and he yanked it out of the trunk, slammed the lid, and practically collapsed, gasping for air.

This couldn't be right. This smell could not be normal. Then again, what experience did he have? What did he know, maybe this was how it went down when you died. If it was, quick mental note: he definitely wanted to eat better and exercise four or five times a week from now on, because death was no party. Okay. When did he fire the last kill shot, what was that, two days ago? Less than that; he'd loaded both corpses into the car at two in the morning on Wednesday—that's forty-four hours. How fast does a body decompose? He actually pulled out his phone and was about to google that very question when the essential insanity of that act somehow managed to announce itself through the fog of his stench-choked brain. He put the phone away and started the walk up the hill with the shovel to dig the grave.

He was ten steps away when he heard the first thump. He turned.

It had come from the trunk of the car.

NINE

Teacake knew from bitter experience that your head could get only so small. Everything else can squeeze, suck in, twist around; people can get pretty sideways when they want to or have to. But with your head there was no negotiation.

Teacake had direct knowledge of this from the fence that had run along the back of his high school. At the edge of the fence there was a pipe, set just a few inches too far off the brick facade, that left a nine-inch gap between the school building and freedom. Determined weed smokers used to be able to get off the bus in the morning, cruise through the front doors of the school, sign in for homeroom, and split out the rear fire doors before the handles got chained for the day (totally illegal, by the way). From there it was just a matter of a shoulder shimmy, a gut suck-in for Big Jim Schmittinger, and a willingness to scrape the shit out of both ears as you popped your head through to the other side. If you did all that, *boom*, you were loose in the open field behind the school building, where you could blaze away in peace. The size of his skull was the main reason Teacake, as toasty a burnout as you would ever find, actually managed to swing a 3.5 GPA in high school—his head was just too goddamn big to get through the fence. So Teacake never got high during the day. It does wonders for your concentration. Some of the math and science even stuck, and when he joined the navy he remembered just enough of it to qualify for duty on a ballistic missile sub. It was a plus. At least he had the same bunk every night.

Nothing he did manage to learn about *Lord of the Flies*, though, was of use in his present situation, where his great big fucked-up head had done him in again. Stuck, he called out to Naomi from the space between the walls.

"What about Vageline? You got any Vageline?"

"Do I have any what?"

"That greasy shit you put on your lips! Get me out of here!"

"Are you trying to say 'Vaseline'?"

"Whatever the fuck it's called, Naomi, get some lotion or grease or butter and get me out of here!"

She'd been trying like hell not to laugh for the better part of the last few minutes, and it was a battle she now lost.

"Oh, yeah, no, definitely, yes, do that," Teacake sputtered. "Yeah, *laugh*, 'cause this shit is, like, *hilarious*."

He was still in the gap in the walls, and he'd wedged himself in good, in the precisely nine-inch space between two I beams. He'd done well up to that point, sliding and twisting and pretzeling his body through the tiny open area toward what looked like an enormous map at the far end of the control panel wall. It was dark inside the gap and hard to tell, but it looked like a map, anyway, and he had been only a few feet from it when he'd gotten stuck between the beams, and the entirety of his high school experience came flooding back to him. Now he couldn't move his goddamn head.

"Lube! You gotta have some lube, right? Throw me it!"

Naomi took a moment to make sure she'd understood him properly before she poked her head in through the hole in the wall.

"I'm sorry, did you just suggest that I carry *lubricant* around with me?"

"I didn't— I wasn't—"

"'Cause that's some offensive shit, Teacake."

"I'd like to apologize and start over."

"I mean, I don't know, you got any dental dams in your pocket?"

"Naomi. Um, ma'am. I'm kind of freaking out here."

She took a step back, looked up and down the length of the wall, and thought.

"Are you good for another twelve bucks?" she asked. "Although we wouldn't have to buy the roll of tape again."

Teacake was in no position to negotiate. "Do what you gotta do, lady. Just promise me you're not gonna pull on me, because at this point

I think if the angle's wrong my left ear is just gonna tear right the—"

The legs of the metal stool crashed through the drywall three feet in front of him and startled him so badly he wrenched his body backward, ripping himself free from the head vise. He fell again, on his ass, in the narrow space that he was now more than ready to evacuate. As he got to his feet, he saw Naomi, standing in the new opening (*that* repair was going to cost more than twelve bucks, by the way; she'd hit a seam right between two panels and they were gonna need three four-by-eights now, minimum). She was staring in amazement at the wall beyond.

"Holy shit."

Teacake got to his feet, rubbing his ears in pain, and slid forward till he was alongside her. The broken panels had opened up a section directly in front of the maplike thing he'd been trying to move closer to, and it was bigger and more detailed than he'd been able to see by the light of Naomi's phone's flashlight. It was an enormous, hyperdetailed floor plan depicting every room, conduit, pipe, and piece of wiring in what must have been the old military storage complex. There were hundreds of LED lights painstakingly placed all over the map marking God knows what, but they were all long since deactivated or burned out.

Except for one, all the way down at the bottom right corner. Its tiny bulb strobed white, in sync with the light on the warning panel nearby.

Teacake came over to the schematic, kicked

out the remnants of the broken drywall, and stepped out of the inner space, moving back into the reception area. He got a few feet away from the thing to get a better look. He stood shoulder to shoulder with Naomi. She looked at him.

"Your ear is bleeding."

He reached up to his right ear, but she meant the left. She pulled another Kleenex from the pack she kept in her pocket, wiped his ear gently, folded it over and pressed it there. "Hold that."

He did. He looked at her.

No one had put a bandage on one of Teacake's wounds with their own hand since he was eleven years old. It almost moved him to tears. In fact, he thought he felt the first sting of a couple of them in the corners of his eyes. That was the last thing he needed, to bust out crying in front of her, *what is the* matter *with me?*

"What's the matter?" she asked. She didn't miss much.

"Huh?"

"You okay?"

"Yeah. Just—ouch. Whatever."

She turned and looked at the map. "It's a schematic."

She leaned through the wall and ran her hands along it, starting at the top, which was the ground floor. "How many levels are there supposed to be in this place?"

"Three. Main floor and two belowground."

"There used to be six. And they *watched* this stuff."

"Yeah, it was military storage, since World War II. You know, weapons and what have you. They cleaned it out and sold it about twenty years ago."

"And they must have sealed up everything below here." She ran her hand down the schematic to the lower levels. "Which was the part they really cared about. See all the sensors? They're all in bunches down here."

She was right. By far the greatest concentration of LEDs was on the lower three levels, the additional sub-basements. SB-2 and SB-3 were apparently sealed off and all their monitor lights were dark. The single flashing white bulb was on the very bottom level, marked SB-4. But there was a large blank space, two feet of map at least, between SB-3 and SB-4. Tiny scribbles of rock shapes seemed to indicate it was earthen.

Teacake studied it, trying to figure it out. "Who builds a sub-basement a hundred feet below the other basements? You'd have to dig the whole thing out, build the bottom floor, then fill in again above it. That makes no sense."

"You wanna go down and see it?"

He looked at her. "How? It's sealed."

"That." She pointed to the far left side of the map, where a thin vertical column rose up from SB-4, through the earthen portion, and skirted along the edges of the other sub-basement levels. It was narrow, with hatch marks drawn evenly between the long parallel lines all the way up.

"What is it?"

"A tube ladder."

"How do you know?"

"It's shaped like a tube, and it looks like a ladder. How else would they get down there?" She pointed to the hatchings. "Look, these are the rungs."

He was impressed. "You must go to college, right? It's a waste if you don't."

"I go as much as I can, yeah."

"Then you should be smart enough to not wanna go down there."

"C'mon," she said. "This is the most fun I've had in years. This is a night out for me."

"Jesus. That's depressing. You don't go out?"

"Not really."

"What about just, like, for a beer?"

"I don't drink."

He persisted. "Not even for one beer?"

"That would be drinking."

"You never go out for one beer?"

"This is getting off the point."

But he was determined. "What about a coffee?"

"I thought you were fun, Teacake. You started out fun."

"Me? I'm totally fun. I'm huge fun. You're the one who just said your best night out in years is vandalizing your workplace."

"I have an inquisitive nature." She held up her phone and snapped a picture of the schematic.

"Yeah, I can see that, and that's cool, and I'm, like, cooperating. You look at me with those eyes you got and say, 'Please throw your chair through the wall,' and you know, I'm on board, I throw my chair through the wall, and then you say, 'Go crawl into that weird space and check it out,' still good, I'm into it, but then you come at me like, 'Go climb down the *tube ladder* a couple hundred feet into the blocked-off part of the fucked-up government shit and see why the *thermistor alarm* is going off,' and, you know, a man's gonna take a second to think things through, you feel me?"

She waited a moment. "You like my eyes?"

"In fact, I do."

"That's very sweet."

"My point is, I'm kinda easy to talk into things, that's why I got the problems I got. People say shit like, 'Wait in the car and keep it running, I just gotta run in and do something,' or 'I know this guy in Dousman needs a favor,' and I say, 'Yeah, sure, I just point the gun at my foot and pull the trigger, is that what I do?' *Bang!* 'Ow! What a surprise, I blew my toe off. Should I do it again? Okay!' But I have spent a lot of time working on my personal self and talking to smart people and learning to ask what's good for me and to not just dive into shit. Which is what I am doing right now, okay? I am taking a fucking moment."

"I understand. I respect that."

"It is very, very important to learn to tell everybody in the whole world to fuck off all the time. It took me forever to learn that."

"I'm not sure that was the exact message you were supposed to—"

But he glared at her, so she stopped and recharted her course.

"I'm sorry. I get you had some bad stuff happen to you. I was not being cool."

"Okay. Good. That's more like it." He took a deep breath and let it out again, then pulled a flashlight off a battery charger on the wall next to the desk and headed for the gate that led deeper into the building.

"You coming or what?"

TEN

Mooney must have stared at the trunk of his car for a solid five minutes. The thumps would come in bursts, just one or two, randomly, then a whole furious burst of them, till it sounded like half a dozen Dutchmen in there with wooden shoes were clogging on the inside of the metal trunk lid. The whole car would rock like crazy, then it'd stop again and everything would go still for ten or fifteen seconds while Mooney pondered the impossible nature of what was occurring. He'd use that moment to question his sanity, his judgment, his ability to correctly perceive reality, his past history with drug use and abuse, and then the dancing Dutchmen would start back up again.

Of course, it was not possible. Not in the slightest. Dead things don't come back to life; decaying corpses don't reanimate. But there was something alive in his trunk, two somethings, wedged in there with the spare tire and the toolbox and the gun case, and they weren't having any fun. In the end, it was Mooney's essential decency that made him open the trunk, his goodness and kindness as a human being. Because the level of suffering going on three feet away from him was intense, and what kind of person allows another living thing to endure that sort of agony? What kind of person stands by and does nothing? Mooney didn't open the trunk because he was stupid, and he didn't open the trunk because he was scared, and he didn't open it so that he could kill them again. He opened the trunk because we are all God's creatures.

Thing of it is, even God would have taken one look at the cat and said, "That shit is not mine."

The trunk was only about six inches open when the first paw came out, claws flexed wide, slashing at the air like it wanted to rip the whole atmosphere a new one. Mooney fell back at that point and the cat did the rest. It leaped straight up, banging into the trunk lid and sending it swinging open the rest of the way. The cat landed on all fours, still in the trunk, and it snarled at him—a look of such profound, intense hatred that Mooney's response came without thought of any kind, a purely synaptic reflex.

"I'm sorry," he said.

Yes, Mooney apologized to the cat, and it really was the only sensible response. The animal was a mess, and it was all his doing. He'd put the .22 slug through the side of the cat's head, and even that small caliber was enough to blow off the other side of its face. Now the half cat would never wow the ladies again. Its fur was dark and matted with blood, its eyes a sickly bright yellow, and, unless Mooney was hallucinating (which he still imagined—hoped, really—was entirely possible), its midsection was expanding as he watched.

But the cat looked good compared to the deer it was standing on.

Tuesday night had started out substantially better than this for Mooney, just over forty-eight hours ago. In need of a little distraction, he'd taken himself to the movies, with a real quick stop at Turdyk's Liquor & Cheese first, where he'd picked up a six-pack of Bartles & Jaymes Exotic Berry wine coolers. He didn't love flavored booze, but they were the only wine coolers that were cold and came in plastic bottles. The plastic ones had screw-off tops and didn't make a racket if you happened to drop, say, the fourth one on the floor of the movie theater. At his last Mooney's Private Movie Night & Wine Party, a bottle had slipped through his popcorn-greased hands, and the excruciating clatter of it hitting the cement and rolling down the sloping theater floor felt like it had lasted half an hour. Just about every head in the place turned, and that kind of silent group disapproval was something he could have gotten at home for free.

So, he was no dummy. Plastics.

Wine coolers go down easy; the problem is the sugar headache, but if you bring five or six Advil, you're fine. Mooney was a big fan of the A vitamin and never left the house without it, so by the time he drove away from the Regal 18 on Highway 16, he was more than fine. He had a nice buzz, and the movie wasn't half-bad either:

mindless enough that you could tune out for whole chunks and not get lost, but not so stupid that you felt bad about yourself afterward. He could have done without some of the language.

But the best part of all was he still had one wine cooler left for the drive home, and it wasn't even completely warm. Life could be kind. He waited till he got through all three stoplights in town before he opened it. Mooney had a hard-and-fast rule: he never, ever drank while driving in the busy part of town, and he rarely texted or went online behind the wheel unless, you know, it was going to be super quick. He was a concerned citizen who cared about his fellow man, so he didn't crack the plastic lid on his sixth wine cooler until he'd hit the long flat dark stretch of 16, where it started the big bend.

You're going to want to, but you just can't blame the accident on the Bartles & Jaymes. That wouldn't be fair. Yes, Mooney's blood alcohol was flirting with 0.15 and his reaction time was down, but 250 pounds of aggressively stupid animal that springs out of nowhere and stands frozen on the center stripe of a dark highway, right in the middle of an unlit curve, I mean, that asshole has to be factored into the equation too. Character is destiny, and that dumbass deer—sorry, that beautiful creature of God— that *thing's* character was drawn within the limitations of a non-sentient brain. It stood there, unmoving, as the car closed the last fifty feet on it; it just hunched there, watching Death come hurtling at it, staring at the car like, well, like exactly what it was, there's a goddamn good reason for that cliché, so maybe it was fitting that the first thing that hit the deer was the headlight.

The rest was a gruesome blur, and Mooney panicked and blacked out most of it, as he did sometimes when things got weird. Next thing he knew he was standing over the wounded animal on the shoulder, staring down at its broken, twitching form and holding his father's .22 pistol. He kept it in the trunk for situations just like this, which, believe it or not, were not all that uncommon around here. Mooney knew what he had to do. It wasn't hard; you point the thing and pull the trigger and put the beast out of its misery, that's what any decent human being would do, and there was no law against it, neither God's nor man's. The animal was clearly suffering, its mouth opening and closing soundlessly, steam rising from its blood as it spilled out onto the asphalt, still hot from the exceptional heat of the day.

Just kill it already, but Mooney had never killed before, never knowingly; he didn't even like swatting flies, it tended to send him off into flights of creepy reverie, reflections on his place in the universe. He'd always figured he was a Buddhist at heart—weren't they the ones who were on about reincarnation all the time, or was that the Hindus? Whichever. The ones who cared, the ones who loved all living things. That was him. But now here he was, faced with the—

BANG. The gun went off while he was still

midthought, and it hit the wounded animal in the gut. It screamed.

Oh, great, now I gutshot *the fucking thing—how can this have happened? I am a warm and sensitive and humane person and— Oh my God, what is that horrible sound this disgusting animal is making at me now? I feel bad enough, what is it, hacking spit at me?* And Mooney filled with some other feeling, not guilt, not tortured reflection, not the milk of human kindness, but a new one, for him.

Rage. Pure, undiluted rage at this senseless animal that had ruined his night, his mental state, and the front left end of his car. He raised the gun again, put it to the deer's brain this time, and blasted away, more than once, way more than once. In spirit it was more of a murder than a mercy killing, if anybody was keeping karmic score.

The crying jag Mooney had afterward in the car lasted a good ten or fifteen minutes. Truth is, it felt pretty good as guilt flooded through his veins again; it was at least a familiar feeling, much better than the out-of-body experience he'd been having before that. Now, what to do? You can't leave a dead deer by the side of the road with three broken legs, a bullet in its stomach, and four more in its head. *That's just, I mean, that's sick.* Mooney needed time to think, which meant that deer had to get off the shoulder of the road and into the trunk of his car.

The sight of Mooney, 180 pounds and half in the bag, trying to get a dead, gangly one-eighth-ton deer into the trunk of his car would have made for some pretty brilliant silent comedy. It may well have taken all night if not for Tommy Seipel, the driver of a 2015 Lexus. Tommy saw what was happening, pulled over immediately, asked one question—

"You loaded?"

—and, sensing Mooney's answer would be in the affirmative, threw his own considerable bulk into helping hoist the mangled deer into the trunk. He slammed the lid on it, wiped his bloody hands on Mooney's T-shirt, spoke a handful more words—

"I'd get the fuck outta here if I was you."

—and went back on his way. Mooney occasionally knew good advice when he heard it, and this was the best advice he'd heard in years. He jumped behind the wheel, slammed his door, and did as told, driving off with the dead deer in his trunk.

As he drove—where to, exactly?—he started thinking about the deer in those last gutshot moments, when it seemed to be spitting at him, and he got enraged all over again. What exactly had gotten to him about that? Was it the temerity of the animal to accuse him of not being able to handle so simple an act as a mercy killing? Was that thing calling him inept, unable, telling him he couldn't hold up his end of the deal? Something had triggered a rush of bad, inadequate memories, but he'd taken care of that, hadn't he? He'd answered any questions quite definitively, with one or two or, okay, fine, four more squeezes of the trigger. *No, I am capable. Quite capable, thank you. I settled that shit but good, and hey, what about my parents' fucking cat while I'm at it?*

Mr. Scroggins was fourteen years old and had been sick for the last, say, twelve of those. He was a diseased and expensive pet; the bills from the animal hospital were about $400 just since the beginning of this calendar year. Though his father would have taken out a second mortgage to keep that ugly cat in the world, Mooney knew the toll the financial strain was taking on his mother. Plus, c'mon, life couldn't be any kind of fun for Mr. Scroggins either, all riddled with disease and shit. Mooney was headed home with a dead deer in the trunk, a loaded .22 that he knew how to use, and a head full of righteous killing fury.

He liked it.

Mr. Scroggins was executed down at the public lake access boat ramp, where the shot might not be heard. Mooney tossed him in the trunk with the mangled deer, and so began the forty-four-hour odyssey of manly pride and horrified remorse that eventually brought Mooney to the grassy knoll here at Atchison Storage. All he wanted to do was give these two innocent dead animals the Christian burial they deserved.

But now Mr. Scroggins was alive again, standing on top of the once-dead deer in the trunk of the car, and he seemed royally pissed off.

The deer, whose mortal injuries had been far worse, flailed all four legs at once, trying to stand up in the trunk, but its broken limbs collapsed underneath it. Mr. Scroggins staggered off him but caught himself on the rear lip of the trunk and clung there, hissing. It had probably been a long ride for these two, and they were sick of each other.

Motivated by something other than normal locomotive powers, the deer vaulted itself out of the trunk. It fell flat onto the gravel, its legs splaying outward, cracking again—there had to be a couple new breaks in there somewhere. Then it hauled itself up on all fours, bounded up the hill, and just kept running upward, disappearing into the night.

Mooney had staggered back when the trunk first flew open, and good thing he'd put six or seven feet between himself and the car, because Mr. Scroggins just missed him when he sprang off the rear bumper, claws extended, half jaw snarling and spitting.

Apparently, Mooney's apology had not been accepted.

Mr. Scroggins landed on all four paws, turned as if in reaction to a sound, and ran up the hill in the same direction the deer had gone. But the cat stopped at the first tree he reached, a tall pine, and threw himself at it, catching hold of the bark and starting to climb. Mooney got up and walked closer, staring in amazement as the cat climbed the tree with incredible determination. There were no stops, no hesitation, no second thoughts, only upward movement. The branches thinned near the top, but still the dead cat climbed, swaying on this one, nearly breaking that one, but losing no speed and no sense of purpose. He reached the top of the tree, the trunk spindly up there, but still strong enough to hold an eight-pound cat. Possibly seven and a half after recent events.

Mr. Scroggins finally stopped at the top when there was nowhere else to go. He paused and took a look around, as if to make sure that this was it, there really were no new mountains to climb, not for him, anyway. Satisfied, he opened his mutilated jaws as wide as they would go. He turned back to the thinning central trunk of the tree, to its tippy-top, and snapped his head forward, impaling himself on the treetop. He squeezed, with a furious might and indignation, sinking his fangs into the bark as far as they'd go, clamping himself down there.

From below, Mooney watched, slack-jawed. You almost never see this kind of behavior from a common house cat.

Thus secured to the very top of the very tall tree by his embedded fangs and his commitment to his cause, Mr. Scroggins began to grow. His remaining cheek billowed, his legs swelled up like four-by-fours, his stomach ballooned out in both directions, and if you were close to him, which thank God you were not, you would have heard his tiny ribs snapping like matchsticks, one after the other, broken by the tremendous gastric pressure from within.

Mooney was unaware of even the existence of *Cordyceps novus*, much less how it had apparently come to penetrate the trunk of his car. He just stared, dumbfounded, at the swollen, once-dead cat at the top of the tree. "How in the name of Jesus—"

Mr. Scroggins burst.

Had Mooney not felt the need to express his understandable amazement in audible terms, his mouth would not have been open when the cat guts hit him in the face.

ELEVEN

The central hallway through the ground-floor level of Atchison Storage was two hundred feet long, with white louvered garage doors running the length of it, thirty per side. There was a pristine beauty to it, if you were into symmetry and the vanishing point, that optical illusion that makes a pair of infinite-seeming parallel lines appear to intersect, far on the horizon. If you had to walk that hallway and a few others like it a dozen times every night for your job, it was boring as shit.

But tonight, Teacake was walking it with Naomi. They were headed for the elevator at the other end, impossibly far away. Naomi had the picture she'd taken of the schematic up on her phone, and she scooched the image around, finding the elevator on the map and sliding it down to sub-basement 1, where the tube ladder's top entrance point seemed to be.

Teacake was nervous-talking.

"Gets down to it, the whole thing is just a terrible idea. Don't pay for storage. Don't *ever* pay for storage. I've seen a half a mountain of shit come into this place, and almost none of it ever comes out, except for the super-short-term stuff. People pay anywhere from forty to five hundred dollars a month, depending on the space and the climate controls, and it's all for garbage they one hundred percent do not need."

"That's a little judgmental, isn't it?"

"Not really. These are sick people, man, most of 'em, and the storage place, they're slick, you know, it's sales, they know what they're doing. They handle it like they're slinging rock on the corner. Take for example, somebody's gotta move, right? They get foreclosed on or whatever. This place gives 'em the first thirty days free. People figure, 'Hey, cool, I don't have to throw nothin' out, I'll just move some of my extra stuff in here, figure it out for a month, no rush, then I can eBay some of it and toss the rest without ever paying a dime.' But that never, ever happens. Nobody moves outta here. So your ratty couch that you don't even like anymore and your old Christmas decorations and your parents' sheets that you kept after they *died* for some reason— now they're all just exhibits in your sad museum. Oh, hey no, that don't fly, fuck nugget."

He'd stopped abruptly, seeing something on one of the white doors. He went to a storage closet, unlocked it, took out a heavy-duty bolt cutter, and returned to the third unit back on the left. There was a brass padlock hanging from the latch, sticking up at an angle—an extra lock put on there by the renter. Teacake snapped it off with one squeeze of the bolt cutters.

"They ain't supposed to add their own locks. Ours are the onliest ones you gotta use, so we have access. Like in case there's illegalness going on in there."

"What kind of illegalness?"

By way of an answer, Teacake pulled his master key out from the retractable key chain reel on his hip, put the key into the main lock on the unit, flicked it open, and cranked up the door. He immediately regretted it and proved the wisdom of the adage "Don't open a door unless you know what's on the other side," if any such adage existed.

Inside the unit, twenty-four fifty-five-inch Samsung flat-screen TVs, still in the factory packaging, were neatly stacked in rows, leaning against the walls.

"My mistake," Teacake said. "Everything's cool."

He closed the door again and they continued down the hall. She looked at him.

He shrugged. "I don't care what they got, they just can't hide it from me. Rules is rules."

She looked at him. "Why do you talk like that?"

"Like what?"

"Like you're from the hood."

"This is how everybody I know talks."

"You know me, and I don't."

"You got any other objections to how I am?"

She thought about it. "Not yet."

They got to the end of the corridor and pushed the button for the elevator. He looked at her while they waited.

"You don't talk much, do you?" he said.

"Not as much as you."

"Nobody talks as much as me."

She looked back down at her phone, moving the image down the ladder, through the earthen part, toward SB-4.

He had more questions. "So you got college, you do this sometimes, what else?"

"That's not enough?"

"Not really. You don't get many shifts."

"How do you know?"

He shrugged. "My job is to watch the monitors."

"Yeah, I see you too."

The elevator arrived, and she got in first. He followed. The doors closed.

"You get, what, maybe two nights a week?" he said.

"So far."

"So, you got another job?"

"Sorta."

"You got people?"

"Do I have 'people'? Of course I have people. Teacake, you're— What's your real name?"

"Travis. Meacham."

"Travis, you're kind of sucking all the fun out of this."

The truth was, he knew she had people, and he knew exactly which people she had, but there was no way to bring it up without seriously creeping her out. Her first night at work had been exactly two weeks ago, and he'd noticed her on the monitors immediately. She was taking a shift usually filled by Alfano Kalolo, an enormous Samoan who had to go three hundred pounds, easy.

The camera in the eastern reception area was placed close to the desk, and Alfano so dominated the screen that his absence one night fairly screamed at Teacake to take notice. Truth, who would *not* notice a thing like that? When Alfano sat on the little metal stool, he was a man-mountain who appeared to be eating a four-legged metal insect with his ass. When, that Thursday two weeks ago, Teacake looked up and saw Naomi there instead, a heavenly choir sang in his head.

He'd stared at her image that night with the intensity of a teenager monitoring his Facebook likes. She sat, she stood, she did her rounds, and always she walked in beauty, like the night. He'd memorized that poem in Ellsworth; they'd had to pick something and learn it by heart for Explorations in Poetry, and that was the shortest of the ones you could pick. He knew the poem, but he didn't *know* the poem until he saw Naomi on the monitor.

When she showed up for work again two days later, he studied her on the monitors for hours, absorbing as much detail as one possibly could from a 540-pixel image. She had a book with her that night. He couldn't quite get the title, but he loved her focus, the way her brow furrowed up at parts. He loved the way she turned the pages; he loved that she even read at all and didn't just stare at her phone like everybody else. When she wasn't back until the following Sunday, he realized that she was a fill-in, that she was grabbing shifts when and if she could get them, and that there was a very real possibility that she would never be back again.

So, he told himself, it wasn't really that he *followed* her after work. Yes, he did leave five minutes early so he could zip around to the other side of the bluffs and be near her parking lot when she left. And yes, he did swing out onto the highway just after she did and keep his car a safe and unthreatening distance behind hers on the road at all times, and yes, he did speed up when she sped up and slow down when she slowed down and make the same turns that she made, until he eventually reached her place of residence. But he knew in his heart it wasn't with weird intent—he was trying to engineer a casual run-in.

It just didn't work out. Once Naomi left the Atchison parking lot, it was kind of hopeless, all country highways till he got to her apartment complex, and then how on earth could he pull up in the car next to her at her building and say, "Oh, hey! Don't you work where I do? Didn't I watch—I mean see you on the monitor a couple times, and man, isn't it weird that you live here, twelve miles away, and I was going that exact same way but my car started making this weird sound so I had to stop right here, in the parking lot of the very same apartment building where you live? Isn't that *bizarre*?"

He couldn't say that. The smoothest motherfucker in human history (arguably Wilt Chamberlain) couldn't have pulled that one off.

So, rather than scare her, Teacake had just sat in the car, waiting till she went in, pretending to be absorbed in his phone. It was a flip, by the way, so if she'd noticed him she might well have wondered what the hell he was staring at. He waited till she got inside, then he waited some more, just to see which light went on, then he waited a teensy bit more, just to see if, well, because he did, and before he knew it almost an hour had gone by, and he really honestly was about to go when the door of the place opened again, and he saw her come out with the little girl.

There was no question that the girl was her daughter. Some things you can just tell. They looked alike, for starters, but also it was the way Naomi held the little girl's hand. Nobody holds your hand like that except your mama.

The little girl was cute as hell and dressed in clean, pressed clothes, a detail Teacake noticed because his own clothes when he was a kid had always been dirty as shit. He blushed, right there in his car, embarrassed, not because he was stalking this poor woman and, now, her kid, but because of all the times that he went to school in filthy clothes and with an unwashed face. But this little girl was what a kid was supposed to look like. She was clean and bright and her mom had given her a good breakfast, he just knew she had, even though she'd come off a twelve-hour shift and hadn't slept since God knows when. Naomi had come home and made breakfast, and maybe even put some cinnamon sugar on the kid's toast, the way she liked.

The little girl was talking a mile a minute, and Naomi was listening. Not "uh-huh, uh-huh, yeah, cool" kind of listening, but trying to actually make sense of what the kid was saying, which had to be nonsense. I mean, how much can a four-year-old say that matters, anyway? He didn't know, but from what he'd heard, the percentage was pretty low, mostly it was just "I want more frosting" or some shit.

They got to the car, the little girl got into a car seat in the back, and Naomi stood there, waiting, her hand on the door, as her daughter finished her pointless point.

Teacake rolled down his window, just a little. He was close enough, just barely, to make out a few words. Not the little girl's—those were all faint and little-girly and coming too fast from inside the car—but he could hear what Naomi said in response, after waiting till her daughter stopped for a breath.

"I hear you, sweetie. That stinks."

And then she closed the door.

That was what killed him. It wasn't "Oh, come on, it's not that bad," or "Honey, please, we're late," or "That's some stupid ridiculous bullshit, you gotta learn to shut up when you talk to people." It was "I hear you, that stinks." It was all he ever, ever wanted from people when he talked to them. To be heard. And this lady gave it to a *four-year-old*, after being up all night.

And all that's best of dark and bright meet in her aspect and her eyes.

So what Teacake wanted to say that night,

while they rode down in the elevator, what he was dying to say was "You're fucking awesome with your daughter," but is there a good way to ease into that when you're not even supposed to know she has a daughter?

So instead, he said nothing.

The elevator doors slid open.

Sub-basement 1 was supposed to be the only sub-basement, and it had never occurred to anybody to question the need for the number. SB-1 looked just fine on the elevator keypad, as good as any other number. The facility's history as a government installation wasn't a secret, so finding out there had once been other, lower levels wouldn't have been much of a surprise, had anybody ever bothered to think about it. But to find out there were three of them, and they were connected by an elaborate series of sensors and alarms to a control panel that had since been walled up behind the reception desk, you know, that would have raised a few eyebrows.

According to the schematic, the top entrance to the tube ladder was located at the end of a short dead-end hallway about a hundred feet from the elevator bank. Naomi reached the end first, stopped, and turned around in the white-painted cinder block space. There was nothing there that suggested an entrance, in fact the opposite—everything about this space said, *This is the end*.

There were three larger storage units on each side of the hallway, the big two-hundred-square-foot jobs that were mostly used by factories storing overstocks. But there was no door or hatchway or obvious entrance of any kind, except for a small, narrow cabinet between two units marked STAFF ONLY.

Naomi looked from the map, to the hallway, to the map. "I don't get it."

"You're sure it's here?"

She held the map out to him. "Look for yourself."

He took the phone, held the map one way, then the other, slid it around a bit. Naomi went to the far wall, the dead end, and smacked it a few times here and there with the flat of her hand. Solid. She knocked, tapped with a fist.

"Cinder block," she said. "If it's behind here, we'd need a sledgehammer. Or a jackhammer."

"Yeah, I'm not down for that."

Teacake turned the phone upside down, looking at the schematic again. He looked down at the floor. *That's interesting, man.*

He zipped the keys out of his key ring again—had to admit, he loved the metallic *zing* that it made whenever he pulled them out, he'd never been a person who had more than one key before this job—and went to the narrow maintenance cabinet. He opened the cabinet, took a claw hammer off a tool rack, and went back to the same spot in the hallway where he'd been standing, about three feet from the cinder block dead end. He moved till his back was against the wall, got down on all fours, and tapped the hammer once on the floor. It made an unpromising *chunk* sound.

"That's concrete," she said.

"Yup."

He crawled forward, brought the hammer down again. Same sound. He kept crawling, tapping the hammer every six inches or so, getting the same sound every time.

"It's a concrete floor, Travis."

"Weird to hear my real name." He kept moving, kept tapping the hammer on the floor.

"Sorry," she said. "It bothers you?"

"Can't decide." Yes, he could, and he already had. It didn't bother him; he loved it. His heart skipped a beat every time she said his name. He couldn't wait till she said it again. *Please say it again, just one more time?*

THWUNG. He'd nearly reached the center of the hallway, and when he brought the hammer down there it produced a hollow, metallic echo.

He looked up at Naomi. She grinned and squatted down on the floor next to him. He held up the phone, swiping to enlarge a certain portion of the screen. "Right there. That semicircle made of dashes, kinda shaded gray, can you see it?"

"Yeah, barely."

"That's the entrance. They just painted over it."

Together, they looked down at the floor. He spun the hammer around in his hand a couple of times, thinking. He sat back.

"Okay, look. There's no way we could hide this shit we're about to do."

"What are we about to do?"

"Wreck some more stuff," he said. "But here's how I see it. Part of our job is security, and there's an *alarm* going off, a'ight? It's too late to call Griffin, he's wasted by now, and he wouldn't know what the fuck it is anyway. He'd just call corporate, but there's nobody at corporate either, it's not like there are self-storage emergencies and they got operators standing by, see what I'm saying? The only other people I can think of to call are the cops."

"To say there's an old smoke alarm or something going off in the basement?"

"Exactly. Ridiculous. But here we are, and there's an alarm going off, and this whole place is stuffed to the rafters with incredibly valuable personal belongings."

"Right! This stuff is *meaningful* to people."

"This is true, what you're saying. I've always felt that way." He was warming up to it now, feeling the creative buzz of getting your story straight with somebody. "There is an *alarm* going off, and we are *guards*. We are people of the security profession."

"We're more like clerks."

"Stay with me. Yes, it is a shitty job, but it is *our* job."

"It's our responsibility."

"Yes!"

"Plus we're curious," she added.

"Yeah, but we leave that part out." She wasn't a natural at lying. That's all right, he knew enough about it for both of them. "A'ight? We in?"

"You know I am."

"Watch your eyes."

She raised a hand and turned away, and he spun the hammer around so it was claw-end down and swung it at the floor, hard. The hollow metallic boom was louder, there was definitely something down there, and it wasn't cement floor. Chunks of dried paint flew. He swung again, two, three, four times in quick succession, and more paint flecked away. On the last blow a two-inch-square section flew off and gave them a good look at the unfinished surface beneath.

There, under several layers of long-dried oil-based semigloss gray floor paint, were the unmistakable metal dimples of a manhole cover.

TWELVE

It had been five or six years since Roberto Diaz had gotten a call in the middle of the night. It was a fluke that the phone even rang on his bedside table; since retirement he'd gotten in the habit of turning the thing off around nine at night and not turning it back on again until he'd had at least one cup of coffee in the morning. He'd been much happier ever since. Mellower, anyway. Annie couldn't quite get there with her devices; she always left her phone on in case one of the kids needed anything, but their youngest was twenty-eight, so chances of that were slim. Still, she liked to check the *New York Times* in bed first thing after she woke up to see if the world had improved in the last eight hours. Strangely, it never had, but Annie was not one to give up hope.

Tonight Roberto had forgotten, left his phone on by accident, and it's funny how the old reflexes kicked in when the thing rang shortly after midnight. He was wide-awake before the echo of the first ring had even faded, had his hand on the phone by the time the second ring started, and was sitting up with both feet on the floor when he answered.

"Hell," he croaked.

Whoops. No voice. Not quite the old reflexes. He cleared his throat and tried again.

"Hello."

"Roberto Diaz?" It was a woman's voice.

"Speaking."

"I'm calling about the 1978 Plymouth Duster for sale."

He didn't answer for a long moment.

"Mr. Diaz?"

"Give me five minutes." He hung up and set the phone back down on the dresser. He just sat there for a few seconds, thinking. He regretted the second glass of wine at dinner, but other than that he didn't feel much of anything at all. That's how you knew you were good, when the call didn't change anything, emotionally. He counted a few breaths, stayed cool, and let the Buddhist mantra he'd discovered in his early fifties float through his mind.

I'm here now.

He wanted a cup of tea before he called back.

Annie turned and looked at him over her shoulder, squinting into the dark. "Who was that?"

"My other wife."

"How can you be funny right away in the middle of the night?"

"It's a gift."

She fumbled around on her night table, feeling for something and not finding it, knocking a few things around.

He looked at her. "What are you doing?"

"Looking for my glasses."

"Why?"

She rolled over and looked at him. "I don't know."

She glanced around the room, as if to make sure everything was still in its place, then turned back to him. "One of the kids?"

"No. Don't worry."

She paused. "Oh God."

If it wasn't one of the kids and he hadn't yet told her that somebody they knew was dead, then it could only be Them. It was more of a tired "oh God" that she let out than a fearful "oh God," the kind of "oh God" you'd say if you found out the cable had gone out again.

"Yep."

"Who?"

"New voice to me. Somebody's having a panic attack."

He leaned over and kissed her on the forehead. He never had cheated on her, or even thought about flirting anymore, after the experience in Australia. He was grateful for that, and for her, every day. "Go back to sleep," he said. "I'll make it quick."

He got up and pulled on the clean shirt and pair of pants he kept hung over the chair so they'd be easy to find in the dark. Talk about old habits.

Annie rolled over and snuggled back into her pillow. "Don't make it too quick. Wait till I'm asleep again, okay?"

"Wasn't born yesterday, gorgeous."

She muttered something sweet and inaudible and was back asleep by the time the door closed. The unexpected was still routine, even after all this time, and the calls had stopped seriously disrupting her sleep years ago.

Roberto loved being in the North Carolina house more than any other place he'd ever owned, rented, or visited. It wasn't a great house, not by a long shot. It was late '80s construction and the walls were too thin; you could hear water in the pipes no matter where you were. They probably should have torn the whole thing down and built a new one ten years ago when they bought it, but aside from the fact that it would have cost a fortune they didn't have, a teardown seemed incredibly wasteful. Mean, almost. The house had behaved well in the world, it had done what was asked of it with minimal complaint for twenty years, and it deserved better than a bulldozer.

They bought it as is, recognizing its flaws, and made plans to repair and remodel in two stages. They fixed and painted the inside first, right after they bought it, and put off the decaying exterior for as long as possible, until the rotting porch and the leaking roof and the patchy siding, riddled with wasp nests, could no longer be ignored. Finally, they took a deep breath, got out the checkbook, and started the exterior work four years ago, just before they both retired.

They ran out of cash with half the roof and none of the porches done.

They didn't actually run out of money, not literally, but there were financial lines they had long ago said they'd never cross, loans they would not take out, T-bills that would not be sold, and dammit if they were about to break their own rules now, when they were so close to having enough to leave a decent college fund for each of the grandkids.

So Roberto learned roofing himself, and how to build a deck, and how to grin and put up with the manly condescension when he went back to the hardware store for the third time in the same day with more dumb questions. Just before Thanksgiving of last year, two and a half years after the last professional help had left the premises, almost four years after they'd started work on the outside, and a full decade after they'd bought the place, the house at 67 Figtree Road was done.

There was a chair on the back porch, a rocker that was good for Roberto's bad back, just to the left of the screen door. It was his favorite spot in the world as he knew it, and he knew a fair amount of the world. That spot was where he sat now, waiting for the kettle to boil, wondering at the warm, misty March air that should have been neither warm nor misty.

Back in the kitchen, he got to the kettle before it had a chance for a full-throated scream. He poured the hot water into the strainer. He stared out the window while he let it steep—$6,200 to move the kitchen window from the driveway side to the backyard side, the most extravagant thing he had ever done, and he regretted it for not one minute since—and poured a few drops of milk into the tea after exactly three minutes. He'd picked up the milk habit while on the London detail. Turns out the milk cuts the tiny bit of acidity in the tea leaves. The things you learn.

He took a sip and went to the broom closet on the far side of the room. It was a funny angled one that wasn't much good at holding anything, but it was the compromise solution to a thorny electrical problem he'd run into when he insisted on designing and building this one corner of the cabinetry himself. He'd allowed no help from anyone else, wouldn't even let anybody in the room while he was working on it.

Now Roberto took the brooms and mops out of the closet, pulled out the tall vases from where they were stored in the back, and took out the small mixer that couldn't seem to find a home anyplace else. He used a hidden key to unlock the lock on the angled panel inside, swung it open, and entered the combination into the safe.

He felt a tiny surge of adrenaline when he threw the safe handle and it made that solid, satisfying clunking sound. It wasn't excitement, far from it, but something more like self-preservation, the old system gearing up in case it was needed. Fight or fight.

The safe was small. It didn't need much in it, just a few currencies and passports that were probably expired by now. It wasn't a proper run box anymore, just a place to put the secure phone and the snow globe, the one they'd bought at a gas station in Vermont, the slightly cheesy one they couldn't resist because it had three kids sledding inside it, two girls and a boy, like theirs. He took out the emergency phone, turned it on, and the screen showed the dull red outline of a battery with a big red line through it. Roberto was surprised it even had that much juice in it. He grabbed the cord, plugged it in by the sink, and looked out the window, drinking his tea while he waited for it to charge up.

After a while, the phone binged and turned itself on. He looked at it for an extra moment, not thinking much but not grabbing it either. He wasn't going to rush; it was just over five minutes now since he'd asked for that many, and the world wasn't going to end if he took an extra thirty seconds. That was one of the nice things about being older, how comfortable you became with the idea of conservation of energy, of deliberateness of style. Youth was all wasted movement and noise production, thinking that the more you looked like you were doing something, the more you really were, when in fact the opposite was most often true. Do you have the patience to remain completely still until the dirty water settles and you can see clearly? Not if you're under fifty, you don't.

When he was ready, Roberto dialed. The phone rang once, and the same woman's voice answered.

"Fenelon Imports."

"Zero-four-seven-four blue indigo."

"Thank you, Mr. Diaz."

"What's up?"

"We're getting a temperature breach alert from a decommissioned facility in the Atchison mines in eastern Kansas."

He paused. *I'm here now.*

"Mr. Diaz?"

"Yeah. I'd wondered about that. Given the weather changes."

"Are you—"

"I wrote a memo in 1997 on that very subject," he said.

"I don't see it in the file."

"And I called, about five years after that. And six or seven years after that."

"So you are familiar with that situation?" she asked.

"Yes."

"Is it something we need to worry about?"

"Yes, it's something you need to worry about."

"We thought, as a decommissioned facility—"

"What time did the alert come in?" he asked.

He heard a pause and some keys clicking while she checked on a computer. "Three eleven P.M. central standard time."

"And you're just calling me now?"

"It took some time to figure out whom to call."

"What if I didn't answer?" he asked. "Who does it say you call next?"

"It doesn't."

Roberto took a breath and looked out the window. "Okay. I'm seventy-three miles from Seymour Johnson. I can be there in ninety minutes. I'll need a plane from there and a car waiting on the other end. I'll drive the car myself. Nobody else goes."

"Is it your opinion that this qualifies as a Heightened Threat?"

"My opinion is it qualified as an Exceptional Threat at three eleven P.M."

She paused. "I'll see what I can do about transportation."

"I'm not finished. I don't have any equipment."

"What do you need?"

"Everything on the list."

"I'm sorry, Mr. Diaz, I'm just not familiar with—"

"I wrote an ECI white paper in '92. It's compartmented and stored in the clean vault. It was twenty-five years ago, you'll need different software to read it, but I archived the program along with it and a floppy drive to run it. Get Gordon Gray to clear you. Only Gordon Gray, you don't need to call anybody else. Read the report and have everything listed in appendix A—I mean *everything*, every single thing—in the car in Kansas when I land. Understood?"

"I can't do all that without multiple authorizations."

"What's your name?"

"You know we're not—"

"Just your first one. Even a fake one. Something to call you."

She hesitated. "Abigail."

Definitely not her real name, the slight rise in

her voice gave that away. She enjoyed the flight of fancy. Good for her, it's probably why she got into this line of work and she didn't get to use it much, handling dead-file outcalls at Fort Belvoir in the middle of the night.

"Okay, Abigail. Remember those good grades you got in high school? And the sports you trained your ass off for? The college you fought to get into. The number of times you said no when people wanted to go out and party and you knew you had to stay in and study. Remember the looks your family gave you when you told them what you wanted to do for a living, the abuse you put up with your first year in the department, and the personal life you've given up for the last, I don't know, from your voice it sounds like maybe ten, twelve years now?"

"Eight."

"Okay, so it's getting to you quick. That happens. But all those sacrifices, all the shit you've had to eat just because you wanted to do what was right for your country? *This* is what it was for, Abigail."

"Yes, sir."

He could tell by the tiny quaver in her voice that he could still give a good *we're in the shit now* speech when he needed it.

"Get the stuff on the list. I'll be at Seymour at two fifteen A.M. EST."

He hung up.

ANNIE WOKE UP, UNPROMPTED, ABOUT TWO HOURS later. Fast asleep one second, wide-awake the next. She came out to the kitchen, where there was one light on, over the sink. She knew what she'd find in there even before she came in the room. Roberto would have washed and dried the mug from his tea and put it away, the same with the strainer. The kitchen would be unchanged from the way they'd left it when they went to bed, except for the snow globe. It would be sitting on the counter next to the coffee machine, on top of a single sheet of plain white paper, on which he would have drawn a heart with a red Sharpie.

That's how it was.

Annie stared at the snow globe for a moment. She picked it up and gave it a shake. Snow fell on the kids and their sleds. On the one hand, it was kind of nice to see the thing again; it had been more than three years since it had been out of the safe.

On the other hand, she wished to hell they'd picked something else to use for the signal.

THE NEXT FOUR HOURS

THIRTEEN

However long most people imagine it takes to chip half a dozen coats of dried paint and a thin overspread of concrete away from the grooved edge that runs around a manhole cover, it was way longer than Teacake and Naomi had figured. If they hadn't found the wide-slotted screwdriver in the tool cabinet, they might never have gotten it open at all.

They took turns with the tools. You couldn't strike more than six or seven hammer blows in a row without needing a break from the painful vibrations that shot through your hands, as if you'd just hit an inside fastball with the thin end of the bat. Twice Teacake hit the screwdriver too hard. He'd thrown both tools down and rolled around on the floor, clutching his palms between his thighs, showing off the breadth and originality of his curse-word vocabulary. Naomi was more methodical, aiming her blows carefully and measuring their impact. Her progress was steady and considered, and hers was the final blow, the one that chipped away the last chunk of paint and concrete and made the cover move a fraction of an inch.

"You got it."

"Get the pry bar," she said.

He grabbed it from the closet, wedged it into one of the four slots evenly spaced around the circumference of the cover. The metal disk came up with a slight whoosh of decompression as the fetid air from below swapped places with the clean air above. Teacake wedged the bar in farther, pushed down on it as hard as he could, and got the handle end almost all the way down to the floor.

"Stand on it!" he told her.

She did, one foot at a time, pinning the bar to the ground once all her weight was on it. Teacake wiggled his fingers into the three-inch gap between the cover and the ground.

"Don't put your fingers in there," she said, but he didn't answer, because they were this far, and there was no other obvious, easy way. Plus she hadn't said it with much conviction, and he knew that what she really meant was "Put your fingers in there!"

But that was okay, because they were on the same page at this point, in it together all the way.

He strained like hell, wishing he'd stayed with the chest and upper-body work he'd done for a year and a half at Ellsworth. He would have dearly loved for her to see some of that now, because he had been cut, man, and he'd been really proud of it, it was such a change, he'd been a skinny kid for as long as he could remember.

But almost the minute he got out he felt puffy and ridiculous, so he'd cut out the gym work and hadn't missed it at all. Well, maybe he missed the feelings right after, when everything was flowing and you felt sort of happy and angry at the same time, that sensation was cool, but really, if she could have seen him then *although you know I don't look that bad now, was she just looking at my biceps a second ago? or, oh shit!* His mind had wandered and he was losing his grip, the thing was slipping, he was going to drop it.

Teacake dug in, snapped back into the moment, bent his knees, and got the cover up past the tipping point. He leveraged it onto its edge and had planned to lay it down the same way he picked it up, but his muscles were screaming at him now: *Why didn't you do this when we were built for it, asshole?!* As soon as he got it all the way up on its edge, he gave the manhole cover a shove and it rolled away, toward the wall.

It didn't go far, though. It must have weighed two hundred pounds, maybe two-fifty, and after six or seven feet it started to tilt over and arc back, rolling right toward them. They danced out of the way, absurdly, as the thing chased them for a few feet, pissed off at having been awakened from its comfortable slumber. The metal rim ground across the floor a few inches from their toes, described one last dying circle in the hallway, and very nearly fell right back into the hole it had just been covering. *That* would have been a scream.

It settled like a spinning quarter on a table-top, making a grinding cast-iron racket until it finally came to a rest, upside down, just in front of them.

When the echo faded, Teacake spoke. "You know, like, looking back? Maybe I could have just slid it to the side a little bit."

"Well, sure, we know that *now*."

If he didn't love her already, he loved her for not telling him he was a fucking idiot the way his old man would have. She didn't say much, but when she did talk it wasn't to give anybody shit, not even as a joke.

Naomi picked up the flashlight, the one he'd grabbed upstairs. She clicked it on. They walked forward to the edge of the hole, got down on all fours, and shined the light down into it.

The light was bright, the batteries fresh, but there isn't much any flashlight can do to illuminate a vertical cylindrical shaft that runs three hundred feet straight down into the earth. The metal ladder ran along one side of it. A ton of newly raised dust floated in the stale air, stirred by the removal of the lid, but other than that there was only the dark.

They looked at each other. Neither one of them wanted to back down, and neither wanted to go first.

"Climb fifty feet down and then we talk again?" she proposed.

"How many rungs is that on the ladder?"

She shined the light down at the corrugated metal rungs and estimated. "Fifty, probably. Why?"

"I don't know, I was hoping it would help."

She shined the light down into the hole again, playing it around the edges this time instead of straight into the black. Some distance below, there was the dim outline of an indentation in the side of the shaft, too far away to see clearly, but there was at least something there, some kind of goal.

"Okay, look. Let's go to that thing—"

"What thing?"

"Over here."

She gestured for him to come around to her side and he did, moving up against her on the floor. His leg touched hers, just barely, but he was keenly aware of it. She traced the light beam around the edges of the indentation.

"There. What is that, thirty feet maybe? We'll climb down to that, see what it is."

"And then what?"

"Then we'll talk. If it's cool, we keep going. If it isn't—"

He waved off the rest of her sentence. "I get it." He took the light from her, swung his legs around, and started to climb down into the hole.

"You don't have to go first."

"I'm a gentleman. I'll go first and shine the light up, so you can see."

"You have to admit," she said. "So far this is cool."

"So far, I have to admit this is cool."

"You really think so?"

"No, I'm just repeating what you told me I had to say. See you in thirty feet."

She laughed, and he started down into the shaft.

Climbing with one hand was harder than he thought, but he was so afraid of dropping the flashlight he didn't even try to use the other. One hand holding tight on the light and the other clamped in a death lock on the vertical bar of the metal ladder, he broke a sweat within ten or fifteen rungs, more from fear than anything else.

Then his mind got the best of him. It started to wander, as it did, and he thought about falling. First a foot slipping off a rung, then his shin banging into it, the painful stretch of tendons as his legs split apart, both hands flailing at the bars, maybe one or two fingers snapping, trying to support his falling weight as his body gained momentum. And then the moment of detachment—the cartoon suspension as his hands flailed at empty space and his feet popped free. Would he scream? Or would he go silent, would all sound drain away as his eyes popped wide and his mouth opened in a horrified, perfect round O shape, making a soundless plea for help as he began to drop, into the darkness, a hundred, five hundred, a thousand feet straight down, until he hit the cement floor at the bottom, feet first, his legs accordioning into his body, the long bones slamming upward into his internal organs, his femur or tibia or whatever the big one was slicing up, through his intestines, piercing his heart and driving itself up into the base of his skull.

Official cause of death: "man killed by own leg bone."

Then another scenario occurred to him, one in which he did not fall free. In this chain of events, one foot wouldn't slip away clean, it'd get hung up in the rungs instead. He'd fall, but his body would flop over backward, bending at the left knee, and he'd hear the ligaments on both sides of the kneecap pop as it wrenched at an unnatural angle, bearing weight and torque it had never been designed to withstand. In this version he'd scream, all right, shriek like a wounded animal as he hung there, his shredded knee holding him, upside down, head banging against the metal rungs beneath him. The flashlight would slip from his hand and fall, the beam throwing crazy, bouncing light over the inside of the shaft as it dropped, finally smashing to bits on the floor far below.

Naomi would shout from above and try to save him. She'd climb down three rungs, loop one arm in, and lean down as far as she could, flailing for Teacake in the near-total darkness. But she'd miss his outstretched hand and lose her own grip. Now she'd fall, and she *would* fall clean, down three feet and right into Teacake. Their combined weight would dislocate his knee and break the tibia of his trapped leg (in both versions the tibia lost big), and the fractured leg would slither, formless, through the rungs of the ladder. They'd both pull free. The ending would be pretty much the same as before, it wouldn't be the fall that did it so much as the sudden stop at the end. Except this time Teacake would land upside down and the cause of death would be changed to "man falls on head," while hers would read "woman dies from hanging out with moron who climbed down a dark, vertical cement shaft with one hand."

Teacake's mind hadn't just drifted, it had gone off on a little *Wanderjahr*, but at least it had killed some time and they'd already gone down thirty-four rungs, reaching the gray indentation they'd seen from above. Crooking one arm through the rungs, Teacake brought his feet together, steadied himself, and turned the light to shine it on the side of the concrete shaft.

"It's a door."

Naomi came down to just above him and looked at it. Three characters, and in retrospect they didn't have to climb down here to hazard a good guess as to what they said.

SB-2.

She nodded. "Yeah, that's what I figured. Want to keep going?"

Teacake didn't think he'd gotten what he'd paid for yet. He hadn't smashed up his employer's wall, hammered through a cement floor, and vividly pictured two distinct and gruesome versions of his own death so he could stare at a closed door with SB-2 written on it in faded black letters.

Without answering her, he shoved the flashlight in his pants pocket, still switched on and with the beam pointing upward so it could light her way. With both hands free, he'd move a lot faster.

They continued down.

FOURTEEN

After Mooney had thrown up onto the gravel behind the tailpipe, after he'd hacked and spit and blown his nose till it was raw inside, after he'd used the dirty beach towel from the back seat to clean every speck of cat gut off his face, he was able to think straight. Sort of. He couldn't get a handle on the whole thing, because it was ungraspable, but he'd at least managed to calm his breathing and get his heart rate down to almost normal levels, and to stop squealing "God, Jesus, oh Jesus, God, what the fuck," or close variations thereof, every few seconds.

As soon as he was clean, a powerful thirst overtook him, and he was relieved to see the lone remaining wine cooler was still mostly full, the cap only loosened in the moment before he hit the deer. He picked it up out of the Exotic Berry puddle it had made on the passenger-side floor mat and finished it in one long gulp. It was warm now, which made the liquor feel stronger, and stronger was what he needed. A little courage washed through his brain, a familiar feeling, but different too. He could feel himself becoming stronger, calmer, better.

He was also becoming a walking dispersal mechanism for *Cordyceps novus*. Mooney was the twenty-eighth human being to be infected by the fungus, but there was an important difference between him and the others. Bartles & Jaymes, like many wine coolers and wine products in general, uses the maximum amount of sulfur dioxide permitted by FDA regulations as a preservative. SO_2 is one of the most effective antimicrobials on the planet and is highly antagonistic to growth. In its gaseous form, SO_2 can be lethal to any air-breathing creature and is in fact the leading cause of death in a volcanic eruption. It's the poison gas that gets you, not the lava.

But in liquid form, and in the right concentration, SO_2 can be quite helpful. It not only prevents invasive microbial growth in human digestive systems, but it can actually clean and preserve a glass wine container itself, during both the fermentation and the storage process.

Mooney's last bottle of Exotic Berry, aside from being tasty and intoxicating, was also a superb growth inhibitor. Whereas the fungus's takeover of its previous human victims had been a blitzkrieg, in Mooney's wine-cooler-besotted state, it was more of a slow and steady infantry assault through mud. The invading army of *Cordyceps novus* was going to win, Mooney was going to lose, but it would take a while.

Having unwittingly bought himself a few extra hours on the planet, he stood back from the car to review the events of the previous couple of hours.

There was a lot to review. The deer had been *dead*, there was no question about it. Same for Mr. Scroggins; the cat was missing half a face and skull. The notion of him surviving that kind of mutilation was laughable. That could only mean that something otherworldly was going on, something unholy. Whatever. The universe was a fucked-up place, with lots of shit he'd never understand.

But what about me? *Specifically, me, Mooney, where do I stand in all this? What did I really* do, *after all?* Mooney had an analytical mind, sometimes, so he put it to use. *What's the worst that can happen to me? Yes, I hit a deer; yes, I pumped it full of lead; and yes, I killed a sick cat, but none of these were crimes.* Burying them on somebody else's privately owned land probably was, but he hadn't done that, he hadn't had a chance. The dead deer had run away, and the half cat climbed a tree and exploded. It's as simple as that, Officer.

So, Fear of Police could be dismissed. He'd done nothing illegal. That left only Fear of Societal Condemnation and Fear of God. Well, the only way society was going to condemn him was if it knew he was a weirdo and an animal killer, and there was no evidence of that other than whatever was left in the trunk. He edged over to the car, the first time he'd come within six feet of it since its occupants decamped. There were no guts in the empty trunk, that was good, but the deer had bled a fair amount. It had also left some weird green-brown ooze that covered half the floor of the trunk. Must be the shit that comes out of you when you die or something.

Whatever, this could all be cleaned up, this was totally doable. This was a garden hose, a couple of old towels, and maybe twenty minutes of his time. Nobody would ever know. So Fear of Societal Condemnation was off the list too.

Unfortunately, that left the biggie. God knew. God knew *all* this shit, and He could not possibly be pleased. It wasn't that Mooney feared for his soul; his personal concept of God was a bit more baroque, more Old Testament. He'd seen enough of life to know that God was big into retribution, and the sicker and more ironic the better. Yes, He was kind and loving, but He also invented colorectal cancer, and is there a super-villain anywhere, ever, who came up with a more diabolical way to take somebody out than that? Don't bother checking, there isn't.

Yes, God had most certainly taken note of what Mooney had done tonight, disapproved, and started unleashing His righteous fury. Bringing the innocent creatures back to life to torture him had been step one, spattering his face with offal was step two, and Mooney knew for certain he didn't want to wait for steps three, four, and five, whatever they might be.

He needed to apologize.

The last time he'd decided he owed God a mea culpa it had cost him almost four years of his life, but he was hoping he could wrap this one up in a couple hours on his knees. St. Benedict's Abbey on Second Street was open all night, and he'd used it before when he needed to atone. The place was run by actual monks, a Franciscan order, and the black cowled robes conveyed a judgmental asceticism that felt pretty legit. The modish wooden pews couldn't have been Vatican approved, but there was a granite slab that ran the length of the floor in front of the altar, and Mooney had spent many hours on his knees there, praying for divine forgiveness of one sort or another. The stone was pockmarked and uneven, so after the first five minutes his knees would start to ache, and by the time a full hour had passed he would be in so much pain he couldn't focus. When his transgression was bad enough, Mooney would stay so long that the skin would grind into the inside of his pants, and when he stood, whole layers of flesh would tear away. By the time he got in the car, the blood would be seeping through the knees of his pants, and that was the sign that he'd done things right and they were square.

Of course, there was the time no amount of penance at the abbey was enough. To all of those prayers, God's answer had been a consistent "Fuck no." Half an hour on his knees, to ask for the strength to resist her? No. A full hour on his knees, to ask for forgiveness after he fucked her and, more important, might I please just this one time have a pass on consequences, could she please not be pregnant? Nope. Another two hours, to ask God to guide her with His wisdom and judgment and convince her to marry him?

Forget it, asshole. And, finally, he'd spent three days on his knees, coupled with fasting so severe that he'd fainted; he fainted so many times that Brother Dennis had asked him to either stop coming or at least use a kneeler.

But the object of those prayers was vehemently denied as well. The baby did not die in utero, the baby was not stillborn, the baby was healthy and was his daughter, his bastard daughter with Naomi Williams. Though the entire rest of the Snyder family had forgiven him, it was abundantly clear that God in Heaven had not and did not intend to do so for a good long while.

Mike—he was still Mike back then—came across Luke 12:48 the day after she'd brought the baby home from the hospital. "But the one who does not know and does things deserving punishment will be beaten with few blows. From everyone who has been given much, much will be demanded; and from the one who has been entrusted with much, much more will be asked."

Clearly, God was not screwing around this time. He was demanding an Isaac-in-the-desert-type sacrifice, and Mike Snyder just had to figure out what it was.

The advantages of joining the Peace Corps were numerous—escape, the chance to serve his fellow man, escape, a settling of accounts with the Lord, and, oh yeah, escape.

Sadly, they rejected him. Turns out the Peace Corps looks for college graduates with decent résumés and real skills. You know, people who actually have something to offer. Who knew?

Service Brigade, Inc., however, would take just about anybody, provided you were not currently under indictment in your country of origin. The brigade had a contract with the Ugandan government to build affordable housing for a modest fee, which in local terms meant a fee that was highly inflated and heavily kicked back to the government officials who distributed it. Whatever, Mike was out of a bad situation at home, Service Brigade was willing to pay him a decent amount under the table, and his family thought he was a saint, so he took it.

Within a few weeks of his arrival in Uganda, the local workers he was teamed with started calling him Muni, short for Muniyaga. He liked the sound of it, so even after he found out that Muniyaga means "one who bothers other people" in some goddamn African language or another, he stayed with his new name.

He was Mooney. It was a fresh start.

He'd returned home to Atchison just a few months ago, was given a hero's welcome and drawn into the uncomfortably tight embrace of his family once again. He'd regretted coming back almost the minute he got there, as soon as he felt their brimming eyes on him, judging the living shit out of him, telling him they forgave him for everything, for his weakness, for his cowardice, for what had turned out to be his complete lack of artistic ability.

They'd tried to get him to take an interest in his daughter, to at least go see Sarah, but that wasn't going to happen. Her mother, sure, that'd be hot, but not the kid, never the kid. But Naomi wouldn't see him at all.

Three days after coming home, Mike had started planning how to get out again. Maybe he'd meet his buddy Daniel Mafabi back in Budadiri, where Mafabi had worked out a sweet deal with the Ministry of Works and Transport to build schools all across the country at double cost. There were a lot of Ugandan shillings sloshing around the budget since Nakadama took office, and Mike knew the people who knew the people. Another couple of years over there and he'd be sitting on enough cash to split on his family for good, to never ever have to hear that they'd forgiven him again.

But God was another matter. *Those* eyes followed him wherever he went, so tonight he needed to get his ass to St. Benedict's, make his apologies, and call this awful night to an end.

He got in the car, turned the key, and it clicked.

Of course.

He tried again.

Not even a grind, just a click. Dead starter. He got out of the car and slammed the door as hard as he could. It bounced open, so he slammed it even harder, then kicked it square in the middle, leaving a good-sized dent. One more thing for the insurance report. He looked around, assessing the middle-of-nowhereness of it all.

The car at the bottom of the hill caught his eye again. It was parked near the entrance to the storage place, just under a mercury-vapor light that lit up the parking lot. In the yellowy haze of the light, he could see the rear end of the car, a ten-year-old Toyota Celica. It rang a distant bell somewhere in his mind. He started walking down the driveway, toward the car, and as he got closer he saw a sticker on the back left bumper. Closer still and he could make out what it said.

PROUD PARENT OF AN AHS HONOR ROLL STU-DENT 2012.

Unbelievable. He knew that car; it was Naomi's parents' car, or it used to be. It was probably hers now. He'd had some good times in that car. He started to smile and walk faster, drawn to the car as if by the ghosts of make-outs past. He'd heard she was going to school and working nights someplace; evidently she was here, right here where he needed her, when he needed her, and if that wasn't Providence speaking to him, what was? Mike took a deep breath of the moist night air, feeling better now, definitely better, thinking more clearly—

go inside and find Naomi, that's what I'll do, find Naomi, find Naomi

—growing more comfortable in his body and mind, improving by the minute. He walked faster, stretching out his neck.

Everything was going to be okay. Naomi would be so happy to see him.

Things were clarifying.

FIFTEEN

Teacake and Naomi had reached the bottom of the ladder, and *damn* it felt good to put his feet on solid ground again. The flashlight in his pocket had been shining upward the whole way and Teacake had long since settled into a kind of trance, his body moving mechanically—step down, slide hands, step down, slide hands, step down, slide hands—no use looking down since it was all just a big black inky puddle down there. Step down, slide hands. He'd hesitated briefly when they reached the gray door for SB-3, but Naomi hadn't even bothered to look down, and if she had he would've grinned and kept on, knowing perfectly well neither one of them would settle for anything less than making it all the way to the bottom at this point.

So they'd continued on, and that's when the climb got long. Really long. From the schematic he would have guessed the lowermost floor to be about a hundred feet below SB-3, but now that he thought about it, that section of the drawing had been broken by a jagged line with a space through it, which must have meant a whole lot of earth was left out. Step down, slide hands, keep going. His mind had gone for a little stroll, a pleasant one this time, since the only thing that was illuminated in the area was above him, and the only thing he could see clearly up there was Naomi's backside. He refrained from calling it or thinking about it as her ass, it was her backside, and it was a very nice one, but hang on, that's exactly what he was trying not to think about, out of respect.

He wondered what they would do if they went out on a date, since she didn't drink. Truth was, he didn't like alcohol as much as he used to; it made his moods unpredictable. He'd get mad when he shouldn't, happy for no reason, and wasted people bugged him more as he got older. Plus there was the waking up in the night—he couldn't sleep twelve hours at a time like he could even a few years ago. Too bad, he missed those days, but he'd noticed the mornings when he was 100 percent clearheaded were kind of cool. So, okay, that's all right, but when people don't drink or get high, like, what do they do around here?

He imagined the two of them jacked out of their minds on coffee, but who wants that?, and then he pictured them working out together and she was very sweaty and glisteny man was she put together tight and whoops, hang on, things were headed off in that direction again, so then he saw them taking her daughter to the movies. And maybe the kid got scared at one point and jumped in his lap, and he'd say that's okay, you're okay, kid, turn your head away, hide your eyes and I'll cover your ears, I'll tell you when it's safe to come out, I'll protect you, and Naomi would look over at him and she'd smile, he was good with kids, he didn't mind them after all, maybe he could actually—

In the end, he did fall. But it was only one step. His right foot hit bottom, hard, he hadn't seen it coming, he lost his balance, and his left slipped off the last rung. He oofed, Naomi turned, and he reached a hand up to help her.

"Careful."

She took his hand, he helped her off the last rung, and they stood together at the bottom. It was colder down here, maybe sixty degrees, and surprisingly humid. He pulled the flashlight out of his pocket and shined it upward, till the light disappeared into the endless black tunnel, now above them. He turned it toward the door in front of them. It was another gray indentation, but this one was bigger than the others, heavily reinforced with a series of bars and levers, and had a black stencil spray-painted across it: DTRA ACCESS ONLY.

"What's DTRA?" he asked.

"Let's find out."

She pulled out her phone to google it.

"No signal."

"Shocker."

He thought. He looked at the door, which was more like a submarine hatch, crisscrossed with a complex latticework of steel slats, all joined together at the corners and leading to a large black handle. Pull on the handle, the hinged slats pull against each other, the door opens.

"You want to do it?" she asked him.

"I'd really like to know what those letters stand for."

"Me too."

"I get the feeling that I'd like to know more."

"What if it's 'Don't Touch, Radiation, Asshole'?"

"Yeah, that would be some amusing shit," he said.

"I'm cool if you want to just go back up."

Yeah, yeah. Like that was going to happen. He reached for the handle, but she put her hand on his arm and caught his eye.

"I mean it."

He looked back at her and thought about that for a nanosecond or two, and really, could things have been going any better at this point? There was a kiss moment coming, there had to be, or at least a gripping-each-other-in-fear moment, and he wondered, these kinds of moments with a woman like Naomi, did he think they grew on fucking trees? Not in the barren, rocky ground that had been his love life, they didn't; the seeds of romance had found no purchase there since, oh God, the middle of high school.

No, he was not going back up. They were going to finish this.

The handle moved so much more easily than he thought it would; the door-opening mechanism was a work of engineering genius. You gave one gentle pull on the black bar and the rest of the pieces glided about their business, each tugging on the other with just the right amount of force at precisely the correct angle. Even after decades of disuse, the high-quality metal had not yielded to rust, even in the humid environment. The dozen moving pieces struck up the music in their symphony of movement, and eight deadbolt locks pulled out of the recessed metal slots in the doorjambs where they had rested for the last thirty years. Teacake pushed the door open.

Something rushed out and slammed into them, but it wasn't anything nearly as horrible as what their imaginations had been conjuring. It was cold air. Cool, really, maybe fifty degrees. After the climb down, they'd both worked up a half-decent sweat, so when the blast hit them it woke them right up.

After the cold, the second thing they noticed was the sound, a whooshing that was coming from right over their heads, like water rushing through pipes. Teacake raised his flashlight toward the source of the sound and saw that was exactly what it was. They were standing under water pipes, a dozen of them, side by side, lining the ceiling of the underground tunnel, and water was circulating through them, fast. It was a low ceiling down here, so Teacake stretched up to reach them, and his hand came away wet. The pipes were sweating.

Naomi looked at him. "Hot?"

"Cold. Freezing."

"I don't hear any pumps or anything."

Teacake looked at the moisture on his hand. "But they're sweating. Must be humid down here."

"It is. I can feel it."

"Why would it be humid underground?" he asked.

"Can I see that?"

She meant the flashlight. He handed it to her and she shined it around the place. They were in another long tunnel, a mammoth, concrete-lined underground space. She looked up at the pipes, rushing with water.

"Where's it coming from?" she asked. "Like, an underground cold spring?"

"Guess so."

From the far end of the corridor, they heard a familiar sound.

BEEP.

The goddamn beep again, accompanied simultaneously by a pinpoint of white light, a superbright strobe about twenty yards away.

Naomi turned and looked at him. "Dude, we are *so* close."

BEEP.

He took the light back. "I carry this."

He started down the hallway, shining the light in front of him, following the pipes as they went. She stayed close. The beeping got louder, the strobe brighter as they moved toward it. Farther in, they could make out the shapes of other doorways; it wasn't just a long tunnel, but another level of a storage complex. There were half a dozen doorways on either side of the corridor,

all heavily reinforced steel with the same kind
of complicated locking mechanism as the entry
door had. There were panels and sensors outside
each door, but they were all deactivated.

Two of the doors had been left open altogether,
but a quick shine of the light inside showed them
to be empty, just blank concrete walls and vacant
space. To be fair, there could have been more to
the rooms than that, but Teacake had little interest in going into them, or even diverting the
light away from the path ahead for long enough
to get a good look. He had a plan, a very clear
plan, both short term and long term—shine
light, walk forward, figure out goddamn beeping, get your ass back upstairs, ask for her number, call it a night.

Steps one and two of his plan were going
fine. The beeping continued to get louder, the
strobing light brighter. As they drew close to the
source, though, step three was looking to be a
real bitch. They slowed to a stop at the last door
on the right, where there was a vertical display
panel similar to the one they'd seen upstairs, but
more detailed and covering only the room beyond this door. Many of the sensors and indica-
tors had been deactivated, but there was one that
still worked, and it was going off now—NTC
Thermistor Breach.

Teacake looked up, because the whooshing of
water through corrugated metal pipes was even
louder down at this end of the hall. He shined his
light up at the ceiling and saw that the pipes, all

of them, made a right turn just over their heads and went directly into this room, through half a dozen specially cut holes in the thick concrete outer wall.

BEEP.

There was only one door left. Teacake and Naomi looked at each other. To open or not to open?

She spoke first. "Nah, I'm good."

"Me too."

They turned to get out of there at almost exactly the same moment, like a couple of synchronized swimmers. Enough is enough. Although he had to admit that *was* fun, of course he'd thought something awful was going to happen, but what do you know, it didn't for once, and no, they still didn't know what was defrosting, but they knew enough and they both felt alive and he was definitely getting a phone number out of this.

That's when they heard the squeaking. It had been there all along, they just didn't pick it up until the moment they turned away from the door. It was the squeak of an animal. Or many animals. Teacake swung his flashlight beam over toward it fast, and the light fell on a lump of fur on the floor a few feet behind them.

It looked just like that at first, a chunk of mohair or animal hide, but this thing was *moving*, writhing on the floor. They edged closer, in spite of themselves, the flashlight's pool of light getting smaller and brighter as they drew up on the thing. There was a lot of movement there; the center of the object was fairly still, but all around its edges there were irregular shapes moving independently, stretching and snapping.

They were rats' heads. There were a dozen of them, arranged in a rough circle around a tangled mass of ropy cartilage in the center. It was like staring at an optical illusion at first, trying to figure out what in God's name this thing could be.

It was a rat. It was one rat, but it was also a dozen rats, fused together into one body at the tails, all screeching and snarling and biting at each other. Two or three of the heads were still, cannibalized by their neighbors. Blood dripped from the rats' teeth and flowed from missing ears. The pile of snarling rodents was bound together at their conjoined tails by a strange greenish sap that had oozed over them.

Teacake expressed his feelings. "Jesus fucking *CHRIST*!"

Naomi was repulsed but also fascinated. "It's a Rat King."

"A *what*?!"

"A Rat King. It's a—well, that." She gestured, because there were no words that could take the place of one quick look at the horrific thing. "They wrote about them in the Middle Ages, during the Black Plague. People thought they were a bad omen."

"No *shit* it's a bad omen! It's called a fucking *Rat King*!"

Naomi leaned in to get a closer look. There was an intellectual detachment to her; she was going to make a good vet if she ever got that far. She could look at pain and deformity and see the clinical side of it rather than the emotional one.

Teacake had no clinical side, he was all feeling and freakout, so he kept his distance. "How do they get like that?"

"Nobody knows for sure. Their tails get knotted and stuck together. Like from pine sap or something."

She looked around and picked up a long piece of scrap metal from the floor nearby. She prodded the mass of fused tails. "If they found a dead one of these, they used to preserve it and put it in a museum."

"Yeah, well, that one's not dead, would you get the fuck back, please?"

"What are they gonna do, run up my leg? They can't even move." She got closer, turning on her phone's flashlight again and shining it on the fused tails. From this close she could see that the dull pink cords of the tails were covered over with a lime-green growth of some kind.

"That's not pine sap," she said. She bent closer. "It's like a—a slime mold."

"Yeah? Cool." He looked around. "Coming up on time to go."

But she moved even closer to the squirming rats. They squeaked louder as she drew toward them, thrashing, trying to get at her or get away from her, it was hard to tell which.

"Um, it seems like you're pissing them off."

Naomi's light was close to the snarl of tails. "No, it's not a slime mold, there's no froth. And it seems like it's . . . moving a little bit. Like a fungal ooze, but God, that's a lot of fungus."

Teacake edged a tiny bit closer, shining the more powerful flashlight's beam on the wriggling mass. Moving the light around to get another angle on it, he noticed that the fungal growth wasn't only on the rats' tails. There was a thin smear of it that ran across one side of the Rat King, covering two or three of the entangled animals, and continued onto the floor below. A jagged ribbon of green led away from the rodents, toward the wall. Teacake raised the flashlight beam, following the trail to the wall, where it had crept up onto—or down from—the wall itself, and then across a groove in between cement slabs, all the way to the edge of the door to the sealed room.

He walked closer and saw that the green trail of oozing fungal matter led into one of the deadbolt slots and disappeared into the room itself. From this close, he could feel something emanating from the door.

Heat.

Slowly, he reached out his hand and laid his palm flat against the metal.

BEEP.

He jerked his hand away from the door and nearly jumped out of his skin at that one, because he was standing just a few inches from the thermistor alarm when it went off, and the sound was right in his ear. He shouted in surprise.

Naomi looked up. "What?"

"Door's hot. I mean, the door is *hot*. And the

green shit is coming out of that room, and there's a fucking Rat King, and curiosity is awesome and everything, but I feel like this is about as far as this shit goes for me."

She stood. "Me too."

"Let's get out of here."

"We can't leave them like that, though." She gestured to the rats.

He looked at her, uncomprehending. "What, you want to take them with us?"

"Of course not. But they're suffering."

"Yeah, well, I don't have any Oxy on me."

"I can do it," she said.

He looked down at the metal pipe in her hand. "Are you serious?"

"You want to leave a dozen animals in agony? To starve to death?"

"No, I would like to get the fuck out of here and not think about them."

"Wait by the door, I'll be right there."

"Fine. Cool. You're weird as fuck, but, I don't know, I'm cool with it." He started to walk away.

"Can I have the flashlight?"

"Hell no."

She looked at him.

He clarified. "I mean, um, wouldn't it be better without it? You know, just get the job done? Not have to look at a lot of gross shit?"

"I'm fine. Go ahead."

He felt like a heel and a coward, but he also felt like getting as far away from the whole situation as humanly possible. As far as the fight between his competing needs went, his need to put some distance between himself and the hot room and its weird fungal shit beat his need to impress Naomi in a first-round knockout. He covered the length of the tunnel in about thirty seconds, looking back over his shoulder only once. He caught just a glimpse of her, bending down over the Rat King, staring at it, enthralled. He reached the hatch at the far end and came out into the dark space at the base of the tube ladder.

He'd never been so glad to be at the bottom of a three-hundred-foot concrete shaft in his life. He closed the door most of the way, just enough to not see or hear whatever it was she felt she had to do, and he waited. It took her longer than he thought it should have. But then he'd never had to put a dozen conjoined rats out of their misery, so what did he know about how much time a person needed to get that shit done?

After a few minutes, he got impatient and opened the door to take a look, but he could already see the weak beam of Naomi's phone light coming at him, bouncing as she walked. As she drew close, she switched off her phone and he waved the flashlight beam in her direction, to light her steps. He raised it to her as she got close.

"You get any of that shit on you?" he asked.

"No."

"You sure?"

"I'm sure." She came through the hatch and he closed it, shoving the big black handle into place. The locking mechanism did its job again; it must have been thrilled to get to open and close twice in ten minutes, after decades of just sitting there minding the store. It sealed up the tunnel with a reassuring *chunk* of metal in metal.

Teacake shined the light up the ladder, assessing the climb ahead of them. "You want to go first this time or—"

He didn't see the kiss coming, and if he had the moment to live over again, of course he would have done his part differently. One second he was looking up and talking, and the next he felt her lips on his cheek and her hand on his other cheek, turning him softly toward her. Then they were kissing—well, she was kissing him, really— and it was a soft and sweet and full-lipped kiss, just the right kind. It was over before he'd had a chance to get his bearings, and maybe for that reason it was the perfect first kiss, the kind that leaves you feeling fresh and alive and wanting another one exactly like it.

Because he could not help himself, he spoke.

"Wait, what?"

She smiled. "Thank you. That was bizarre and cool."

Without another word she turned away and started climbing back up the ladder toward the top.

Teacake grinned. Some things you just couldn't call.

"So are you, lady."

He shoved the flashlight back in his pocket and followed her. He smiled all the way up, and he did not look at her ass, not even one time.

SIXTEEN

The moment he pulled onto the base, Roberto knew that Abigail hadn't called Gordon Gray after all. If she had, they wouldn't have stopped him at the back gate on Andrews and sent him around to the main entrance on Pope. He wouldn't have had to wait ten minutes for the two base security lunkheads to put him in a jeep and drive him to the runway, and STRATCOM certainly would not have put him in the care of the 416th Fighter Squadron, with a priority clearance and a passenger manifest that showed up on every screen in Omaha.

Gordon would have moved with speed and with stealth. Roberto would have taken off fifteen minutes ago on an already scheduled flight of the 916th Air Refueling Wing, just another retired officer hitching a free ride west to see the kids. He would have been the kind of old duffer the pilots barely even notice and certainly don't chart. Instead, he was alone in the back of a C-40A, as obvious and traceable as the air force could possibly make him.

Darn it. It was such a good speech to Abigail too; he'd really thought he'd put the fear of God into her. Six or seven minutes after takeoff, the phone rang in the burnished walnut cabinet next to his absurdly comfortable leather chair, and he picked it up.

"Hello."

"Designator, please?"

"I had such high hopes for you, Abigail."

"Could you please tell me your designator?"

"I guess I might have done the same thing at your age. All right, we can recover. Makes everything a little harder, but we'll fix it."

She hung up.

Of course, he'd known she'd hang up. She had to. He was just having a little fun with her. He had to admit, even though he was tired and even though the fate of everybody he could possibly think of was hanging in the balance, it was nice to feel useful again. Retirement had been a little disorienting so far. He'd looked forward to it for years, but he hadn't really prepared. He knew deep down that all the work on the house had been something of a dodge. And now even that was done. You can't just go from forty years of movement and activity and forced but enjoyable camaraderie with an unbelievably varied cast of characters from all over the world to— well, sitting in a chair. Not overnight, and not without motion-induced nerve damage from the sudden stop. No matter how nice the chair is. He adored his wife, any day spent in conversation with her was a good day by him, but a person's got his habits, and Roberto Diaz was used to being in motion.

The phone rang again. He was still holding it, so he tapped the button with his thumb and answered midway through the first ring. He spared her the fucking around this time.

"Zero-four-seven-four blue indigo."

"Thank you."

"*Qué pasó*, Abigail? I was very specific."

"Is there a problem with the transport? My screen has you over Fayetteville already."

"You didn't call Gordon Gray," he said.

"He was unavailable."

"Of course he's unavailable, it's two A.M., everybody's unavailable, until they aren't. You found me, I'm sure you could have—"

"Mr. Gray passed away in January."

His brain processed that statement in three distinct steps. The first two were achingly familiar, because they'd happened so often over the past ten years. Step one was the absorption of the information. Gordon Gray was dead. The man who had once refused to cross a casino picket line out of moral principle was gone. "Gordon," Roberto had said at the time, "you're drunk as a skunk, you're gambling with your rent money, you just broke a guy's nose because he stepped on your foot, and you're in *Las Vegas*. Why exactly are you making a stand here?"

Gordon had just smiled at him and shrugged. "I'm full of contradictions."

There were a thousand other memories, most of them far less benign, but that was how he always chose to remember Gordon, as a pretty amusing bundle of nonmatching character traits. Now that particular molecular combination of soul and folly no longer existed. Once Roberto forgot about that endearing moment in Las Vegas, it would be gone into the ether. It would never have occurred. That was step one, the sudden and vertiginous emptiness of death.

Step two came close on the heels of that feeling, and it was compassion. He was sad about the hole that Gordon's death must have left behind with his family, his friends, his brothers and sisters in arms. Roberto now had some people to belatedly console, a few phone calls to make.

And that was what brought on step three, which was an entirely new thought, one he hadn't had with any friend's death till this moment. Roberto had the grim feeling that he'd just moved into a new phase of proximity to death. Because no one had called him to say, "Gordon's dead." When you're young, the reaction is "Holy shit, so-and-so is dead, can you believe it?" Then you get older and start glancing at the obituaries to see if there's anybody you know in there, but that stage doesn't come as a surprise, because every middle-aged person you've ever met tells you they do that. Then, when you're older still, starts the sad litany of phone calls coming in as nature's sniper starts picking off your friends and family one by one. You buy a funeral suit and then a couple of different ties for it so you don't have to wear the same thing every time. You get used to all that.

But this thing, this was brand new—at sixty-eight, Roberto had reached the age where somebody died and nobody called, not because they didn't care, but because it's Too Fucking Depressing.

That was a new one.

He didn't say any of this to Abigail. To her he said, "I see."

"In January," she repeated.

"Who did you call instead?"

A man's voice answered for her. "Thank you, Belvoir, you can clear the line."

Roberto kicked himself for imagining they'd been alone on the line. Only a few years out and his edges had been dulled already. There was a faint click as Abigail disconnected, and Roberto could hear the colonel breathing on the other end.

"Hello, Roberto."

"Hey, Jerabek, how's that rash?"

"Your wife said put some cream on it, it's fine now."

Why did men talk like this to each other? Why not just agree to meet up and punch each other in the face until they felt better about things?

Jerabek went on, enjoying the role reversal. When Roberto had retired, the colonel had moved up, and that was the spot from which he looked down at this time. "I thought you put this one to bed thirty years ago."

"Apparently it woke up," Roberto said.

"Sounds like a broken thermistor to me."

"That would be nice to think."

"I'll be frank with you, Roberto. You're on that airplane as a gesture of respect to Gordon Gray. No other reason."

Again, why the fuck had *no one* called to tell him Gordon was dead? People sucked.

"Threat assessment and sober report. That's what I want, and that's all I want. Clear?"

"Gotcha," Roberto said. "Hey, you got a cell number for Loeffler?"

"See, you're saying that to irritate me, Roberto, and I understand. I would do the same thing. That is the sort of jocular back-and-forth I so enjoy with you. But I'm not kidding around. This is going to go quietly and quickly. Assess and report. No off-the-books stuff."

"Phil, I'm fucking with you. It's probably nothing. I'll check it out and go home. And by the way, you're welcome. I'm not exactly on the clock anymore."

Jerabek took a moment, deciding whether or not to trust him, and opted for some of both. "I know that. Thank you for making yourself available."

"You should probably take me off the file."

"I will do that. Keep in touch."

The phone went dead. Roberto held it for a moment, thinking. He looked out the window, at the lights of Charlotte down below, off to his right. Broken thermistor my ass.

Fuck that guy. Off the books was exactly where he was going.

He'd be on the ground in Kansas in less than two hours. That would make it tight, but if Trini answered he had an outside shot at it. The trick would be coding the call, and he certainly couldn't do it on the plane's phone. He reached into his flight bag, took out the MacBook Air his son, Alexander, had given him for Christmas (too much, makes everybody uncomfortable, tone it down, Alexander), and turned it on. The plane's Wi-Fi signal was half-decent, and he called up Tor2web without hitting a DoD net nanny, first stroke of luck. JonDonym and the two or three other .onion rerouters he knew were already dead. The dark net had pretty fast-moving currents, and he wasn't surprised to see he was already out of date. He was trying to think of next steps when something in his jacket pocket buzzed.

It was the satellite phone, the one he'd taken out of the safe back in his kitchen. He looked at the screen, didn't recognize the number. He made an educated guess.

"Abigail?"

"I can talk for two minutes." It *was* her. Roberto was genuinely delighted.

"I think you have the wrong number," he replied, and hung up the satellite phone, which was most certainly monitored. He tapped a few keys on the laptop, accessed a DeepBeep site he trusted—thank God that one was still there—and leached into the first number with at least ten nodes of encryption that scrolled by. He called her back and she picked up on the first ring.

"I'm on my personal cell in the ladies' room." He could hear the echo of her voice off the tile.

"I take it you read my white paper."

"I did," she said.

"And you believed it."

"What do you need me to—" She stopped, and he could hear that the door to the bathroom had just opened. Someone had come in.

Roberto took over. "Okay, I'll talk, you listen. Even with encryption, airplane Wi-Fi won't be secure enough for the conversations I need to have, so you'll have to make the calls for me. Find a reason to get yourself out of there on the double, go buy a burner, and call a former agent named Trini Romano. I'll repeat that name before I hang up. When she answers, tell her 'Margo is under the weather.'"

"Margo is under the weather? I'm sorry to hear that." Still with the stilted voice—she wasn't alone in the bathroom.

"That's it. Then tell her what you know, she'll help you with the list. Even number seven. Especially number seven. We're under two hours, so you have to move fast."

In the background, he heard a toilet flush. He continued.

"Text your burner number to me through a Mixmaster and I'll call you when I'm rolling."

Water ran in the bathroom. Someone was washing her hands.

Abigail sighed. "I understand, Mom, I just think it's kind of soon after your knee replacement."

Roberto smiled. She was pretty good, all things considered. "I'm dying to know why you decided to believe me, but that can wait. Doesn't matter, I guess." He could hear the bathroom door open and close again.

Abigail's tone changed. "Is it as bad as what you wrote in the report?"

"Every bit. And none of the people who understand that are in power anymore. Jerabek is not going to bed, he'll keep an eye on things, and he will not be helpful. But believe it or not, I've done all this before."

"Including item seven?"

He didn't answer that. "Trini Romano."

He hung up.

SEVENTEEN

When Teacake was fourteen, he fell in love for the first time. Patti Wisniewski was seventeen and he never really had much of a shot with her, but he'd started hanging around with seniors when he was a freshman, thanks to his overpowering sex drive. Like any fourteen-year-old boy, Teacake had powerful erections and he followed his dick wherever it led him. One day it dragged him to auditions for the school play, of all places. It was the last thing a frankly thuggish kid like Teacake would have done under normal circumstances, but he had an angle to work. The whole school had to watch the fall musical one afternoon, and he would have been blind not to have noticed that there was an inordinately high percentage of attractive young women up there onstage, almost entirely surrounded by losers. Three weeks later, he went to auditions for the new play.

Because he was a human male and alive on the planet, he was cast immediately. It was some shitty old play about a bunch of actresses sitting around a New York City apartment waiting for their big break. He barely knew the name of it then and certainly couldn't remember it now. He'd played Frank the Butler and had exactly two lines:

"Shall I call a taxi, Miss Louise?"

And, in the second act, the kicker—

"Taxi's waiting, Miss Louise."

One night he screwed them up and switched the order around, which should have brought the play to a crashing halt, but nobody really noticed. He never talked loud enough anyway. The other two shows he managed to deliver both lines at the right times and without laughing.

But his real accomplishment was getting himself accepted into the sex-and-drug-filled paradise of seventeen-year-old life. He was kind of cute for his age, smart enough from hanging around his older brother to know what to say and what not to say, and the seniors took him under their wing as a sort of mascot. He wasn't fully developed, so his sexuality wasn't particularly threatening, and that gave him all sorts of access to older women. He worked it as hard as he'd ever worked anything in his life, and at the cast party on opening night, Patti Wisniewski gave him a mercy hand job in the bathroom of Kres Peckham's stepdad's house. The only shame was that he was too drunk to remember it.

That was the thing. If asked, Teacake would be hard-pressed to come up with a single sexual encounter or romantic overture in high school that wasn't fueled by booze or drugs. He started smoking weed in seventh grade, like most people he knew, but that was the sort of thing you did with your buddies, when you didn't care how stupid you came off. With women you wanted to be drunk. Coke was nice if you could get it, but there was such an ugly price to pay for it, some creepy twentysomething asshole you'd have to hang around with, or cash that had to be scooped out of the till at work or stolen from somebody's parents. Too much hassle involved. Rock was cheaper, for sure, but you didn't have to be a genius to see that smoking that shit would take you no place good. That kind of high had nothing to do with getting off, anyway; you lost interest in sex almost immediately.

Things in his romantic life didn't change all that much after high school, when he got the job at the asphalt place. By that time his moms had split, and his dad was enjoying his own intimate relationship with the sauce. He'd always drunk a lot, his old man, but Teacake didn't think much of it, because everyone around here drank too much. Atchison was fucking *bleak* in the winter, dark side of the moon, there wasn't anything else to do besides get loaded, and then it's not like you're going to give it up for the spring and summer. At best, his dad's drinking became a little more joyful as the weather improved; he could at least hide it under the cover of celebration.

Teacake didn't care. If he were his old man, he would have gotten wasted every night too. The guy was a loser with a series of shit-ass jobs that kept going away, he was a cuckold who couldn't hang on to a wife, and he was stuck raising a son to whom he could find nothing that he wanted to say. The closest they got to bonding was when his dad would stumble across a Three Stooges marathon on TV when he was half in the bag and shout upstairs to Teacake, "Get down here and watch this shit with me! I love these assholes!"

They tried to stay out of each other's way as much as possible, and mostly succeeded. Both of them got fucked up. A lot.

What was there to stay sober for? Atchison had been nice once, but now it was your basic deserted Main Street with 30 percent unemployment. The majority of the populace saw inebriation of one kind or another as a valid survival mechanism. They weren't wrong. It works. At least in the short term.

A few months after high school Teacake got his own place with a buddy, covered his end of the rent okay most of the time with a few different jobs, and got shit-faced. Of dates, there were none; hookups, a few, but always under the influence. Within a year and a half of graduation he was in front of the judge for a drunk and disorderly and resisting arrest, and that was when the judge said it's the military or jail. Teacake said, "Hello, Drill Sergeant." Although since he picked the navy, it was "Hello, Recruit Division Commander."

Then it was two years moving from port to port overseas, where there were a surprising number of women and opportunities. The lady journalists in particular were always down for it, but they liked to get blitzed even more than he did.

Now Teacake was twenty-four. Ten years of romantic history were a cloud, a haze, a rush of dulled sensation only dimly remembered.

And then this. March 15, 2:26 A.M., standing at the bottom of a three-hundred-foot-deep concrete shaft. That was the time and place, that was the moment.

It was the first time Travis Meacham had ever kissed a woman sober.

There was an awful lot to be said for it.

For Naomi, the kiss was a momentary impulse that had been building for several hours. She'd come to work that night in a mood most foul, stuck in the fog of anger and despair in which she'd awakened that afternoon. She'd had a shift the night before, making this a rare and welcome two shifts in a row, which meant a better paycheck but worse sleep. After a night shift, she'd come home, get Sarah ready and take her to school, and with any luck she could be in bed by 8:30 A.M. That meant about five and a half hours of sleep, because she had to be back at the school to pick her up at 2:50. That was on a day with no classes for herself. A year ago, she would have been able to put Sarah in the after-school and not have to pick her up till 4:30 (luxury!), but the school lost its federal grant for that program at the end of last year. Now the after-school was called Extended Learning Opportunities, and it was run by a for-profit group that charged forty dollars a day. That was half a day's after-tax wage for Naomi and made no economic sense what-soever. She might as well not do the extra work.

Point is, today she woke up tired at two in the afternoon, and the last thing she needed was for one of the dark moods that had haunted her for the past several years to come roaring back. But she knew the moment she opened her eyes that the Black Dog had returned. That was Naomi's private nickname for the depression that periodically engulfed her, and this thing was no friendly Labrador. It was a mangy, skeletal cur, all bones and teeth, and when it came she could see it loping at her out of the woods, tongue lolling off to one side, yellow eyes fixed on her.

The Black Dog would stick around, on average, three or four days. Sometimes there'd be a day of false hope in the middle, a day when she'd feel okay and assume it had gone back into the primordial forest where it lived. But no, the mutt had only been hiding, the better to screw with her head, and it would come back to finish its run of despair the following day. She knew she was impossible to be around during those periods, but she didn't care. It was everyone else's fault anyway; they were the ones who'd called the dog in the first place. How, exactly, she did not know, but rationality was in short supply when she was in a mood. She learned after a few years that the best thing was to just stay away from people as much as possible during those times, to hide in her room, curled up on the bed with the door shut.

"If you can't be a pleasant part of things," her

mother used to say to her when she was little, "then you need to go somewhere else and leave us alone."

That was before her mother decided that she herself could not be a pleasant part of things and went somewhere else for good.

So the Black Dog had followed Naomi to work that night, and it stuck around until the moment she started talking to Teacake. That hadn't ever happened before; no one person could make the darkness go away—hell, fifty of them couldn't. But Teacake had; she'd sensed it the moment they started chatting on the loading dock. She'd gone with him to check out the beeping sound in part because she was curious, but also because being around him made her feel better. The Black Dog in her mind had skittered away, back into the trees, and disappeared further and further into the forest the longer she talked to Teacake. Why? He wasn't impossibly sexy and he wasn't impossibly smart and he was, not to put too fine a point on it, an ex-con.

But he made her laugh and he kept the dog at bay. Whatever that mysterious thing was, Teacake had it, and Naomi wanted to be around it, at least for tonight, to see if it was real.

So, yes, a kiss is just a kiss, but this one meant something to both of them. Ground had been broken. More was expected.

They exited the top of the tube ladder through the open manhole in the floor of SB-1. They were laughing, exhilarated by the brush with weirdness down below. They'd talked about it all the way up, fast and excited. The obvious next move was to call Griffin. The broken wall was something they were prepared to live with, because they actually *had* found something, there was a real problem down there, and it would likely involve the police and corporate and God knows who else. They might even be rewarded for having found a gas leak or animal infestation or some other nightmare scenario in the making.

Naomi was first out of the manhole. She swung her legs around so they were out of Teacake's way and sat cross-legged on the cement floor while she waited for him. She had her phone out of her pocket in a minute and typed in the four letters that were stenciled on the door down at the bottom of the tube. DTRA.

The first hit she got off Google was the Dirt Track Riders Association, but she didn't even have to think about that one to know that wasn't it. It was never a serious candidate, not even for the split second it took for her eyes to skip down to the second link on the page.

"Defense Threat Reduction Agency," she read.

Teacake, just coming out of the manhole, didn't respond right away, but she wouldn't have heard him if he had, because she'd already hit the link and was scrolling through the U.S. government's home page for the DTRA. Her attention was fully consumed by unreassuring headlines like "Stepnogorsk Biotoxin Production Facility Briefing Notes" and "Joint Improvised Threat Defeat Organization Links with DTRA" and

"Death by Nerve Gas: Two Arrests, Many Questions."

"Holy shit," she said.

"Holy *shit*," he replied.

They'd said the same thing at more or less the same time, because they were each looking at something unexpected. For Naomi it was the DTRA website.

For Teacake it was the bloated deer.

The animal was standing at the end of the short hallway, just staring at them. This in itself wasn't a big deal, that was sort of what deer did, they stood there and stared at you, frozen, wondering how it's all come to this. But this deer's insides were *moving*, you could see it in every breath it took. Either it was about to give birth, or it had eaten something that seriously disagreed with it.

Naomi saw it and stood, slowly, phone in one hand and the other held out to the deer as if to say, *Wait. You don't make sense.*

The deer lifted its chin and made a grotesque hacking sound at them.

Teacake climbed out of the manhole, slowly, and stood next to Naomi.

"What's the matter with it?" he asked.

"It's sick. Distended belly."

The deer took a couple of steps toward them, hacking some more. Teacake picked up the pry bar he'd used to open the manhole cover.

"Don't," Naomi said.

"Tell it not to come any closer."

She looked at him. "Like I talk to animals?"

"Wait a minute," Teacake said. The deer froze again, as if obeying him. Teacake thought. So, okay, sick deer staring at them, but *this* sick deer was in an underground storage facility, all the way down in sub-basement 1. There's only one way it could have gotten to SB-1. The elevator.

"How the fuck did it get down here?"

The deer cocked its head suddenly, as if called, then turned around and trotted back toward the mouth of the hallway, throwing a look back over its shoulder to hack at them one more time. It rounded the corner, only a bit unsteady, considering deer hooves were not at all made for concrete, and then clattered off and out of sight, its steps echoing off the walls.

Teacake and Naomi glanced at each other, but neither one needed any convincing. They followed it.

They came around the corner but were falling behind the thing. It had picked it up to a trot and was just now turning a second corner, at the far end of the hallway. They walked faster. They turned a final corner, and this one came to a dead end at the only elevator. The deer trotted toward it.

Teacake and Naomi slowed, approaching it warily.

"Uh, what do we do once we catch it?" he asked.

"I don't want to catch it," she said. "I want to help it get out of here."

The deer reached the elevator doors at the far

end and stopped, looking back over its shoulder at them.

Teacake walked even slower. "I'm not getting in an elevator with that thing."

At that moment, the elevator doors binged and slid open. The deer turned, as if fully expecting that, click-clacked its way into the elevator, turned back around to face them, and, swear to God, it glanced up at the floor numbers as the doors slid shut.

Teacake and Naomi stared.

Teacake spoke first. "The fucking deer just took the fucking elevator."

Naomi looked around, as if seeing the walls on either side of her for the first time.

"What the hell *is* this place?"

EIGHTEEN

Consider the night the deer was having. After the animal's execution by Mike's handgun at the side of Highway 16, it had gone through a period of blackness from which it abruptly awakened in the trunk of a car with a lunatic, half-faced cat standing on top of it. *Cordyceps novus*, having pulled off the seemingly impossible migration into the trunk of the car, had spent more than eight hours marinating inside the helpless creature's brain. The fungus had gone to work to repair damage from the bullets, in the process rewiring neural connections to alter the animal's behavior. The amygdala was expanded; the frontal cortex was inhibited. All the animal's basic instincts—eat, reproduce, run away—had been subordinated to the primary goal of helping the fungus sporulate and disperse.

The deer didn't have much in the sense of wonder, so it had no interest in trying to puzzle out how a pathogenic, mutating fungus that had been stored in a sealed subterranean environment ended up aboveground in the trunk of a

'96 Chevy Caprice in the first place. Still, it's a question worth asking.

By the early 1990s, the *Cordyceps novus* sample that had been recovered in Australia and stored at Atchison was brutally unhappy. When you have one biological imperative and that imperative is thwarted, it gets pretty depressing. But even though the temperature inside the bio-sealed tank was fourteen degrees below zero and the fungus was nearly inert, fourteen below zero is still a lot warmer than absolute zero. And nearly inert is not at all the same thing as completely inert.

Deep underground, sealed in a tank that was shut in a box that was locked in a crate, the fungus continued its pattern of consumptive evolution, albeit slowly, given the temperature and the inhospitable chemical composition of the stainless steel tube itself. Manganese and aluminum were abundant in its makeup, but they were of almost no use, given their nonreactive nature. A full 16 percent of the tube was chromium, which was actually a growth inhibitor for *Cordyceps novus*, so that was a downer, and carbon, which was what the fungus truly craved, made up a scant 0.15 percent of its chemical surroundings.

The fungus did grow. But barely.

Still, time marched on. By 2005, after almost twenty years of ceaseless effort, the fungus had managed to transform and occupy an area of the tube a few microns square. Through that tiny opening the fungus trickled out into the larger storage container in which the tube rested. It

picked up a little nourishment from the polyure-
thane foam in which the tube was nestled—at
least poly had more than two reactive hydroxyl
groups per molecule, a fungus could work
with that—but it wasn't until it made its way
through the portable sample kit's outer shell, in
late 2014, that *Cordyceps novus* hit its digestive
stride.

Because the outer box, the big one, the crate
Roberto and Trini had watched so carefully in
the back of the truck twenty-seven years before,
was made of carbon fiber.

Superfood.

The fungus was out of containment and loose
in the sealed room at this point, but still slowed
by the underground temperature. Slowed, not
stopped. The powerful cold spring, fed by the
deeper undercurrents of the Missouri River, had
spent most of the twenty-first century warming
up along with the rest of the planet. The river
surface got hotter; the spring got hotter. The
ambient temperature inside sub-level 4 had risen
seven degrees since the fungus had first been in-
carcerated, and the temperature only went up as
the fungus produced its own chemical reactions.
Its conquest of the sealed room was completed
by midsummer of 2018.

The fungus oozed through the wiring in the
wall in the autumn of that year and spread into
the main corridor of SB-4 in November. An un-
usually cold winter delayed its growth briefly,
but when a record-breaking heat wave hit in
early March of this year, *Cordyceps novus* got the

few extra degrees it needed to crank up its metabolic machinery. It infected organic matter again for the first time since its birth in Australia.

That was when it found the roach.

The American cockroach has several impressive evolutionary characteristics, besides its ability to survive a nuclear winter. One is that it can live without its head for up to a week. Respiration occurs through small holes in each of its body segments, so even after the first *Cordyceps novus/*cockroach hybrid was decapitated in a snarl of mayhem with a dozen other infected roaches who attacked and tried to consume each other, C-nRoach1 was able to continue on its purposeful way.

And it *did* have a purpose. From the moment of its hijacking, C-nRoach1 became imbued with a biological purpose greater than any roach in history. That's saying something, for a 280-million-year-old genus.

Cordyceps novus was driven. Over thirty-two years of isolation, it had changed very little, except to note that its growth environment was for shit. Its epigenetic memory of its initial expansion, back in Kiwirrkurra Community, was one of extreme fertility. The first living thing it had come into contact with was Enos Namatjira's uncle, whom it had entered through a loose flap of skin under a torn fingernail on his right hand. The warmth and fetidity of the inside of a human body had caused explosive proliferation.

Human beings were also highly mobile and, as a species, had a tendency to congregate. It was as if God had drawn these creatures up specifically to make life easy for the fungus. The complete takeover of twenty-seven human fleshpots was fast and easy; oh, how glorious things had been back then, before the fungus was jailed inside this tin can. If there's one thing prison gives you, it's plenty of time to sit around and long for the good old days.

Cordyceps novus had tasted humans, and it wanted more.

First it had to get out of here, and C-nRoach1 was a means to that end. The headless insect had moved methodically back and forth across the floor of SB-4 for four days, skirting a path around the shrieking, cannibalistic Rat King, until it reached the far end of the corridor. There the roach discovered a four-centimeter tube opening at the base of the wall, covered by a small metal grille. The tube was required by law in any underground structure more than fifty feet below ground level, in order to prevent the type of CO_2 buildup that had killed so many mine workers in the nineteenth century. From a containment point of view, the opening was a terrible idea, but the sub-level had never been designated for storage of biohazards, and the opening was just small enough to have escaped the notice of the team that had entombed the fungus thirty-two years ago.

C-nRoach1 didn't care why the tube was there; it just sensed fresh oxygen, crawled inside, and followed an upward curve in the pipe, which rose gradually to vertical.

The insect climbed.

Two days later, nearing the end of its life but about to achieve its greatest success—and late success really is the sweetest—C-nRoach1 reached the ground-level grating of the ventilation tube's emission port and wriggled out onto the surface of the hot, loamy earth. It was fifty yards from the entrance to Atchison Storage on a warm late-winter afternoon.

What a piece of work was this roach! It had endured infection by a hostile fungus, it had survived its own decapitation, it had methodically searched for and found a way out of a prison specifically designed by intellects far superior to its own to allow no escape. But little C-nRoach1 had done just that. Headless, dehydrated, and dying, it had climbed 323 feet, straight up, on a slick surface. Given its tiny size, this feat was the human equivalent of climbing Kilimanjaro on your knees right after going to the guillotine. The tiny roach had performed perhaps the greatest act of physical conquest in the history of earthly life.

Then a car parked on top of it.

C-nRoach1 died with a squishy pop beneath the right rear tire.

The car was Mike's, and this was this afternoon, when he'd come to Atchison Storage, looking to bury the cat and deer he'd murdered. While Mike walked up to the hilltop and searched for the right spot, *Cordyceps novus* faced the latest obstacle in its thirty-two-year journey: 10/32 of an inch of thick rubber car tire. But it had been confronted with something similar once and knew just who to call.

The sheen of *Benzene-X* that lived on the surface of the fungus activated almost immediately. It invaded the rubber in the tire, ate its way through, and opened a doorway for the fungus to pass into the airy interior of the wheel. *Cordyceps novus* floated upward, and the fungus and its endosymbiont repeated the penetrative process through the tread at the top of the wheel. From there they rode along a bit of wiring that led into the trunk of the Chevy Caprice, where *Cordyceps novus* discovered abundant consumable organic matter in the form of a dead deer and Mr. Scroggins, the former cat.

That was more like it.

NINETEEN

The fucking deer just took the fucking elevator."

Naomi, who was still staring at the closed doors in amazement, didn't even look at Teacake, still trying to digest what had happened. She murmured, "You said that already."

"I think it is a hundred percent worth repeating. *The fucking deer just took the fucking elevator.*"

Naomi looked back at the phone in her right hand. She didn't know exactly what the Defense Threat Reduction Agency did, but it was a safe bet that a Rat King and a deer that knows how to work an elevator were probably right up their alley. She turned her phone around and showed him the website. "We need to call this place."

"Be my fucking guest."

"Do you mind, with the language?"

"Sorry." He was. Anything for her. "Please call them."

Naomi scrolled to the "Contact Us" header, clicked on it, and a list of phone numbers popped up. "There's gotta be a hundred numbers listed here."

"Like what?"

Naomi thumbed her phone again, rolling past the numbers and job titles. "'Director,' 'Deputy Director,' 'Command Senior Enlisted Leader,' 'Counter-WMD Technologies'?"

Teacake looked around, nervous as hell. "What about, like, green shit leaking everywhere and animals acting all fucked up?"

"'Chem/Bio Analysis Center'? 'DOJ Radiation Exposure Program'?"

From the elevator shaft, they heard an inhuman caterwauling echoing off the concrete walls. They took a step back.

"Or," Teacake offered, "maybe we put a couple miles between us and this place and *then* we call them."

"I'm cool with that." Another howl came from inside the elevator shaft. "Stairwell?" Naomi suggested.

"This way." He led her down the hall at a run, around the first corner, and they reached the locked stairwell. Teacake zipped his key off the ring (still loved that sound, no matter what else was going on), unlocked the door, and they pushed through. They bounded up two flights of stairs, reached ground level, and he used his key to open the door there. They stepped out into the all-white hallway, never so grateful to be aboveground in their lives. He took her by the hand (*Damn, she's got some soft skin, soft but strong hands, you can feel it, I wonder if that's from carrying her kid around?, nah, that'd make your arms strong but not necessarily your hands, how come she's got such strong hands?, wait, focus, man, we gotta get out of here*) and led her down the hallway, headed for the lobby.

Not far away, the deer stood in the elevator, awaiting further instruction. It's not that the deer was sentient; it had no sense of selfhood. What it had was a clearly articulated purpose. As long as it was moving toward fulfillment of that purpose, the pain in its belly was not as intense. The deer didn't have the faintest idea why any of this should be the case, but then it didn't under-stand much of what had happened to it in the last forty-eight hours.

THE ELEVATOR DOORS OPENED AT THE FAR END OF the ground-floor level of Atchison Storage and Teacake and Naomi both screamed. They had taken the stairs specifically to avoid the dis-figured, resourceful deer that seemed to know how to operate an elevator, and now that deer was standing right in front of them.

"How the *FUCK*?!" Teacake shouted at the deer, which took three shaky steps toward them, making a phlegmy hacking sound at the back of its throat.

Teacake and Naomi stared in horrified fasci-nation. From this closer perspective they could see the deer had numerous gunshot wounds to its head, and one hindquarter appeared to have been completely crushed and then reinflated, somewhat off-shape. The deer's belly seemed to expand as they watched, and its once-spindly limbs had taken on the shape of piano legs.

Naomi held her hands out, one toward the deer and one toward Teacake. "Just—just—just—"

Teacake looked at her, his voice an octave higher than usual. "Yeah?"

"Don't—don't—don't—"

"Are you talking to me or the thing?!"

She wasn't sure.

The deer took another few steps toward them, and they, in turn, took a few steps back. They continued to back away, moving toward the T-junction of the hallway.

Inside the deer's head, a civil war was taking place. Every one of the animal's natural instincts was screaming at it to turn and run away from these scary two-legged creatures, but an even stronger instinct, a new one that had taken hold only recently, insisted on just the opposite. And this new voice was loud and firm.

Move forward, the new voice said, *get as close as you can, go to them, go to them, walk, walk, walk. And then the pain will stop.*

Cordyceps novus knew what it wanted, and it wasn't a cockroach, cat, or deer; it was the intelligent, highly ambulatory, communal creatures that were ten yards away at the end of the hall.

The deer kept moving toward them, and Teacake and Naomi continued to back up, until they reached the cinder block wall at the end of the corridor. They could have turned and run in either direction, but that would have meant tearing their eyes away from the unnatural spectacle that was unfolding in front of them, and that they could not do.

The deer was still swelling, its body creaking and groaning and snapping on the inside. It was puffing up like a water balloon at the end of a hose; there were just a few seconds left before its gut let go. Naomi and Teacake were directly within its spatter radius and didn't realize how close they were to a certain and painful death.

But at the very last moment, Naomi's four-year-old daughter, Sarah, stepped in and saved both of their lives.

For the last three months, Sarah had been deep in the throes of a *Willy Wonka* obsession. Sarah, and therefore her mother, had watched the 1971 version of that movie, in whole or in part, more times than Naomi cared to count. Sometimes Naomi was awake, actually watching it with her daughter. Sometimes she was asleep, dreaming it, or folding laundry in the other room, the audio bouncing off the walls and into her head. Naomi knew every line, every lyric, every part of it by heart, and the parts she knew best were the parts that scared Sarah. The parts where she needed her mama to come over and sit down and pull her onto her lap and stroke her hair and tell her it was all just pretend.

Naomi didn't mind. She actually liked her kid best of all in those moments, because those were the times she felt like a halfway-okay mother. The scary parts of *Willy Wonka* were some of the most peaceful moments of Naomi's life, which of course made her feel guilty. *Does my kid have to*

be terrified and clingy in order for me to be happy?
Well, no, but sometimes it helps.

What mattered now was the part of the movie
that scared Sarah the most: when Violet Beauregarde stole the Three-Course-Dinner Gum
and began to swell and blow up into an enormous blueberry. Sarah would cover her eyes and
scream in panic, "She's going to pop! She's going
to pop! *Mama, she's going to pop!*"

The deer was going to pop.

Naomi grabbed Teacake by the arm and
hauled him to the side, pulling him around the
corner and slamming them both up against the
wall, hard, just as the deer's overtaxed frame
gave out. It isn't accurate to say that the deer
burst, like Mr. Scroggins and Enos Namatjira's
uncle had. This was different. One second the
deer stood there, swollen nearly to round, like
Violet Beauregarde. And the next second, the
deer was *not* standing there, but the ceiling,
floor, and walls of the hallway were painted with
thick, foamy green fungus. Naomi held Teacake
pressed firmly against the wall, inches out of the
line of fire, safe behind their blast shield when
the goo flew.

There was a second there where Teacake
could look into her eyes from up close without
coming off as creepy, a second where it was just
gratitude and connection. The first half of that
second was thrilling—her eyes were home, they
were the only place he ever wanted to be, and
the last lines of the only poem he knew flitted
through his mind—

A mind at peace with all below,
A heart whose love is innocent.

But then came the other half second, and his mind was no longer at peace, it felt only sorrow. Because he knew no matter how she felt tonight, no matter the thrill or danger or exhilaration of discovery, inevitably tomorrow morning would come, those feelings would fade, and she would realize they couldn't possibly be together. A single mother—no, an *outstanding* single mother— would not, could not, choose to be with a minimum-wage worker with a prison record.

Specifically, she would not choose to be with him. If she did, she wouldn't be her, and he wouldn't respect her. He'd spare her the awkwardness of telling him once they got out of this; he'd just slip away. She wouldn't know why, but maybe she'd know he'd saved her the trouble.

From around the corner, they heard the elevator doors open again, and the sound of footsteps on the hard cement floor.

What *now?* Naomi pulled back from Teacake, and they looked at each other in confusion and alarm. Still hidden around the corner, they stayed silent, gesturing to each other. Her furrowed brow and cocked head asked, *Who the hell is that?* and his upturned palms and quick shake of his head answered, *Like I know?*

The footsteps drew closer and louder. They were definitely human, but there were no other workers in the place at this hour, and neither one of them had buzzed anyone in.

Teacake called out from around the corner. "Hello?" He tried to sound authoritative, but stayed where he was, hidden from view.

The footsteps paused, then started walking again. They heard a soft gush as the feet must have hit the edge of the wet carpet of fungus in the middle of the hall and kept coming toward them.

Naomi's turn, louder: "Who is that?"

The footsteps stopped again, but only for a second before they resumed, faster, splatting through the fungus. They were just around the corner now. Teacake and Naomi backed up a few feet into the middle of the hallway, a safe enough distance away to still turn and run if they had to.

A man came around the corner and stopped, staring at them.

It took Naomi a moment to comprehend the weirdness of what she was seeing.

"Mike?"

Mike pulled back his lips and showed his teeth, which was not at all the same thing as a smile, but it was the best he could do. "Hi, honey."

Teacake looked back and forth between them, three legitimate questions in his mind. He elected to skip two of the more mundane ones— *You guys know each other?* and *"Honey"?*—and move immediately to the more mysterious issue. "You were in the elevator with that thing?" he said to Mike.

Mike turned his head, as if noticing Teacake for the first time. "I was in the elevator with that thing."

Teacake looked at Mike, then at Naomi. *He's your weirdo.* But he pressed on, turning back to Mike. "So, *you* pushed the buttons?"

Mike blinked. "I pushed the buttons. A deer can't push buttons."

Teacake squinted. He had an odd conversational style, this guy, and he ended every sentence with that weird, half-open mouth, like he was trying to smile but his lips kept getting stuck to his teeth.

"What are you doing here, Mike?" Naomi jumped in. "What the hell happened to that *thing*?" She pointed to the mass of goo that Mike had just walked through, then looked back at him, noticing the sleeves of his shirt were soaked red with blood that oozed out of a series of long, jagged cuts running up the lengths of both arms. "And what the hell happened to your *arms*?"

That was way more interrogation than whatever was left of Mike's brain could handle. He'd been feeling pretty good outside, especially when he saw Naomi's car and realized there was another human being in the immediate vicinity. Not just any human, but one whom he knew and could get close to. *That's something I should do, right?* he asked the feeling in his head. *That's something I should do right away, isn't it?*

Oh yes, the feeling told him. *Cordyceps novus*, after the failure in Australia and the limited success with Mr. Scroggins, had lost interest in height as a prerequisite for contagion and had now seen the wisdom of *lateral* mobility.

Yes, get as close to them as you can as soon as you can, yes, please.

So Mike had moved. He was confident, he had a purpose, which was more than he'd been able to say for a long time. The locked front door of the storage facility hadn't deterred him; he'd found a side door with a glass panel in it, smashed it with a rock, and wriggled through. The broken glass didn't hurt that much when it sliced up his arms, and when he landed on the other side of the door and stood up, he'd been delighted to see the deer through the broken window, standing at the edge of the woods ten yards away, staring at him.

Mike was thrilled. He'd felt bad about the deer for two days, but there it was, alive, and—somehow he knew this—it was on his side. He'd opened the door, held it wide, and the deer trotted inside the building. Together, they walked the halls of Atchison Storage for a good twenty minutes, looking for Naomi but not finding her, or anyone else for that matter. They'd moved on, wordlessly, to the basement, taking the elevator down a level to continue their search. She had to be here somewhere. Mike and the deer had the same imperative—*find a human and infect it, repeat as many times as possible until you're dead*—and goddammit they were going to carry it out. He was going to be *good* at something.

It was when they'd reached SB-1 and the elevator doors opened that Mike had frozen up. Because there he'd heard her voice, coming from around the corner, talking to Teacake, and the 49 percent of his brain that still contained useful human feelings like guilt and remorse kicked into overdrive. He remembered what he'd done and that he'd fled, and that he had a child, some- where, whom he had failed to father. As Naomi's voice drew closer, Mike had pressed his body back, against the wall of the elevator, out of sight next to the control panel, and prayed to be anywhere but here. Prayer is a powerful psychic force, more powerful even than *Cordyceps novus*, or at least it was for those sixty seconds or so. Mike cowered in the elevator, out of sight, able to temporarily fight back the urge to go get them.

When the deer walked back into the elevator and Mike was able to push Door Close, a wave of relief washed over him. He wouldn't have to see her again, he wouldn't have to face the weight of his sins. They'd reached ground level and the deer—*God bless you, you beautiful, intrepid creature!*—had stridden out of the elevator to- ward the pair of humans, swelled up, and done its level best to coat them in fungus.

But it failed. And the religious rebellion in Mike's brain was quashed under the boot heel of *Cordyceps novus*, which simply said, *Next man up!* and pushed Mike forward to do his biological duty.

Now Naomi waited for him to answer her questions. Any of them, really.

He blinked, just looking at her.

Teacake tried like hell to figure this out. "Are you okay, man?" he asked Mike, but Mike just opened his mouth and then closed it again. Teacake turned to Naomi. "You know this guy?"

"Yes." She hesitated, because she hated saying it.

"Yeah?" Teacake was waiting.

"He's my kid's dad."

Mike opened and closed his mouth three times, clicking his teeth.

Teacake took that in, then turned back to Naomi. "Uh—for real?"

Mike moved toward Naomi. "Open your mouth."

She took a step back. "*What?*"

Teacake stepped in front of her, holding a hand out to Mike, palm out. "Whoa, dude, what kind of shit are you talking, what's the matter with you?"

Mike opened his own mouth wide, as if stretching out his jaw muscles, then clicked his teeth at Naomi again. "Open your mouth."

Of all the unpleasant things Naomi had seen and heard tonight, this was perhaps the unpleasantest. What the hell was wrong with her that she had ever given this jerk the time of day, much less conceived a child with him? Why was he now heaving his stomach in and out, like a cat trying to bring up a hairball? And why was he reaching around behind his back?

Teacake had been around guns in the military and spent his fair share of time on the rifle range, but mostly he saw a lot of movies, and he knew there was only one reason to make that gesture, ever. It wasn't because you had a sudden itch at the top of your butt crack. While Mike sucked his gut in and out and closed his right hand around the handle of the .22 he'd shoved into the waistband in the back of his pants, Teacake studied the geography. Mike was between them and the exit, but just behind them was the open hallway that led to units 201 through 249, and at the end of that was the jog to the right, maybe that would buy them enough time, some units had dead bolts on the inside and they both had phones, so maybe—

Mike wedged words in between the heaves. "Open"—*heave*—"your"—*heave*—"mouth"—*heave*.

The gun came out, but Teacake had already turned and taken off, pulling Naomi along with him. The vomit that Mike finally succeeded in dredging up from his gut spewed a good eight or nine feet, but fell short, splatting on the cement in the spot they'd just vacated.

Teacake and Naomi turned the corner as Mike raised the gun, fired a shot at them, and took a chunk out of the cement block near their heads.

Neither one of them had ever been shot at before. It was not enjoyable. They raced down the corridor, no words, just flight, and could hear the anguished, angry cry of Mike as he chased after them. The only way out of the building was back the way they'd come, back where the guy with the gun and the barf and the exploding deer were, so that wasn't happening. Teacake's mind did the mental math and didn't like the numbers, not one bit, these hallways were *long*, and wasn't nobody could outrun a bullet. He'd be willing to take his chances if it were just him—what were the odds that pukey weirdo could actually land a shot on a moving target while running? But that wasn't a risk he was willing to take with Naomi's life.

He took the next corner hard, pulled them both to a stop in front of unit 231–232, a sweet combo unit eight feet wide and sixteen feet deep. He zipped the master key up off his hip, flicked the lock open, and yanked the door up a couple feet off the ground.

Naomi knew the only option when she saw it. She dropped to the floor and rolled under the door, into the darkness on the other side. Teacake didn't open the door any farther; he didn't want to in case he had to close it quickly and lock her in, which he was fully prepared to do. If Mike had been rounding the corner already, he would have done it and fought the fucker one-on-one, gun or no gun, but when he looked back the hallway was clear, though Mike's semihuman cries of rage were coming this way fast.

Teacake dropped to the floor. As he hit the ground, he saw Mike's feet come around the corner, they were only about ten feet away, and he heard the sharp cracks of three wild gunshots and the *clang* of bullets hitting metal. Teacake's view of the feet spun over, upside down, as he rolled under the door and into the storage unit, then the feet were right outside the door and Mike's hands were reaching down to rip the overhead door open the rest of the way, and Teacake knew he'd miscalculated, just by a few seconds, but it was enough, he'd fucked this up, he was in no physical position to get up and pull the door down before Mike succeeded in ripping it open the rest of the way, *shit*, great plan, asshole, he'd led them straight into a dead end, a sealed storage unit, they were cornered.

But Naomi was on her feet already, of *course* she was; she'd leaped to her feet as soon as she'd come through. She was up and braced and had both hands on the door's center handle—*She got leverage on you, motherfucker*, Teacake thought—as she put everything she had into it and slammed the door down so hard the *clang* echoed all the way down the hall.

Mike howled in agony, his hands crushed underneath the metal lip of the door, pinned there for a moment. Naomi pulled it back up three inches, not out of sympathy, but just to let him get his sorry-ass hands out of there. Mike yanked them back, Naomi slammed the door again, and Teacake, now on his feet, threw the metal locking pin at one end of the door, then darted over and threw the pin on the other.

The two of them stood in the pitch dark for a few seconds, breathing heavily, listening while Mike yowled and raged in the hallway outside. He banged on the metal with both fists; it rattled and clanged. He fired another half dozen gunshots at it, and dimples bloomed on the inside of the door as bullets slammed into the thin metal. Mike kicked it, then he tried like crazy to open it again. Light from outside streaked underneath as the door lifted and fell, but it would rise only a half inch, and the steel pins at either end had no intention of ever giving more ground than that.

Teacake spoke first, still out of breath. "So that's Dad, huh?"

"I know, right?"

Outside the door, it went quiet. They waited.

After almost a minute, they heard footsteps as Mike walked away. They waited another thirty seconds, then they both pulled out their phones and the screens lit up their faces.

Teacake looked at his first. "Griffin called me eleven times."

"Do you really give a shit right now?" she asked.

"Yeah, just, I need to keep this job."

"You've mentioned." She squinted at her phone, which was still showing the DTRA website. "There's a number for a place called Fort Belvoir."

"Fort Belvoir? That's an army base."

"Should I call it? Or the cops?"

Outside the door, they heard the faint patter of footsteps approaching again, fast. Someone was running straight toward them. The footsteps abruptly stopped as the someone launched himself into the air, there was a split second of silence as he sailed toward the door, and then the corrugated metal shuddered with a tremendous vibration as he slammed into the middle of it, denting it inward ever so slightly. But the door held fast.

They could hear Mike's body crunch to the

cement floor outside and he let loose an animal cry of frustration, a shriek that sounded unlike anything produced by human vocal cords.

Teacake looked at Naomi. "Yeah. Call the fucking army."

TWENTY

The runway rushed up at him and Roberto stretched one last time. He'd moved around as much as he could on the flight, but at sixty-eight his body stiffened up a lot quicker than it used to, and in surprising areas. *Wait a minute, I pulled a muscle in my* ass? *How does that even happen?* He and Annie talked about it all the time; they'd started to strain muscles in odd places or trigger back spasms by doing formerly uncontroversial things like, oh, standing up or opening a jar of peanut butter. That was the last thing he needed tonight, some pop-up infirmity to slow him down, and thirty thousand people die as a result.

The plane landed and taxied toward the far hangar, the one the airstrip at Leavenworth saved for visiting dignitaries and emergencies. *Thanks a lot again, Jerabek, way to keep it all low profile.* Roberto couldn't wait to get off the government plane, drop his cell phone in a Faraday bag to block signal detection, and fail to call in for a good four or five hours. Until this was sorted. "Sorted"—he'd picked up that expression in London too and always loved it. Sorted. Handled, dealt with. Everything put in its proper place, quietly and efficiently, like a clerk in an office. Well, this one wouldn't be quiet, but it would be thorough as hell, if all went according to plan. Permanent. Sorted.

He looked out the window and saw the open doors of the far hangar. The lights were on inside, but it appeared to be empty, just a large expanse of gleaming floor. There was a van parked in front and a figure in a dark coat standing beside it, a cloud of smoke curling up above the person's head, backlit by the fluorescents inside.

The pickup truck with the airstair reached the plane just as it came to a stop. Inside, Roberto was already at the door. The copilot met him there with just a nod, no loose talk. That was one thing he missed about the service. Pleasantries were kept to an absolute minimum, which felt honest, and God knows it saved time. They both waited a few seconds for the *tap-tap*-pause-*tap* from outside, then the copilot flicked a few switches, pulled the handles, and the door sucked inward and rotated open. The copilot gave another nod and a tight "Good night, sir," and Roberto stepped out into the four A.M. Kansas mist.

He hurried down the metal stairs, returned a salute from the airman at the bottom, and walked across the tarmac toward the van. He closed the distance between himself and Trini, and each of them was struck by how much older the other one looked. He hadn't seen her in fifteen years, which meant Trini was in her seventies by now.

Her health habits had never been good, and they had not improved, judging by the bright red glow at the end of the Newport Menthol King she was inhaling. The cigarette didn't stand a chance.

Roberto reached her and stopped. He looked around the empty tarmac. "No base security escort?"

"Told 'em to buzz off and go back to bed."

"And they did?"

She nodded. "I'm persuasive." She went into a hacking cough and held up a finger—*Hang on*.

Roberto waited until she finished. "How is it possible you're not dead yet?"

She shrugged. "Too mean." She turned, opened the driver's door, got in, and slammed it shut. Roberto walked around, eyeing the boxy white Mazda minivan with disdain, and got in the passenger side.

He settled into the white fake-leather passenger seat. "Cool wheels. This is your personal ride, right? You don't expect me to drive it."

Trini shook her head and put it in gear. "Oh, you're a real beauty." She hit the gas, cut the wheel, drove right through the open airplane hangar, and came out the far side. She took a left and headed for the Pope Avenue exit from the base.

"Seriously, Trini, I'm concerned. Didn't you get lung cancer about ten years ago?"

"I do not have lung cancer, you inconsiderate prick, and I never have. I have emphysema, which is completely different and a hundred percent survivable." She took another drag on her cigarette.

"Could you at least open a window?"

She opened his, and it sucked all the smoke right past his face.

"Come on."

"Sorry." She closed it and opened hers instead. "That tootsie from Belvoir sounded like you put the fear of God in her. What did you tell her?"

"Tiny bit of the truth."

"Yeah, well, that'd do it." She gestured toward the rear of the minivan. "It's all there."

Roberto turned and looked in the back. The rear seats were folded down and there was a tarp thrown over several storage crates that looked like about the right size and amount. "Including number seven?"

She shook her head. "We have to stop and pick that one up."

He looked at his watch. "Are you kidding me? You know we're critical, right?"

There'd been a shift in their power dynamic about twenty years earlier, when Trini stopped advancing in rank and Roberto continued his upward trajectory. He'd given the orders to her after that, not that she really cared all that much.

She turned to him now, offended. "The balls it takes for you to complain. Two hours ago, I was asleep. Now I'm driving you around at four A.M. with half a dozen contraband items that could get me sent to prison for the rest of my life."

"So, what would that be, like three or four days?"

She laughed until she hacked so hard she almost had to pull over.

He smiled at her. "Do you miss it?"

"Like crazy."

"Which part?"

She gestured back and forth between them. "This stuff. The bullshit."

He enjoyed it too and hadn't realized how much he'd missed her. "Gordon's dead," he said.

"Yeah, I know. It was a beautiful service."

He looked at her, annoyed. "How does everybody know this except me? Why didn't you call me?"

"Not my job to call around every time somebody dies. I'd never get off the fucking phone."

Well, that was true. Roberto looked out the window for a moment, trying to remember the last time he'd seen or talked to Gordon, but he couldn't call it up. He returned to the present and turned back to Trini. "You know, you actually look pretty good, kid."

"I look like hell, fucker, and you know it. *You* look great. Sorta over-the-top handsome, as usual. Like a Mexican Ken doll. I picture you with no private parts."

"Don't picture that."

"What should I picture?"

"Why do you have to picture anything at all?"

She shrugged. They reached the main gate and she opened her window the rest of the way, throwing a stern glance at Roberto. "See if you can shut up for a minute."

While Trini signed them out of the base and discharged a wave of Newport smoke into the guard shack, Roberto took the Faraday pouch from his jacket pocket and opened the double-grade, military-tested fabric. Just as he was about to drop his phone inside, it buzzed. He looked at the screen. The number had a 703 area code. He plugged one ear, hit Answer, and listened for a moment.

A woman's voice spoke. "Hello?"

Roberto listened. He heard the sound of wet tires on pavement on the other end.

"Two minutes," he said into the phone. Then he hung up.

He went into the weather app on his phone, entered Fort Belvoir, Virginia, and saw that it was raining there. Satisfied the call came from where it said it was and had not been put through a rerouter, he dropped the government-issue cell phone into the Faraday bag and zipped it shut. He pulled his laptop out of his backpack, slipped a card into one of the free USB ports, put in a Bluetooth earpiece, and called up the DeepBeep site he'd accessed on the plane. He typed in the phone number that had just called him on his phone. It was answered on the first ring, but Roberto spoke first. "You're outside now?"

Abigail's voice replied. "Yes. In the rain."

"Trini was here when I landed, and heavy. Well done. I don't need anything else." He was about to hang up, but Abigail spoke again.

"There's been a development."

Roberto tensed. "What kind of development?"

"On the ground in Atchison. Someone made a call to Belvoir from inside the facility."

"Who?"

"A civilian. Twenty-three-year-old woman."

"That's too bad. How'd she get your number?"

"She googled DTRA off a door."

"Okay, she's not stupid. What'd you do?"

Abigail paused, and Roberto could hear voices on the other end as people hurried past her in the rain. When they faded, Abigail went on. "I hung up on her, came outside, and called her back on one of the burners I got. I have her on the other line now. Want to talk to her?"

Roberto continued to be impressed by Abigail, but this was going to be even more complicated than he'd thought, and he knew he'd need her again. He was careful not to overpraise. "Yes. What's her name?"

"Naomi."

"Toss your burner into the back of a moving truck when we're done and text me a new number."

"Will do. Hang on."

Roberto waited. Trini looked at him and inclined her chin: *What's up?* He covered the phone's mic with his thumb. "Civilian. Inside the mines."

Trini winced. "I hope she's enjoyed a full life."

The connection worsened, and the frightened voice of a young woman came through Roberto's earpiece, trying hard to sound authoritative. "Okay, who is this *now*?"

"Hello, Naomi. My name's Roberto. I'd like to talk to you about what's going on."

"Okay, why did that first lady hang up on me?"

"Because she cares about your situation and

wants to see it resolved in the right way, like I do." In the background, Roberto could hear shouting, a man's voice, something along the lines of "Ask him what the fuck is going on!" or words to that effect. "I hear someone there with you. What's his name?"

"Travis. We're security guards here."

"Okay. Could you do me a favor and ask Travis to shut up while I'm talking to you?"

Her voice was fainter as she turned her head and said, "He says you should shut up." Then a pause, some mumbling, and she spoke into the phone again. "We have a serious problem here. There's this virus, or a fungus—"

"Right on the second one. I know all about it. I know more about it than anyone else. Are you somewhere safe right now?"

"We're locked in a storage unit."

"Okay. Could be worse. Stay in there."

"No kidding. For how long? Are you sending people?"

"Has anyone come into direct physical contact with it? You'd know if they had because they'd have—"

"Yes."

Roberto mouthed *shit* silently. Trini looked at him as often as she dared while driving at seventy miles per hour over Centennial Bridge.

"Hello?" Naomi asked.

"Yes, I was just calling something up on my screen," he lied. "How many people have been infected?"

"Just one, I think."

"And is that person still inside the facility?"

"Yes. He keeps trying to get in here. Where we are." In the background, he heard more shouting—the ranting guy was at it again. Naomi conferred with him quickly, said, "Okay, okay, *okay*," and came back on the line. "Also, there was a deer. A deer was infected."

"Where is the deer now?"

"It blew up."

"Outside or inside?"

"Did you hear me? I said it *blew up*."

"Yes, I heard. Can you tell me where it blew up?"

"In the hallway." Her tone said *like that matters*, but Roberto breathed a tiny sigh of relief that it was still inside the building.

He continued. "Okay, listen to me, Naomi. You're going to be all right. You called exactly the right place, and you're speaking to exactly the right person. You have some excellent instincts, and they've served you well so far. Now it's time to trust somebody else. I'm on my way there, and I know what it takes to resolve this situation. There are several of us who have encountered this before, and we've planned for a situation where we might have to deal with it again. I'm going to be there in—" He looked at Trini.

"Less than an hour," she said.

He spoke back into the phone. "A little over an hour. Stay right where you are. Don't open the door. Don't call anyone else. Not even Fort Belvoir. The woman who put us in touch will call you every ten minutes. Speak only to her or to me. Don't pick up your phone again unless it rings. Do you understand?"

"What are you going to do?"

"Tell me you understand."

"I understand."

"Who should you call?"

"Nobody. You'll call me every ten."

"There you go. A-plus. Keep Travis calm, he sounds like the type who might want to try to leave. Don't let him."

"The deer exploded."

"I know, some crazy shit, right? I'll tell you all about it when I see you. You're going to be fine. One hour." He closed the computer, took out the earpiece, and rubbed his head.

Trini looked at him. "Three people and a deer?"

"One person infected, still in the building. The other two are clean, locked in a storage unit. The deer burst, but it was contained."

"I guess that's workable."

He looked at her. "Are you kidding? It's a gift from God. Let's hope it lasts an hour."

Trini nodded, eyes on the road, weighing it all. Finally, she spoke, just a few words. "They're dead, aren't they?"

He thought. "Probably."

He didn't like that answer, so he thought some more. He thought it all the way through but came up with the same conclusion.

"Probably."

TWENTY-ONE

The hour's first fifteen minutes had gone pretty well. Mike had settled down outside, just sitting on the floor across the hall from unit 231–232, staring at the metal door. He didn't know much anymore, only that he had to get in there.

I have to get in there the door is closed I have to get in I have to door closed

As for a solution to that problem, his complex reasoning and problem solving weren't firing on all cylinders, but they were grinding away as best they could and had come up with a few different approaches. The first strategy had been based on a fragment of a song his father used to love that was bouncing around somewhere in Mike's subconscious, something about throwing yourself against a wall, but that strategy hadn't worked out very well. He'd likely separated his shoulder when he crashed his body into the metal door, and for sure he broke two fingers underneath himself when he fell to the cement. The pinkie finger on his right hand stuck out at an angle Mike had never seen before, but he didn't give it much thought. He didn't have the thought to spare.

have to get in door closed get in

Strategy number two involved more vomit, this time by lifting up the garage door a crack and trying some target-specific barfing through the half-inch space underneath it. But the appeal of that approach had been dimmed by the sensory memory of his fingers, which had been crushed beneath the door when Naomi had slammed it down, and he never tried it. Strategy number three was, as they say, still in development.

While Mike waited for that idea to come, he sat and stared at the corrugated metal door, dead-eyed. He'd wait.

Behind the door, Naomi and Teacake were considerably more comfortable, but their minds were no more at ease. The unit in which they'd taken refuge was a lucky choice: it looked like someone's overflow furniture from when they'd had to move to a smaller house. Maybe the renters were sure the move was only temporary, that they'd be back on top one day soon and they'd need all their stuff again. The extra couches and chairs had been in there for a few years now, but they didn't stink, the owners had covered them loosely and loaded the cushions up with silica packets, the way you're supposed to. There was even a dehumidifier plugged into one of the outlets. Naomi and Teacake had thrown the cheap sheets off a couple of the armchairs, shoved them toward the back of the unit, to stay as far away from the door as possible, and even found a lamp with a bulb in it that still worked. They sat there, armchair to armchair, lamp on a box between them, and they stared at each other, wondering how it had all come to this.

Teacake, who abhorred silence, was the first to speak. "So that's Dad."

"Please stop saying that."

"Sorry, it's just kinda hard to get my head around, that's all. How does *that* guy have a chance with you?"

She looked at him. "He wasn't always like that."

"Well, yeah, obviously I get that, I don't think anybody on earth has ever been quite like that. But, I mean, he had to be some version of that, right?"

"I guess so."

"And you're, you know, you."

"Thank you." She wished he'd stop talking.

"And she's a beautiful kid."

Oops.

Naomi tilted her head, looking at him, thinking.

Oh God, how he wished he could snatch those last five words out of the air before they found her ears, how he wished he could go back in time, just three seconds would do it. But he couldn't, he'd said it, she'd heard it, and she understood what it meant.

His mind sorted through options. His ordinary instinct would have been to keep talking, to paper over it with more and more fulminations, to bury the slip of the tongue so deeply in blather that she might not notice or would forget that he'd just announced he not only knew she had a child prior to tonight, but had actually seen that child, a clandestine event she had most certainly been unaware of till now.

He was about to turn on the fire hose of lies, but something stopped him. This had been a long and bizarre night, and Naomi was different, and it occurred to him that maybe his instincts all these years had been the wrong ones. Maybe those instincts were the reason he had a shit job and no girlfriend. Maybe, Teacake thought, he should go with the truth for once, maybe he should admit an unpleasant reality before it became impossible to do so, maybe he should speak frankly and self-deprecatingly and forthrightly as soon as it was necessary. He could actually show a little fucking *class* for once, he thought, maybe he could speak with such charm and grace, such wit and style, that this moment, this admission, this candor, might actually win her over rather than drive her away.

"I followed your ass home one morning it was fucked up sorry."

Or, you know, he could do it that way.

Naomi's phone buzzed. She picked it up immediately, glanced at the number, and answered. "Hello." She paused, listening, staring at Teacake. She continued the perfunctory conversation, her eyes pinning him to his chair the whole time.

"Yes. Yes. Same as ten minutes ago. No, he hasn't tried. I assume he is, we haven't heard him walk away. Yes. Okay." She hung up.

Teacake tipped his chin for information. "She say anything new?"

"No."

"So, like, are they getting here soon, or what?" He made an exaggerated show of checking the time on his phone, profoundly grateful for the change in subject. She'd forget, maybe she forgot already! He kept talking. "Like, forty-five minutes from now? So, okay, it was, like, around four when you talked to the guy, so—"

"You're flip-phone guy."

She hadn't forgotten.

He sighed. "I apologize, Naomi. I get—I do dumb stuff sometimes. I wasn't, I didn't . . . ah, shit."

"In the parking lot of my building, right? About a week ago. Staring at your flip phone."

"You saw me?"

"Yeah, I saw you. I knew you looked familiar tonight, but I couldn't figure out where I saw you before. I should have got it when you pulled your phone out. Nobody has those anymore."

"I'm sorry, I—"

"Are you a stalker, Travis?"

"No. I swear."

"Because that's creepy."

"I know. I apologize. I never did that before."

"I would hope not."

"I just wanted to talk to you. And then I got—in a jam, and I didn't know how to get out. I am sorry."

She looked at him for a long moment, analytically, as if evaluating every piece of him, dissecting his entire character based on the look on his face in that one moment. Finally—

"Okay. Don't do it again."

And it was *done*. He was stunned. This was not how he'd expected this to go. She was letting him off the hook. She was really, truly, for serious letting him take a pass, she wasn't repulsed or any shit like that. He'd told the truth and *it worked*. He smiled, and for nearly a full minute, the two of them had forgotten where they were and what was happening.

Then they heard it. It was faint and far away, but it was so deep and down low that it vibrated through the entire cement-and-metal building. The overhead door rattled in its tracks ever so slightly. They both looked at it and then at each other at the same time. *Is this what it sounds like when the cavalry arrives?*

Teacake stood, almost involuntarily. "They're here!"

Naomi checked the time on her phone. This didn't feel right. "I don't think so."

On the other side of the metal door, Mike had heard it too. It'd be impossible not to, it was louder out here, the *brrrrap* echoing off the cinder block. The dull roar was getting louder fast and coming from outside. There were vehicles approaching, Mike knew that much, and vehicles meant there were people in them, and people meant grouping and spread and migration. That was all good and much easier to deal with than the metal door that made his whole body hurt just from looking at it.

I don't have to get in there after all don't have to other people

He turned and walked away down the corridor, toward the sound.

OUTSIDE THE ENTRANCE OF THE BUILDING, HEAD-lights swept down the driveway and splashed across the front facade. There were nine lights in all, a pair from the black half-ton pickup and one each from the seven Harleys, which were the ones making all the noise. Griffin's Fat Boy, outfitted with the straight-pipe exhaust, was the loudest of them all, so loud that even his fellow riders would have told you that it was a little over the top. You know, dude, there *are* other people in the world.

Griffin banked the bike around in a semicircle by the front door, got off, tossed his goggles over the handlebars, and spit in the gravel. He'd been drunk for nearly ten hours at this point, which wasn't that big a deal for him, but along with the weed he'd smoked and the half-pound beef burrito he'd wolfed down around two A.M., things were starting to repeat on him a little bit. Even a fat gut has its limits. The other Harleys rolled to a stop around him and the drivers got off one by one—Cedric, Ironhead, Wino, Cuba, Garbage, and Dr. Steven Friedman.

Dr. Friedman, like Griffin, was the sort of person who was impossible to nickname. Nothing seemed to stick, ever. There was just something about him that screamed Dr. Steven Friedman, and so Dr. Steven Friedman he remained, a reasonably nice dentist who liked to ride and wear leathers. Shorty and the Rev got out of the truck. Most of them were in various stages and types of inebriation, with the exception of Dr. Friedman, who had his eighteen-month chip, and Shorty, who was straight-edge.

The night had started innocently enough at Griffin's rented house, a sparsely furnished two-bedroom ranch-style near Cedar Lake that was down a long driveway at the end of a cul-de-sac. The neighbors were far enough away that they didn't complain about noise, and Griffin didn't care what happened to the place or what you did. You could get wasted, pass out, score just about anything you wanted, and Griffin had fifty-five-inch curved Samsung Premium Ultra 4K TVs in the living room and both bedrooms, all three hooked up to bootleg cable, which meant nobody ever had to fight over what to watch.

They'd come to the storage place at four in the morning because of the TVs. After five months of sitting on a stash of two dozen hot Samsungs, Griffin had finally sold half of them tonight. It hadn't been easy; he'd been working on this group since midnight, and it wasn't until he brought out the last of his meager supply of coke and passed it around that they all agreed to give him a hundred bucks each and take a TV home tonight in the Rev's truck. That was one TV for everybody and five for Garbage, who thought he could unload them to his buddy in the electronics department at Walmart for sale out back. That would be pretty hilarious, as Griffin was pretty sure the Walmart resupply depot in Topeka was where the TVs had come from in the first place. But he knew better than to ask questions.

Griffin had agreed to store and sell the stolen TVs back in October and had grown to hate the things. They retailed for $799 and were supposed to be this big deal when they came out, but then nobody gave a shit that the screen was curved. Or that it was 4K, or LED, or Ultra any of that shit, because you could get almost the same TV anywhere for half the price and the picture looked exactly the same. The deal Griffin and the guy made was they would split any sales Griffin could make fifty-fifty, which meant that tonight, for his troubles, he would clear all of $600. It was barely more than the cost of the storage unit for the five months he'd had it, but at least he wouldn't be underwater anymore, and he'd be halfway out of this problem.

He'd arrived at the storage place angry. He must have called that little turd Teacake a dozen times in the past hour, to tell him he was on his way with some Serious People, and if Teacake knew what was good for him he'd piss off to the other side of the complex and not see things he'd wish he hadn't. But the kid never answered his phone. The shithead had apparently gotten the message, though, because as Griffin stomped to the door, he could see the front desk was unoccupied. But then he froze, passkey in midair, when he saw the wall. His already bulging eyes bulged out even farther.

There was a *hole* in the wall behind the desk. *Two* holes, as a matter of fact, big ones, messy four-foot-wide gashes in the drywall. Griffin's entire bald head flushed crimson, hot blood rushing into it. "What the *fuck* that little shit what the fuck what the *fuck*?!" he wondered. He swiped his card through the reader, the door buzzed, and he stormed inside. He hunched like a boxer getting ready to throw a punch and stalked over to the desk, staring at the holes, aghast.

Ironhead stepped up beside him. "Whoa, Griffin, your shit's fucked up. What kind of place you run here?"

"I'm gonna fucking rip him a new one what the fuck did that little fucker do to my *fucking place of business*?!"

Cedric and Garbage seemed to think it was kind of funny. Ironhead hopped over the desk, drawn by the blinking lights behind the wall. "There's a whole bunch of electronics and shit back here. What is this?"

Dr. Steven Friedman stepped up next to Griffin, sober and sympathetic. "Looks like you have some personnel problems, Darryl." Griffin hated Dr. Friedman, even though he was the only one who used Griffin's Christian name.

Griffin pulled out his phone and stabbed a thick finger at Teacake's number again, but the Rev's voice boomed through the lobby, impatient. "We doing this, or what?"

Griffin hung up. He would kill Teacake later. "Yeah. This way." He walked to the gate that led to the storage units and swiped his card again. The gate buzzed, and they pushed through, headed into the back.

As they made their noisy way down the corridor and into the depths of the storage facility, Cuba heard a sound to her left and turned to look. They were passing the open mouth of another hallway. She got a glimpse of a person: not a security guard, but a slightly puffy guy in too-tight jeans and a work shirt that was green-spattered and strained at the buttons, as if he'd put on a lot of weight recently and refused to buy new clothes. The guy was looking their way as he walked through another intersection a hundred feet away. They made eye contact and she found his look disconcerting, his face as swollen as the rest of him and his stare a bit too intense. She saw him only for a second or two and then he passed out of sight, moving parallel to them in the same direction, as if following them from one corridor away.

Cuba—who had not one ounce of Latina blood in her but did enjoy *ropa vieja*—wondered what kind of weirdo would hang out in a self-storage place at four o'clock in the morning.

She hurried to catch up with the others.

TWENTY-TWO

Trini turned off the lights when they were half a block away and rolled to a quiet stop on the suburban street. Roberto, who'd known enough not to ask questions of Trini until they were immediately relevant, asked the obvious one now. "Where are we going?"

Trini killed the engine, unzipped her purse, and rummaged around until she found a small rolled leather pouch. "Where item seven is." She got out of the car, looked up and down the deserted street, and headed off, staying just beyond the throw of the infrequent streetlights.

Roberto got out, closed his door softly, and caught up. He didn't say anything, just kept pace with her as she counted off the houses. The lights were out in all of them, no respectable person up at this hour. Trini stopped just before a pleasant-looking two-story, stepped up off the street, and started across the grass toward the house. She didn't bother with the front door; instead she went into the narrow yard, about fifty feet of space between the house and the one next to it. She reached a side door, dropped to her knees on the cement slab just outside it, and unrolled the leather pouch on the ground in front of her. "A little light, please?"

Roberto pulled out a key chain with a tiny Maglite on it and bent down, to contain the beam. He clicked it on and held the beam on the pouch. As it rolled open the light glinted off a pick set, half a dozen metal tools of varying shapes and sizes. "Forget your keys?" he whispered.

Trini didn't answer. The less he knew the better, so she offered nothing. She skimmed her fingers over the torsion wrench and the offset pick, glanced up at the style of the lock on the door, and selected an L rake. She wiggled it into the lock and maneuvered it carefully, listening.

Roberto looked around, then back at her in mild annoyance. "This is really the best storage plan you could come up with?"

"Worked for thirty years, didn't it?" She kept wiggling the L rake but wasn't getting anywhere, so she pulled it out, switched to a diamond offset pick, and went back to work with that. "Only pain in the ass was when they moved. Took me six weeks of very creative lying to get them to let me pack the basement by my— There we go!"

The lock had clicked. She turned it gently, using the pick. The door opened a crack. She slid the tools back into the leather roll, tied it quickly, and shoved it in the back of her pants as she stood up. She looked at Roberto, expecting praise but not getting any, then shrugged.

There's no pleasing some people. She opened the door and stepped inside. Roberto followed.

They were in a kitchen, a busy family one, from the looks of it. Even in the dark they could make out the counter, crowded with olive oil jugs and spice bottles and half-read books and somebody's homework and assorted plastic crap. Trini nodded her head and Roberto followed her across the room, silently, to a section of the wall that was covered by a pinboard filled with kids' drawings and ribbons and schedules and reminders. Trini reached down to a half-hidden handle, turned it, and opened the door. "Light again?"

Roberto shined his tiny Maglite ahead of them, revealing a staircase that led to a basement. They glided down the stairs. He kept his light on this time, shining a path ahead of Trini as she moved through the half-converted downstairs space, past the ratty sofa and the broken, permanently reclined recliner, around the bumper pool table, and to another door at the far end of the room.

She turned the handle and pushed into an unfinished storage room. The family had lived there for quite a while and there must have been a number of kids, spread out over a fairly wide age range, because there was everything down here from old Big Wheels to a rack of frequently used skis. The back half of the storage room was curtained off, and whatever was piled back there bulged, threatening to push right through the curtain. Trini pulled it aside.

The character of the stuff in the back half of the room was different. There was no kid paraphernalia back here, just a lot of beat-up old crates and cases packed on top of one another, unsentimental keepsakes like camp trunks and an old snowblower. There was a narrow path through the cases, a definite method to someone's pack-rat madness, and Trini held her hand out for the light. Roberto gave it to her and she turned sideways, making her way between the cases toward the very back of the very back.

There was a large storage container there, locked in three places along its front edge. Trini pulled out a set of keys, handed the light back to Roberto, and opened the locks, then the lid. Inside the trunk was a large, flat wooden tray with divisions of all shapes and sizes, filled with colorful pieces of paper. Roberto's first thought was that it was currencies—maybe Trini had a run box down here—but on closer examination the paper wasn't money at all, it was much too small and square. Trini drew her breath in sharply, as if she'd forgotten what was in the box, and he flicked the light up to her face.

She was grinning like a six-year-old. "My stamp collection!" She ran her fingers lightly over the rows of neatly mounted stamps, sorted by country and continent, each one on a tiny piece of stiff cardboard, its date and origin neatly lettered beside it. She picked one up, fascinated. "Kampuchea! That's rare!"

"Maybe not right this second?"

"Sorry. Forgot it was here." She spread her

arms out, reaching all the way to both sides of the five-foot-long box, and locked her hands around the wood frame of its top tray. She wiggled it a little and lifted, pulling the whole tray out, the way you would the top level of a foot-locker. She turned, found a flat place nearby, and while she set it down, Roberto turned the light back to the trunk. Beneath the top shelf was a mountain of bubble wrap. He started pulling it aside, Trini turned back and pulled the rest out, and finally they uncovered what they'd come for.

The thing was big and shaped like a water barrel that had been cut in half vertically. The flat portion had a series of straps and ropes and buckles and clamps, and they wrapped around the barrel itself with three or four leather straps. As a container it was meant to be lightweight, but with that size there wasn't much of a chance it actually was. The exterior was covered in a light-colored canvas, with some kind of hard shell underneath.

It was exactly as Roberto remembered it from thirty years ago. He wasn't sure why he'd thought it would be any different. "Looks old."

Trini shrugged. "So are we. We still work."

True, but they were human bodies, meant to age and decay and malfunction from time to time, and the half-barrel backpack was a T-41 Cloudburst, a selectable-yield man-portable nu-clear weapon. If Trini's or Roberto's body broke down, they'd die, and a few people would cry for a while. If the T-41 broke down, everybody within a ten-mile radius died.

The T-41 was a product of the Operation Nougat tests in the early 1960s, after Eisenhower had first authorized and implemented the concept of battlefield nuclear weapons. Subsequent models were refined and deployed throughout the late '60s, most of them to various Western European hotspots. The idea behind the weapons was that they could be used to stave off a Russian invasion. They were to be delivered where needed by U.S. Army Green Light Teams, elite squads of soldiers specially schooled in the care and activation of portable nuclear weapons. The weapons were designed so that they could be carried behind enemy lines by a one- or two-man squad, set with a timer or radio detonator, and used to destroy strategic locations such as bridges, munitions dumps, or tank encampments. They could also be delivered by parachute or into water, or buried to a depth of up to twenty feet, although detonation was significantly less reliable than when accompanied by a technician.

The T-41, like most of the W54 series of special atomic demolition munitions, SADMs, could be adjusted to a yield as low as ten tons or as high as one kiloton, which was enough to destroy either two city blocks or the entirety of the country of Lichtenstein. In the latter circumstance, the safe escape of the Green Light Team was highly in doubt, and the soldiers who had taken the job had been told to view it as a kamikaze mission.

This particular T-41 had been built and deployed in 1971, for use in the Fulda Gap in West

Germany. Strategically critical for most of the modern era, the Fulda Gap contains two corridors of lowlands through which it was feared Soviet tanks might drive in a surprise attack on the Rhine River Valley, their entrance to Western Europe. To prevent a drawn-out tank battle, the idea was that a single T-41 would remove the threat in a controlled burst of destruction. Nuclear weapons, in those early days, were viewed by some in the Pentagon as just bigger and more effective versions of conventional bombs. By 1988 sentiment had changed, the INF Treaty had taken firm hold, and the last three hundred SADMs were removed from Western Europe, decommissioned, and dismantled.

Except for this one. For three years after confirmation of the success of the Kiwirrkurra firebombing, Roberto, Trini, Gordon Gray, and two other cohorts in the DTRA had been on a fruitless and frustrating quest to warn their superiors of the need for a contingency plan should *Cordyceps novus* ever escape its confinement beneath the Atchison mines. The nature of the storage facility was ideally suited to a controlled detonation of a nuclear device, they'd argued. With proper planning and placement, they could closely limit loss of life. Even an underground nuclear blast would be impossible to conceal, they granted, but after all, this was a break-the-glass scenario that would likely never have to be used. Still, shouldn't they be ready for it?

Rebuffed or ignored at every turn, they had finally taken matters into their own hands. As disarmament activities swept through Western Europe, they falsified movement records within the Joint Elimination Coordination Element, and, thirty years later, here it was. The contingency plan, in a box in a basement, underneath Trini's stamp collection.

Roberto started to lift the unit out of the crate and felt a twinge in his back. He stopped immediately—*Don't push it, moron*—bent his knees, straightened his torso to vertical, and lifted. The T-41 weighed fifty-eight pounds, heavier than he expected or remembered. He set it on the edge of the crate and looked up at Trini. "Hold on to that for a second, will ya?"

She reached out and steadied it. He turned around and squatted down, facing away from it. He looped his arms through the straps, tightened them as much as he could, exhaled, and stood up again. He could feel it in his thighs already. This thing was *heavy*, and he was not the man he used to be. "Okay to go."

She turned, shined the light on him, and laughed.

"What?" he asked.

"The shit we get ourselves into."

"Keeps retirement interesting," he said. "After you."

They headed off, back to the other side of the curtain in the unfinished storage area, around the bumper pool table, past the broken recliner, and to the stairs that led to the kitchen. She was on the fourth step up and Roberto had his foot on the very first one when the basement fluorescents all switched on.

They froze, momentarily blinded. They looked up, wincing at the light, and could make out the silhouette of a man at the top of the stairs, a guy in boxer shorts and a Kansas City Chiefs T-shirt, pointing a shotgun at them.

Roberto's mind flicked through options and found none, not with this *refrigerator* strapped to his back, and not in this position, second up at the base of a flight of stairs facing a guy who already had the drop on him with a twelve gauge. For the first time in a long while, he searched his mind, instincts, and experiences and came up with exactly nothing. "Uh," he said.

The guy at the top of the stairs sighed. He pulled the gun back, looking at Trini. "Mom. *Really?*"

Trini smiled. "Hi, sweetie." She looked him up and down. "You look heavy." It was true, Roberto noticed; that T-shirt was a little clingy in the paunch.

The man came down a few steps, cautious with the shotgun and even more careful with his voice, keeping it low. "What are you *doing*?"

Trini continued up the stairs toward him, and Roberto followed. "Oh, just grabbing something," she said. "Out of your hair in two seconds." Remembering she wasn't alone, she turned around. "Sorry, Anthony, this is my friend Roberto—"

Roberto came up another step, reaching a

hand past her to shake. "We met. I think you were about three years old."

Anthony took it reflexively. "Uh-huh." He turned back to Trini. "Janet would kill you. And me."

Trini made a zipping motion across her lips, gestured up the stairs, and Anthony turned. He trudged back upstairs, reached the kitchen, and stepped out of the way, letting them pass. He couldn't help but see the enormous military-looking thing Roberto had strapped to his back, but he just rolled his eyes and looked the other way. He went to the kitchen door and opened it, showing them out wordlessly. Trini turned back to him when they got outside.

"Maybe Thanksgiving?"

"Maybe. I'll work on it."

"Love you, sweetie."

"Love you too, Mom."

The door closed softly. As they made their way back across the darkened lawn to the mini-van, Roberto couldn't take the silence.

"Seems like he turned out nice."

"Yeah, good kid."

Roberto looked at her as they approached the van. "I'm just wondering . . ."

"Yeah?"

"Well, the, uh, location. That you chose to store this."

"What about it?"

"Um—the children?"

Trini rolled her eyes. "Oh, come *on*. It's not

like they know how to activate it. Jesus, you're overcautious."

Roberto dropped it. Trini was Trini, and that's what he liked about her.

TEN MINUTES LATER, THEY WERE PARKED OUTSIDE Trini's house, her work done. Roberto was behind the wheel now, item number seven in the back. He'd been on the ground in Kansas for thirty-two minutes.

Trini gestured, pointing down the street. "Turn right here, second left after that, you hit the on-ramp in about half a mile. It's a straight shot up the 73."

"How long to Atchison?"

"Twenty-five minutes. Sure you don't want me to—" She cut off, going into a hacking cough that sounded painful.

Roberto looked at her. The night had drained her almost completely, and they both knew there was no way she could or should go with him. "I'll be okay," he said. "You still got it, you know."

She shook another cigarette out of the box and lit it. "You will try to get those two out, won't you?"

He thought for a moment. "I don't know if I can."

"Try. Okay?"

He looked at her. "You're getting soft in your sunset years."

Trini smiled. "Sun's already down, *guapo*. The fireflies are out." She took a deep drag off the cigarette and blew out a big, billowy cloud. It swirled and wrapped around her head in the still night air.

Roberto reached a hand out the window and rested it on her shoulder. She tilted her head toward it, grateful for the human touch. "You call me up any time you want," he said. "I'll sling all the bullshit you can handle."

She smiled. "That'd be nice."

TWENTY-THREE

Mary Rooney had fallen asleep on the daybed in her storage unit hours ago and might well have slept there all night, if it weren't for Mike's gunshots. It wouldn't have been the first time she'd spent the night in good old SB-211; in fact, she'd found that lately it was the only place she slept well at all anymore. She'd started with short naps every once in a while, just taking a few extra minutes to spend with her lifetime of memories. But once she'd moved the daybed out of the guest room at home and into storage, things got awfully cozy in here. The naps got longer and longer. Where else was it completely peaceful, where else could she be surrounded by her loved ones' things, and where else did she feel as safe? Certainly not in her apartment, with the ill-advised roommate she'd taken in at the insistence of her kids, who were worried about her living alone. Mary had come in today with the last of Tom's things, a couple of shoeboxes filled with his mementos and certificates of meritorious service from his time on the force. As she'd set about putting it all in its proper bin, the walk down memory lane became exhausting, and she'd lain down and drifted off.

She was awake now, that was for sure. The first report from the .22 had done the trick. This place was an echo chamber and there was no mistaking a gunshot. Mary had sat up, wide-awake for the next half dozen shots, which fully answered the question *Did I dream that?* No, she had not. Someone was shooting out there from somewhere up above her. Who the hell was robbing a storage facility in the middle of the night, and why were they killing people to do it? That made no sense to her at all.

Or maybe, she thought, it was one of those crazy mass shooters you see all the time, but that made even less sense—didn't they want to kill a *lot* of people? Wasn't that sort of the whole point? She'd never seen more than two people in this place at a time. Mary had sat stock-still for the next fifteen minutes or so, not daring to leave her locked storage unit, but there was no way she was going to be able to go back to sleep either.

When the roar of the motorcycles echoed from outside, she'd heard voices in the hallway, a lot of voices, and she'd started trying to come up with a plan. Staying in here all night until the situation resolved was probably the best idea, but what if there were people in danger? What could she do about it? A better question—what would Tom do? She looked at her husband's things, sorted and piled so neatly and lovingly on the metal-and-particle-board storage racks she'd ordered off Amazon and assembled all by herself. She tried to put Tom in her shoes.

Because Tom would definitely do *something*.

TWENTY-FOUR

Nearby, Teacake and Naomi had been sorting through plans of their own ever since they'd heard the sound of the Harleys. They'd heard Mike's footsteps as he headed off down the hallway, apparently drawn by the sound himself. Teacake had come to a conclusion about it all that he was unwilling to be moved off of.

"This is like some kinda zombie shit."

Naomi was feeling more reasonable. "Okay, first of all, zombies are not real."

"Zombies are real. Zombies are a hundred percent real."

"No, they're not, Travis. That's TV. That's movies."

"Yes, and some really fucking excellent TV and movies, I'd like to point out, but that's not what I'm talking about. Zombies are totally real, they're based on this shit in Haiti, it's like common knowledge or whatever. It's dead bodies they make into slaves with magic. I cannot *believe* you don't know that. And you want to be a vet?"

She looked at him. "Do you actually believe that is what's going on here? Haitian magic?"

"What? Fuck no. I'm not an idiot." He was getting impatient.

"So what is your point?"

"I said this is *like* some kinda zombie shit, as opposed to *exact* zombie shit, which I understand is, like, not a thing in Kansas, okay? Whereas, i.e., that is to say, in reality here tonight, there is some growing green fungus and a Rat King and an exploding deer and a dude that wants to throw up in your fucking mouth." He made a gesture that said his point was proven.

"Right. And?"

"The *thing*—whatever it is—it's spreading. It *wants* to spread. Call it whatever you want, but the thing is in here, in this building, and it wants to get out there, into the world. So what are we gonna do about it? Twenty years from now, when you and me are sitting around the fire and our great-grandchildren are asking us what we did way back in the great big zombie war, what are we gonna be able to tell 'em?" She opened her mouth to speak, but he held up a hand to stop her and kept talking. "And yeah, I know, my math doesn't add up on the great-grandchildren thing, so don't even start."

She wasn't going to quibble with his math; she had been about to point out that he had just assumed they were going to have children together. But that seemed beside the point, and kind of sweet anyway, so she let him keep going.

"We gotta go out there and stop that dude before he throws up in somebody *else's* mouth."

"Why do we have to do it? The guy on the phone said he'll be here in twenty minutes."

"Yeah, and who is that, exactly?" he asked. "A guy on the phone who talks a big game? A lady at Fort Belvoir who had to hang up on you and call you back on her cell phone? Why would she do that? These are fucking amateurs, man, they're just as scared as we are. I don't know why, but they are. Now, if you'd talked to Colonel Dick Steel or whoever, and he said there were a half a dozen Sikorskys flying in here with missiles armed and playing 'Don't Fear the Reaper' on big speakers, I'd maybe wait around and let that happen. But I don't think we have time to sit here hoping a couple freelancers show up and don't get eaten before they get out of their own car. We gotta go out there and *do* something."

The debate bounced back and forth for another minute or two. Teacake had by now played Griffin's messages and knew it was him and his lowlife biker buddies who had arrived, probably to pick up the stolen merchandise. It was all Teacake's fault, of course, because he'd been unwilling to bend the rules, yet another example of doing the right thing and getting screwed because of it. But he and Naomi finally agreed that Griffin and his friends, though admittedly detestable, were human beings and didn't deserve to die. Or, if they must, it would be great if they didn't spread a deadly fungus to the rest of the

world on their way out. They agreed that starting with a phone call made sense.

Teacake hit Call Back on Griffin's last incoming call to him and waited. The phone rang
twice before Griffin answered. He was talking
before the phone got to his mouth, so it picked
up midsentence. "—you fuckwit you ever ignore
my calls again and I'll fucking fire you think this
is some kinda fucking game I promise you it—"
and then his voice faded away again as he lowered the phone and hung it up, also midsentence.

Teacake looked at the phone. "Wow."

"What?"

"He's just such an asshole. I'm always kinda
taken aback."

"He hung up?"

Teacake nodded and called again. It went
straight to voice mail. Teacake lowered his
phone, stumped. "I have to admit, I did not see
that coming."

"Did he sound all right?"

"Well, he sounded like a jerkoff. So I guess it
was him and he's all right. Let's get to him before
your friend does."

"He's not my friend," she said, indignant.

"Whatever. The guy you had a baby with.
Let's stop him." He went to the door and threw
the bolt on one end. She stepped in front of the
bolt on the other end, not done talking about
this yet.

"He has a gun."

"He has a .22. Yes, a .22 can fuck you up, but

the magazine only holds ten rounds, and I think he used them all."

"How do you know?" she asked.

"Because while we sat here for the last fifteen minutes I counted 'em in my head. One in the hallway, when we were running away from him. Three outside the door, when I was rolling under it. And six that he shot at the door after we had it locked. Look, you can see where every one of 'em hit."

She looked up and, indeed, there were six little dimples, spread out over a three-foot area in the metal door, where the slugs had dented the outside. She was impressed.

Teacake continued. "So, he can't shoot us, right? He can only barf at us or blow up on us, but if we stay far enough away that's not gonna matter. We get Griffin and whatever shitheads he showed up with to clear out, keep your baby daddy inside this place—"

"Please stop that."

"—and wait for the cavalry to come. If they know what they're doing, then boom. We saved the world. Or at least eastern Kansas." He paused. When a good salesman knew he had a kicker, he always saved it till last and used as few words to express it as possible. Teacake knew he had it, so he took a suitable pause and then deployed it. "And your kid too."

Naomi looked at him, touched.

Teacake went on, and this was the part that meant more to him than all the rest. It was the part he hadn't realized until he got almost all the way through his speech and understood why he was selling so hard, why he was campaigning for the right to open the door and go risk his life when he didn't absolutely have to. This bit came from the heart.

"Look, I know they pay us for shit here, but this place hired me straight outta jail, and nobody else would do that. I'm supposed to take care of it, and for once in my life, it would be nice to not fuck something up. This is my one job, and yes, it's a shitty one, but it's the only one I've got or that I'm gonna get. You don't have to come with. I'll leave, you lock the door, I'll come back and get you when it's clear."

Naomi looked at him, and she thought, *It's funny. Some things improve with closer inspection. He sure did.*

She threw the bolt on the other side of the door and, together, they pulled it up over their heads and stepped out into the hallway.

Immediately, Teacake was proven right about one thing—the gun must have been empty, because Mike had left it behind, on the floor where he'd sat. They started down the corridor. They'd taken only three or four steps when Naomi's phone buzzed.

She signaled to Teacake, stopped, and answered it, whispering, "Still here."

It was Abigail, ten minutes on the dot since she had last called. "Good. Just checking. Is your situation unchanged?"

Naomi hesitated. "Not exactly."

"What does that mean?"

"We left the locker."

Abigail paused, thinking. "I am at a loss as to why you would do that."

"There are more people here now. We gotta tell 'em."

"How many people?"

"I don't know. Call me back." She hung up and looked at Teacake. "She was not happy."

Teacake shrugged. "Who is?"

THE LAST
THIRTY-FOUR MINUTES

TWENTY-FIVE

The loading of the Samsung boxes had gone pretty well so far but was taking longer than Griffin wanted. The renegotiation had slowed everything down. After all the work of finally selling these bozos on the TVs, that prick Ironhead had tried to lower the price to $75 at the last minute. And it wasn't like he did it quietly either—everybody heard, and everybody wanted the same. Ironhead was good at this; they didn't call him Ironhead just because of the bike he rode. He worked in sales at IRT and negotiating was second nature to him, so he'd waited till they were standing in the unit, took one look around at the overstock, and knew he had Griffin over a barrel. They haggled for a couple minutes, but Griffin's head was throbbing by this point, and the idea of everybody walking out of here and *leaving* these things was unthinkable. So $75 it was, the grand total take-home for the night was going to be $450 instead of $600, but whatever, Griffin took it.

The TVs were heavy and awkwardly shaped, so it took two people to carry them out, one at a time. Cedric and Wino had taken the first one out, Cuba and Garbage the second, Shorty and the Rev the third, and Griffin and Dr. Steven Friedman had made two trips already. Ironhead had somehow managed to cast himself in more of a supervisory capacity and was leaning against the inside wall of the unit grabbing a quick vape when Mike showed up in the doorway.

Mike stood there for a long moment, his breath wheezing in and out. He stared at Ironhead, who looked back at him. "What the fuck do you want?"

Mike didn't answer, just stared. Ironhead blew out a cloud of smoke. "I asked you a question, dickhead."

Mike still didn't answer. Ironhead took a step forward. "You are about to have a serious problem, man. Privacy of the eyes, motherfucker, either you take two steps back and look away from me right this fucking second, or I will bounce your head off that wall till it goes pop. You understand?"

Mike turned away and looked down the hallway, not because Ironhead told him to, but because he heard voices. Cedric, Wino, Cuba, and Garbage were headed back from their first load to the truck, coming for more, and they were drawing close. They saw Mike, but he took a few steps back, giving them plenty of space. Ironhead assumed he had managed to intimidate the psycho who'd been staring at him.

"That's what I thought," he said to Mike as

the others came back into the unit to get another TV. Cuba looked over her shoulder, recognizing the weirdo who had watched them earlier. His shirt was even tighter than before, two of the buttons already popped over his swollen midsection, and a couple others looking like they were about to give way.

"What does that guy want?" she asked Ironhead. "I saw him before."

"Fuck if I know. Don't worry about him. Just keep going, we don't got all night."

Cedric had seen enough of Ironhead's bossy behavior over the years to be sick of it. "When are you gonna grab one, you lazy piece of shit?"

"Hey, I'm *coordinating*. You should be thanking me. I should be charging you a commission for the money I saved you."

From outside, they heard shouts, two voices somewhere far away, and they looked again, past that weird staring guy, but didn't see anybody. Ironhead turned back to the others, waving them along with some urgency. "Get a TV, come *on*, let's get the hell out of here."

There was a low tearing sound, like a sheet ripping in half, and they all turned at the same time. Mike was back in the doorway, and the sound had come from his midsection. His stomach lining, stretched beyond its elastic capacity, had finally separated from the stomach wall and was now a free-floating mass of viscous jelly inside his abdomen.

He had less than ninety seconds to live.

Jaws dropped open, but only Ironhead managed to get a couple of words out. "What the f—"

He cut off, because all at once Mike's stomach collapsed inward as his body forced his insides up, through his throat, into his mouth, and out into the air at twenty-five miles per hour. That's not very fast for a car, but for puke it's super quick, and it covered the distance between Mike and the rest of them in less than a second. Certainly, it was less time than any of them had to react, and the spray of the droplets was wide, so they were all caught and contaminated by the blast. They screamed, staggered back, and Mike reached up, slamming the overhead door and slipping the padlock back through the hole—he wasn't exactly sure why, but he knew he had more work to do and needed them to stay out of the way.

The evolved form of *Cordyceps novus* inside Mike was racking up one positive growth experience after another, and now it had learned the value of *not* detonating a host's body at the very first opportunity. Mike's spread of the fungal mass had proven just as effective via vomit as it would have been by the fruiting burst of his entire body, plus it had the additional advantage of leaving him somewhat intact and mobile for at least another sixty seconds.

The fungus was an excellent student. It learned.

From inside the storage locker, Mike heard shouts and screams, but they were contained. They just needed to stay that way for a minute or two. Mike didn't have much left inside; he was consuming and expelling himself rapidly, and he had to make sure that what little there was left of him went to a good cause.

The other humans.

He turned toward where the shouts had come from.

LESS THAN TWO MINUTES EARLIER, NAOMI AND Teacake had come out of the storage unit. Naomi had answered Abigail's call, hung up on her, and they'd pressed on, making their way cautiously down the corridor. Naomi's phone buzzed again, but she ignored it this time, hit the button on the side and sent the call to voice mail. From up ahead, they heard voices. Teacake moved to an intersection, leaned around the edge, and looked down the next hallway, where he knew Griffin kept the storage unit with the stolen TVs.

The unit was about fifty feet away, and he could see the door to it was wide open. Mike was standing in the open doorway, looking inside, and Teacake could see shapes inside the unit, four or five people. They were doing something, but they sure as hell weren't paying attention to Mike, which was what they should have been doing. Naomi came around the corner as Mike started to suck his gut in and out. They both knew what was coming next and shouted at the same time to the poor bastards inside the unit—*look out, get away, get the hell out of there*—but they were too late. They could only watch as Mike's stomach emptied itself and the fungus sprayed into the storage unit. They watched as he reached up, slammed the door, locked it, and turned to them.

He stared at them for a moment.

Then he ran at them.

From the looks of Mike's decomposing body, it didn't seem like he'd be capable of running, but he was, in a rapid, shambling sort of way, coming at them hard and fast. He was already too close for them to turn and run themselves, and Teacake realized, with some regret, that his grand heroic plan had consisted of almost zero real ideas. Leave the unit, tell the others, save the earth? Honestly, that was a for *shit* plan, it didn't deserve the word *plan*, it didn't deserve to be mentioned in the context of real plans. He'd convinced Naomi, this totally decent woman and awesome mother who actually mattered on this earth, to leave the safety of their hiding place and step out into a danger- ous situation with no concrete strategy and no- body but him, the Planless Wonder, to protect her. Teacake heard his father's voice in his head, telling his idiot son the same thing he'd told him for the last fifteen years.

"If you didn't have shit for brains you'd have no brains at all."

Mike was only a second away from them now and Teacake squatted low, to lunge himself at their attacker, to at least block him long enough so that Naomi would have time to run. He tensed his legs, ready to spring forward.

Naomi heard the gunshots first, because they came from a foot and a half behind her left ear.

They were so loud they burst her left eardrum and temporarily deafened her in the right.

A Glock 21SF .45 automatic has been standard issue for the Kansas Highway Patrol since 2009. Nobody really had any idea why they felt they needed quite that much firepower, but the last people who would complain tonight were Teacake and Naomi. Six slugs from the .45 whistled past Naomi's head, over Teacake's shoulder, and slammed into Mike's chest with such force that they reversed his course of motion. They lifted him off his feet, blew him back two yards in the air, and dropped him to the cement floor, dead. His fungus-riddled body was in such a state of disrepair and disarray that he nearly disintegrated on impact.

Naomi, completely deaf in her left ear and overwhelmed by a loud ringing in her right, turned and saw the woman standing behind her, holding the smoking weapon.

Teacake rose, looking at the woman with eyes wide.

"Mrs. Rooney?!"

Mary Rooney lowered her dead husband's service weapon, the one she had reported lost rather than turn in when he died, the one she'd brought to the storage unit in the shoebox that very day.

She turned from Mike's scattered remains and looked back at Naomi and Teacake. "That boy just wasn't right."

THE GUNSHOTS WERE STILL ECHOING IN THE LOBBY when Shorty and the Rev turned on their heels and took off for the pickup truck. The situation wasn't the sort of thing you needed to stick around and try to figure out. Six gunshots—like *cannon* shots, these things—coming from what sounded like a semiautomatic weapon somewhere a hundred feet ahead of you, while you were in the process of loading stolen merchandise into your truck in the middle of the night? Yeah, you go ahead and get the hell out of there as fast as you can.

They jumped in the truck, Shorty threw it in reverse and stomped on the gas, and gravel flew so hard and so far that it left a spatter of cut marks in the glass entry doors. She spun the wheel, the truck skidded around in a neat 180, and they took off up the driveway without a look back.

Griffin and Dr. Steven Friedman weren't positionally advantaged in the same way, however. They were already on their way back to the storage locker for another load of TVs, just around the corner from it when they heard the blasts. Dr. Friedman ducked low and threw his hands up to cover his ears, a biologically useless response that left him a sitting duck in the middle of the hallway, but his years in dental school included no training for this sort of predicament.

Griffin was different. Griffin had gamed out this kind of scenario a hundred times while playing *School Shooter: North American Tour 2012*, a modification for *Half-Life 2* that he'd downloaded off the internet. He responded instinctively, joyfully, flattening himself against the wall and pulling the Smith & Wesson M&P 40C from the shoulder holster under his jacket. Before the shots had faded, he'd done a quick recon, left-right-left, and saw the hallway was clear except for Dr. Friedman, who was still crouched in the middle of it. Griffin took one step forward, grabbed the dentist by the collar with his hammy left hand, and dragged him back against the wall.

Dr. Friedman looked up at him, still crouched, terrified. "What the hell is going on?" he asked in a trembling whisper.

"Active shooter," Griffin said.

He hadn't felt this good in years.

TWENTY-SIX

Roberto was on Highway 73, just eight miles outside of Atchison, when Abigail's call came. His cell phone was still sealed in the pouch, so he'd left his laptop open on the passenger seat, using an AT&T card to stay connected to the internet. He put in his Bluetooth, hit the space bar to answer, and listened while she explained the latest development from inside the storage place.

He wasn't quite sure he actually understood. "They left? What do you mean they left?"

"They're not in the unit."

"Why the hell not?"

"She said there were others inside the facility and they had to warn them."

"Great. They're noble. How many others?"

"She didn't say."

"Can you get her back on the phone?"

"I've tried four times. She doesn't answer."

"How long ago was this?"

"Less than two minutes."

"What about the other person?" he asked. "The infected one, outside their door."

"She didn't say."

"You didn't ask?"

"It was a very short conversation. She hung up on me. You know everything I know."

"Okay," he said, thinking. "Okay. Okay." He repeated everything she'd just said, because that's what he'd been taught forty years ago. "Naomi told you she and the other clean body were leaving the storage unit because they heard others had arrived. She did not say how many. You have not had contact with her since. This was about two minutes ago. Do I have that right?"

"Yes, sir."

"Do you know their names?" he asked.

"Yes."

Roberto thought quickly. Damage assessment, diminishing returns, risk versus reward, evaluating the rotten situation and deciding on the least rotten course of action. He had an idea, but it meant widening the circle. Could help, but it would have to be a cloudless night. He put down his window, stuck his head outside, and looked up. The sky directly overhead was clear, a brilliant canopy of stars. Okay, they got lucky on the weather. He put the window back up.

"I'm going to need some aerial help," he said into the phone.

There was a pause on the other end. "I don't see how that's possible."

"Anything's possible, Abigail. Some things are just more possible than others."

"I don't have those types of resources."

"I know exactly what kinds of resources you

do and do not have, okay?" He didn't mean to snap at her, and he softened his tone. He had exactly one ally at the moment and couldn't afford to lose her.

"You want satellite reconnaissance." She said it the way someone would say, "You want a billion dollars."

"I *want* a Global Hawk directly overhead at ten thousand feet, but we'd never get one here from Edwards in time. I'll settle for a Keyhole. A ten-minute redirect would do it."

"That would require attorney general approval."

"Yeah, if we were going that route. But we're a little more informal on this one."

"You're crazy. Operationally, I mean. You're almost delusional."

"No, I'm ambitious, Abigail, and so are you. Come on, who do you know at the NRO?" The National Reconnaissance Office handled coordination of surveillance satellites and dissemination of data within and among the NSA, CIA, FBI, and Homeland Security.

"I don't know anybody there," she said with irritation.

"Can you please lose the attitude? I will be on-site in nine minutes." He looked down at his speed and saw he was over eighty. He lightened up on the gas.

There was another pause on the other end of the line, then Abigail's voice came back, still tentative, but he could almost feel her mind engaging with the problem. "My friend Stephanie dates a guy at the ADF-E." The Aerospace Data Facility–East was located just on the other side of Fort Belvoir and was the operational hub of reconnaissance satellites all over the world.

"See?" Roberto said. "You see what you can do?"

"But I'd have to wake her up—he'd have to be on duty—"

"We'll need a few things to break our way, no question."

"I'll call you back."

"Wait," he said. "Have you ever met this guy?"

"No. I saw a picture of him once."

"Who's better looking, him or Stephanie?"

"I don't know. Do we really have time for that?"

"Stephanie, I mean, Abigail—goddammit." He was getting tired and seriously cranky. "Please just answer the question. Who is better looking?"

"Stephanie is gorgeous. She's way out of his league."

"That's our first break right there. Wake her up. You have the coordinates already. I need eyes overhead in five minutes. If any infected people leave that place, I need to know how many there are and where they go. Got it?"

"Got it."

"And get me some personal information on both of the people inside that place. The clean ones. Work history, favorite ice cream, whatever you can come up with, I might need it. Understood?"

"Understood." Abigail hung up to get to work.

Roberto pulled out the earpiece and closed the laptop. He allowed himself a tiny sigh. This was sort of, possibly, maybe going to work out. He'd forgotten how many people he knew and how good he was at getting the best out of the ones he didn't. Wrinkles appeared, and he ironed them out. There's just no substitute for experience. You take a lifetime of acquired skills, season it with the wisdom of age, throw in some good instincts and reflexes—you can't learn those, you have to bring 'em to the party—and you've got yourself a pretty damn effective operative. Hell, maybe he never should have retired in the first place. He'd be there in eight minutes and have this resolved within the hour. He smiled.

Then the cop popped his lights.

Roberto looked up into the rearview mirror, a familiar sinking feeling in his stomach. The cop was so close behind him and the flashing red cherries so bright they stung his eyes. He looked down at the speedometer. The needle was pushing ninety. Speeding? He was *speeding*? *Yeah, you're a real genius, Roberto.*

He banged a fist off the steering wheel and drove on for a moment, his mind racing in eighteen different directions, every single one of them a dead end. The cop double-tapped the siren, and the *whoop whoop* almost made Roberto jump out of his skin.

He had no choice. He pulled over.

The gravel shoulder crunched under Roberto's tires and he brought the minivan to a smooth and responsible stop. He looked up into the rearview to see if there was anything he could learn. The cop's car was a standard four-door sedan, probably a Chevy Impala. It had a red light bar on the roof, square headlights with alternately flashing high beams, and a blue zipper light in the front grille. This information, taken as a whole, was of absolutely no use whatsoever.

A look back over his shoulder was too much an admission of guilt, so Roberto switched to the side view, where the angle would mean he was a bit less blinded. The police car hadn't pulled as far onto the shoulder as he had, so he could make out the cop's silhouette through the windshield. The man was looking down, radio in hand, probably just ran the plates and was waiting for a response. Roberto steadied his breathing, running through options. There weren't any good ones. Taking off was the worst—you can't outrun radio waves. He'd end up in a high-speed chase that he would lose.

He thought about throwing the minivan in reverse and slamming into the cop's front end, hoping he'd get lucky and pop a tire, but he was just as likely to blow one of his own, which would make it a real short chase. And even if he got lucky and disabled the police car without damaging his own, see section regarding radio waves.

Reluctantly, he thought about killing the cop. Even if he could get his head around murdering an innocent officer of the law who was just doing his job, he had no weapon on his person. The nearest gun would be an unloaded M9 in one of the trunks in back. Trini would have left a full clip in the foam packing beside it that he could slap in in a second, but getting to it would be a problem. If he made the slightest move toward the rear of the car, that cop would be out of his own vehicle and crouched behind his door with his weapon drawn in seconds.

And then there was that part about killing an innocent cop. He'd never done that before.

The door of the police car opened, and the cop got out. He was tall, maybe six feet four inches, and he had his round-brimmed hat in one hand. He paused, closed his door, and took a good long time putting on his hat and adjusting it just so. Great, he was a dick on top of everything else.

He started to walk toward Roberto's car. Roberto watched in the side view, still thinking. A bribe seemed unlikely to have any effect, and he had only a few hundred dollars in his pocket anyway. As the cop reached his window, one last desperate thought popped into Roberto's mind. Maybe try the truth?

Never work in a million years.

He opened the window. The cop glanced at him, bent down ever so slightly, and checked to reconfirm that Roberto was the only passenger. "License and registration, please."

"Was I speeding?" Jesus, that was it? The skilled professional, and that was what he came up with, the exact same thing that every single motorist who has ever been pulled over in the history of the interstate highway system said? *Was I speeding?!*

"You were. License and registration?"

"I'm going to open my glove compartment," Roberto said. *See? I'm a good citizen. I'm a reasonable guy like you. You can trust me. See?*

"Go ahead," the cop replied.

Roberto leaned over and opened the glove compartment, having no idea what he would see inside. It occurred to him, as he pushed the button on the front, that there very well could be a weapon in there. Trini was thorough, and she would have sent him out into that good night fully prepared for any situation that might arise, including a sudden need to arm himself. He hesitated, his finger on the button of the glove compartment, and thought about how mistakes can cascade on you. He let it hang there for a second while he thought. Revealing a gun in the glove box was going to deteriorate this situation in a big hurry.

"Sir?" Roberto's head was turned toward the glove compartment, so he couldn't see the cop, but he could feel his presence, and he could hear the rustle of the man's shirt as his arm moved. There was a very subtle creak of leather, and Roberto knew the cop's right hand was now resting on the butt end of his sidearm, moving it infinitesimally in its holster to make sure it wasn't stuck.

Things were falling apart fast. Again, he had no choice. He had to open the glove compartment and hope. He released the button, it clicked, and the door fell open.

There was no gun. He closed his eyes and

willed himself to breathe. Still okay. Not only was there no gun, but there was a neat yellow rental car jacket, the paperwork exactly where it should be. Roberto picked it up, turned, and offered it out the window to the cop. "It's a rental."

The cop took the papers. "Your license?"

"Inside my jacket." He held up his hand, just outside his jacket—*May I?*

"Go ahead."

Roberto reached into his jacket, took out his wallet, removed his license, and handed that out the window too. The cop took it.

Roberto waited while the cop inspected the documents. If Trini had rented the car in her own name, he would have some explaining to do, but that was the least of his problems at the moment. That one he could talk his way out of. He looked at the dashboard clock. He'd lost three minutes already, he needed to be rolling in another two or the satellite window he'd asked for, which he had no reason to think Abigail was even going to be able to open, would be closed by the time he needed it.

How could everything be so much worse now than it was just 180 seconds ago?

"Thank you, Mr. Diaz." Roberto heard a slight pause and the tiny bit of spin the cop put on his last name, tried to think about whether that casual racism would help or hurt matters, and concluded it made no difference. The policeman handed him back his documents, saying nothing about the rental car registration. Damn,

Trini was a star, she'd even put the car in his name. Roberto took the papers.

As the cop turned his focus from the documents to the inside of the car, his gaze stopped abruptly on the back. The tarp that Trini had thrown over the military crates wasn't big enough to completely conceal them, not with the addition of the half-barrel-shaped T-41. To anyone who had any experience at all, or even watched the right kind of TV shows, the stuff in back looked exactly like what it was—crated weapons.

The cop pulled a flashlight from his belt and clicked it on. He couldn't look in a trunk without permission or cause, but he could sure as hell look into a car through an open window. Roberto glanced up at the cop, taking advantage of the momentary distraction to size up his opponent. He thought briefly about throwing open the driver's door, slamming it into the cop hard enough to knock him over or wind him or get a lucky door handle in the guy's balls. If that went his way, he'd keep his momentum going, lunge out of the door, disarm the cop, and pop him twice in the head with his own gun. That was a lot of ifs, and most likely it ended with Roberto dead by the side of the road or stuck in a Kansas jail cell while a plague-like fungus ravaged the land.

So, not so good, that one.

But then he saw the tattoo. Because the cop had to keep his right hand near his weapon at all times, he'd pulled the flashlight with his left and had to reach across his body to shine it into the back of the car. The warm weather meant he was wearing his summer uniform, a short-sleeved light blue shirt that cut just below the biceps. His arms were big, worked, and as the cop moved his arm around with the light, the sleeve slipped up over the curve of muscle, revealing an extra four inches of bare skin.

Roberto saw the thick black X tattooed there, meant to fall just above the line of the uniform, discreetly kept under the fabric. But tonight, at this moment, in this position, it was revealed, lit by the red flashing lights of the cop's own cherries.

The X was just two thick bars, their tips pointed into triangles at either end. Nothing fancy, nothing colorful, just black ink, but Roberto was reasonably certain it was a southern nationalist flag symbol. The bars were meant to evoke the St. Andrew's Cross and the blue star-spangled X of the Confederate battle flag. But the color and stars had been removed for those who wanted or needed to keep their alt-right political views to themselves in certain situations. Like being at work, when you're a police officer.

The cop shifted the flashlight back to the front seat, momentarily shining it right in Roberto's face as he put it away. "What have you got back there, Mr. . . . Diaz?"

Aha! The pause was longer this time, and the tiny emphasis on Roberto's last name confirmed any lingering suspicions. *Aha, you racist son of a bitch, I got you figured out now. You're a white nationalist.* Okay. That was something. Roberto could work with that.

"You got me, brother."

The cop looked at him. Brother? That was starting out awfully strong, but hey, when you've got only one card, you play it for all it's worth.

"I got you doing what, Mr. Diaz?" The cop's face was unreadable. He gave nothing away.

"Being ready."

"For what, sir?"

"For when the day comes."

The cop stared at him for a long moment. He gave no reason for Roberto to feel encouraged, but he didn't ask him to get out of the car either. Roberto took that as license to continue. He shoved the rest of his chips into the middle of the table.

"Saw your tattoo. If we lived in a free country, I'm guessing you'd put III% on there, am I right?"

The cop just held eye contact, thinking.

Over the last seven or eight years Roberto was at DTRA, there had been a sharp increase in reporting on weapons acquisitions by well-armed domestic militias. He'd read those sections of the daily security briefings only cursorily, as his purview was almost exclusively overseas, but he knew enough to know the names of a few of the more prominent nationalist movements, which included the Three Percenters. An American paramilitary movement, its members pledged armed resistance against any attempts to limit

private gun ownership by a tyrannical government. The name was derived from the claim that
only 3 percent of the population of the original
thirteen colonies fought against and defeated
Great Britain in the Revolutionary War. In
truth, the number was closer to 15 percent, but
who's counting when there's a rhetorical point to
be made.

The Three Percenters counted among their
numbers a fair amount of law enforcement, and
in fact a group of Jersey City police officers had
been suspended in 2013 for wearing patches that
read ONE OF THE 3%. Since then, members in
public roles knew better and kept their beliefs on
the down low. The southern nationalist flag tat
was a popular and subtle marking.

Roberto had no doubt the cop was in. The
only question was how far.

The cop held eye contact with him for a good
ten seconds. Roberto looked back steadily. "The
day's coming, my man. The country we love and
honor needs us to be ready."

The cop turned the flashlight on again, playing it over the military crates in the back, taking
one more look.

He turned back to Roberto. The only question was: Did Roberto look white enough to
this prick to overcome his last name? The cop
thought for a long moment.

"Drive safe, patriot."

Apparently, he did. The cop clicked off the
light, turned, and walked back to his car, his
shoes crunching on the gravel.

Roberto didn't stick around for confirmation. He put the minivan in gear and pulled away, not too fast and not too slow, lifting his hand up into the beam of the cop's lights and giving a little thank-you wave as he put distance between them.

In his mind, he reverted back to his original position. *I am* very *good at my job.*

He'd be in Atchison in seven minutes.

TWENTY-SEVEN

Within thirty seconds of when Mary Rooney fired six shots into the chest of the weird guy who'd exploded, a thought occurred to her. She'd just killed a man. The unreal fact that he'd burst in a haze of green goo was less relevant to her than the objective reality of her situation. She had committed murder—okay, possibly manslaughter, depending on how you slice it, and he had been running at them at the time. But he was also clearly unarmed, and she was holding a weapon that, in the law's eyes, had been stolen from the State of Kansas. You didn't have to be a legal scholar to know this would not hold up well in a courtroom.

Naomi was doubled over, holding her ears in pain, some blood seeping between her fingers. Teacake turned to Mrs. Rooney, eyes wide. "Mrs. Rooney Jesus thank you God where the hell did you get that?!" he asked, all at once, his eyes fixed on the smoking cannon in her hand.

"I have to get out of here," she said.

"No no no, you're fine, you're cool, you had to, this guy, he's infected with, like, this horrible zombie shit, there was this deer that blew up, and weird shit in the basement, and he was—he was trying to barf on us, and . . ." She was just staring at him. He trailed off, hearing how he must sound. "You're right. You gotta get out of here."

From around the corner ahead of them, they heard voices, low and muttering. Teacake thought he recognized Griffin's guttural grunting. He turned back to Mrs. Rooney, took her by the shoulders, and talked fast. "Not the front, go back that way, turn right twice, go out the side door." He pointed to the gun, still in her hand. "Dump that in the river." She didn't move.

From around the corner, Griffin raised his voice. "I'm armed, motherfucker!" He was full of bravado, but Teacake could hear the quaver in it.

He turned back to Mrs. Rooney. "Go!"

"Thank you," she said. She took off in the direction he'd indicated.

"You hear me?!" Griffin shouted again. "I'm all loaded! I'm coming in strapped!"

Teacake turned and shouted back, "Griffin! Be cool, man, it's me! Teacake!"

Griffin yelled, "I got a gun, shithead!"

Teacake bent down next to Naomi and pulled her hands gently from her ears. Naomi looked up at him. Her whole head hurt, but the left side had a strange numbness to it, a total, disorienting silence that felt like a weight. The loud, sharp ringing in her right ear more than canceled out any quieting effect the silence might have had, and her whole head throbbed. Her vision was fine; she could see Teacake was just in front of her, his eyes full of concern. His mouth was moving—he was saying something to her. She couldn't hear a word, but she could read his face, every expression heightened and more easily understood with her attention focused on it.

Maybe not hearing him was just the right thing for her at the moment. She watched his lips; she looked into his eyes and registered every minute change of his features. She didn't know what he was saying, but better than that, she knew what he *meant*. That she was going to be okay. That he would not let her down.

She saw him turn and shout angrily back over his shoulder, at someone around the corner— maybe the police were coming? She saw the smear on the floor that had been Mike, and it was moving, seething, as if still alive. It was inching toward them.

Now Teacake was pulling her to her feet, urging her to do something. To leave? Yes, that was it, he wanted her to leave, in the other direction. Whatever the danger or whatever had to be done, he didn't want her to be a part of it. Naomi was moved, maybe because she could only feel him, and his feelings were so powerful. He was saying one thing over and over again; she was no lip reader but could recognize her daughter's name—he was telling her to get out of there *right now* because maybe he didn't matter and maybe she didn't either, but her daughter did, and she had to take care of her.

Teacake turned and shouted something over

his shoulder again. Naomi couldn't make it out, but whoever was at the other end of the hall was coming this way, and there was danger. Teacake turned his body and shoved Naomi behind him, pushing her down the corridor in the other direction. She could tell by the strength of the shove that he would not be argued with. She staggered back and moved around the corner, just out of sight of whoever was going to come down the hallway.

She lingered there for a moment, hidden, unsure what to do next. She couldn't hear, her head felt like it was going to split in half from the pain rattling around inside it, she had no idea who was coming, and the only person who could explain it to her had just told her in no uncertain terms to get the hell out of there. Naomi froze.

A second later, Griffin came around the corner at the other end of the hall from Teacake, gun in front of him. His body was hunched, coiled in a SWAT team crouch. He swung the gun from side to side, as if expecting someone to lunge from one of the units and go after him.

Teacake shouted to him from his end of the hall. "Griffin, you asshole, put the fucking gun away!"

Instead, Griffin put both hands on the grip and extended it in front of him, pointing it at Teacake's head as he advanced. "Hands in the air!"

Teacake put his hands up. "It's *me*, okay?!"

Griffin kept coming, stalking forward on bent

legs, both hands on the gun, unconsciously mimicking the movements and posture of his avatar in his copy of *School Shooter*. "Drop the gun!"

Teacake looked up at his own hands, which were both empty. "What gun?"

"Drop it!"

"Griffin, *I don't have a gun*, okay?"

From behind Griffin, Dr. Friedman peeked out, assessing the situation. "It's true, Darryl, he does not appear to have a gun."

Teacake, trying to keep his hands in the air, pointed at the mess on the floor that had been Mike a short while ago. "Don't get any closer to that, man."

Griffin stopped, staring down at the remains. Revolted, he looked back up at Teacake, pointing the gun at him again. "Down on the floor!"

"Why?"

"Against the wall!"

Teacake, who had been about to get down on the floor, stopped. "Which?"

"Do it!"

"Seriously, you want me to get down on the floor or up against the wall?"

Griffin, hearing something behind him, whirled around with the gun. Dr. Friedman, whose right boot had squeaked on the floor, barely got his head out of the way as the barrel swung toward him, aimed wildly around the empty hallway, and then swiveled back to Teacake.

"Where is the shooter?!" Griffin shouted, bringing some focus to his ever-changing list of demands.

"He's gone," Teacake said, lying only in the sense that he used the wrong pronoun. "Took off as soon as he shot."

Griffin looked down at Mike's body again. "Who is that?"

"That's what I'm trying to tell you," Teacake said, taking a step forward.

"Don't come any closer!"

Teacake sighed and stopped. The night had been weird, then exciting, then terrifying, and now with Griffin in the mix it was just annoying. "I don't know. He's got some kind of disease or something. It's contagious. It'll kill you. The fucking army's coming, or at least some guy who knows the army or— Can I put my hands down or what?"

"You called the cops?"

"Yeah. Sorta. DTRA."

"What the hell is that?"

Before Teacake could answer, a sharp banging sound from the right startled Griffin and he swung the gun around again. Dr. Friedman dove out of the way faster this time, doing a good job of not getting his head shot off, and Griffin pointed the gun at the storage unit right next to them. "What's that?!"

Voices shouted from inside the unit, more fists pounded on the door. Griffin recognized them. "Ironhead?! What the fuck are you doing, man?!"

The voices shouted some more, the door rattled and banged, and Griffin noticed the lock, hanging unlocked in the hasp. It was enough to hold the door closed, but it wasn't clicked shut,

so if the door rattled long enough it was bound
to be dislodged.

Griffin turned the gun back on Teacake.
"What'd you lock 'em in there for?!"

"I didn't. That guy did." He pointed to Mike's
residue. Griffin frowned, his reptilian brain trying to process it all. Keeping the gun on Teacake,
he moved toward the locker.

Teacake took a step forward. "Don't, man."

Griffin stopped, swinging the gun back on
him. "Why not?"

"They're infected."

Dr. Friedman stepped out of Griffin's shadow,
recognizing he might have some role in this conversation after all. "Infected? With what?"

"*I* don't fucking know!" Teacake said, his patience nearing an end. "Bad shit! For the last
time, will you put that fucking gun down already?!"

Griffin squinted at him. There was a dead guy
on the floor, his friends were all locked in a storage unit, and Teacake was the only one in the
hallway. No, he would not put the fucking gun
down, no goddamn way. He took two steps back
from the storage unit, gesturing with his gun
from Teacake to the door. "You open it," he said.

Teacake looked at him. There was no reasoning with this lump. He looked over at the door.
He saw the lock, dangling in the hasp, clicking
against the sides of the metal loop as the people
inside the storage unit continued to pound on
the door, demanding to be let out.

"No fucking way," he said.

"Now!" Griffin shouted, taking a step forward with the gun. As he moved, his sweaty right index finger tensed on the trigger, which he'd adjusted for maximum sensitivity. He inadvertently squeezed off a round, which leaped from the barrel and sliced through the very outer edge of Teacake's left ear, drawing a spurt of blood before it flew the rest of the way down the hallway, ricocheting off two metal doors and finally burying itself in a cement wall.

Teacake screamed and grabbed his ear in pain. "What the *fuck*, man?!" he shouted. He pulled his hand back in amazement and saw it was now smeared with blood. It wasn't much of a gunshot wound, more like a razor slice, but it was a *gunshot wound*, Griffin had definitely shot him, the fuckwit had *shot* him.

"You *shot* me!" Teacake pointed out.

"You *shot* him!" Dr. Friedman confirmed.

Griffin did everything he could to conceal the fact that he had in no way meant to do that. He took a second to erase the stunned look from his face, then stiffened, pointing the gun back at Teacake. "And I'll do it again if you don't open the goddamn door! Those are my friends in there!"

They were also his customers, but he didn't bother with that detail. In his mind, there was a chance, admittedly an outside one, but at least a tiny chance that the rest of the stolen TVs could still be moved out of here before the cops or the army or whoever showed up. There was still $450 on the table, and Griffin intended to take it home with him.

Teacake needed time to think. He wiped the blood from his ear on his pants and walked forward toward the door, as slowly as he could. He kept an eye on Griffin, who was following him with the gun and an increasingly unhinged look on his face—he'd never shot anyone before—and on Dr. Steven Friedman, who was backing up, putting a bit more distance between himself and Griffin. Teacake looked back at the lock, dangling there, unlocked. The sounds from inside, which had stopped for a few moments after the gunshot, had resumed, frantic voices calling, hands pounding on the door, people demanding to be let out. Their tone of panic was rising.

Teacake got closer. He reached out to the lock. He closed his fingers around it.

From the other end of the hallway, a woman's voice cried out. "Hey, Griffin!"

Griffin turned, and then everything happened at once. Foam exploded from the spout of the fire extinguisher Naomi was holding from about thirty feet away, and it sprayed Griffin and Dr. Friedman in the face, momentarily blinding them. Griffin swung his gun crazily and another shot went off, again by accident.

Teacake reached out to the lock and snapped it shut, and Dr. Friedman, who'd had enough of Griffin's reckless bullshit, grabbed Griffin's gun hand and tried to wrestle the thing away from him before he actually killed somebody.

That was all the opening Teacake needed. He turned and took off, racing down the hallway toward Naomi. She was turning as he got to her, dropped the fire extinguisher with a noisy *clang*, grabbed his hand, and they took off into the other hallway. They headed for the side door through which Mary Rooney had just escaped.

At the storage locker, Griffin wrestled his gun hand free and gave Dr. Friedman a ferocious shove, knocking him on his ass. "The fuck is the matter with you?!" he shouted at the dentist, wiping foam from his eyes. He turned back to the locker door and pawed at the lock. There was more pounding from inside the locker, frantic now, and the voices were changing, rising in pitch and intensity. There was panic inside the locker, the situation in there was changing, something was happening, and it wasn't good.

Griffin shouted at the door. "Ironhead! You got my key! You got my key, shithead!"

From inside the locker, there were sounds of a struggle and a body slammed up against the door, hard. Griffin stumbled back. Something else hit the door, something heavy, maybe another body, and the door dented outward. The struggle seemed to intensify, the shouting and screaming accompanied by unfamiliar sounds now: a low gurgle, a wet slap, the sound of a Samsung Premium Ultra 4K smashing into a million tiny pieces.

And then it went quiet.

Griffin and Dr. Friedman just stared at the door for a long moment.

"Ironhead?" Griffin asked, sotto voce.

There was no answer.

"Cedric?"

Nothing.

But then the door lifted an inch. A shadow moved inside. And with the soft scrape of metal on cement, a key slid out from inside.

Ironhead's voice came from the other side, calm now. "Griffin?"

Griffin didn't answer.

"You there? Griffin?"

Griffin picked up the key. He looked at Dr. Friedman.

Ironhead's voice came from the other side of the door again, a low chuckle. "All's cool, man. Just got a little hairy there for a second."

They didn't answer.

"Hello? Griffin?"

Griffin hesitated.

"You there?"

Griffin and Dr. Friedman just looked at each other, no idea what to do.

Ironhead spoke again. "Griffin? *Griff?*"

Griffin turned back to the door. He had waited thirty-one years for someone to use his self-chosen nickname. Hearing it was a balm on his soul.

He put the key in the lock.

TWENTY-EIGHT

Roberto answered the phone on the first ring. "I'm a minute and a half out."

Abigail replied, puzzled. "I had you there six minutes ago."

"Bit of a snag. I worked it out. I'm just west of the Missouri River and about to make the turn onto White Clay Road. What have you got?"

"I got ahold of Stephanie."

"And?"

"The name of the guy at ADF-E is Ozgur Onder. He's not on duty right now."

"Shit."

But Abigail wasn't done. "Better than that. He's in bed with her, at her place. And he can redirect a KH-11 from his laptop."

Roberto closed his eyes and promised God that if this worked out, he would never take His name in vain again. "God*damn*!" You know, after tonight. "That's great. Will he do it?"

"He's not happy, but he's doing it. Apparently, it's something he's done before, to impress her. On their third date, he grabbed video of them in front of her house, waving up at the sky."

"Our national security is in good hands. I hope he got laid."

"It would seem."

Roberto slowed, his headlights revealing the entrance to a long gravel driveway through a break in the tree line up ahead. "Do we have visual yet?"

"Yes. Nine minutes left of a look-down before we lose orbital view and control passes off to Canberra."

"Anybody leave the place?"

"One, a little over a minute ago. A woman, late sixties, driving a late-model Subaru Outback. Do you want the license number?"

"If she was able to drive a car, I'm not worried about her. Let it go. Anybody on foot, I need to know immediately." He turned into the driveway and approached the crest of a hill. He could see the lights of the storage facility glowing just over the rise. He slowed. "I'm pulling into the driveway now. You have Ozgur live?"

"Yes, sir."

"Stay with him. Anything you know, I need to know, when you know it." He reached up to his earpiece to end the call, but then had another thought. "Hey, Abigail?"

"Yes, sir?"

"You know what I have to do, right?"

"Yes, I do, sir."

"You're okay with that?"

She paused. "I read the white paper, sir."

There were good, smart young people out there. Roberto hoped they'd get to stick around to be good old people. It wasn't so bad, being old. As long as you were with the right person. But better not to think of Annie right now. Don't tug on that thread, the whole sweater'll come apart and you won't do what needs to be done.

"Tell me quick what you found out about the people inside," he said. Abigail told him what she knew, he made mental notes of what he could remember, and wrapped it up.

"I'll have to use my cell. That means Jerabek will know I'm here and he might get curious. Watch your back."

"I always do, sir."

Roberto hung up. Over the crest of the rise now, he saw the front entrance of the storage place, sticking out from the hillside like a fat lip. Up at the top of the hill, just to his right, he saw a car pulled over at the side of the drive, its trunk hanging open. Not a good sign. In its trunk he thought he detected a slight phosphorescent glow, and traces of more of it scattered out on the hillside behind it. It was faint, damn faint, and he could have easily been wrong about it, but he had a feeling he wasn't.

Down at the bottom of the drive, a Honda Civic and half a dozen Harleys were parked in front of the main entrance. He turned off his headlights and pulled to a stop a hundred feet short of them. He was halfway between the entrance and the car with the open trunk.

He took a breath, let it out slowly, and got out of the van.

TWENTY-NINE

Teacake and Naomi banged through the broken side door of the building, took a sharp right turn, and ran toward the parking lot. "My car's right here!" Teacake shouted. Naomi could hear his voice, just barely, over the ringing sound in her right ear, but her left ear was still dead. They raced along the side of the building, triggering the motion-detector lights all along the upper part of the wall as they ran. They came around the front, past the Harleys, and were just reaching Teacake's Honda when a halogen beam flicked on and a commanding voice shouted from fifty feet away.

"STOP."

The order was clear, and the voice was the kind you don't argue with, so without even thinking about it, they stopped. They turned toward it, raising their hands in the air.

The flashlight beam was brilliant, piercing, and they both winced, blind to whoever was behind it. There was another light coming from the same spot, and this one was a sharp red beam. Teacake looked down and saw the laser dot right over his heart. As he watched, it flicked over to Naomi and centered up on her chest.

Shoes crunched on gravel as the figure walked toward them, cautious. As the man drew closer and came into the light, he slipped the flashlight into his belt but still held the gun on them. He had a pair of green, owl-like goggles on his head, but not down over his eyes. He was holding an M16 with a laser scope.

Naomi spoke first. It came out more of a shout, as she could barely hear herself. "Roberto?"

Roberto stopped. "Naomi?"

Teacake wiped more blood from his dripping, injured ear. "Do you *mind*?" he said, gesturing down at his chest, where the red dot had recentered itself over his heart. "I've had about enough of fucking guns pointed at me, okay, fucker?!"

Roberto lowered the rifle. "And you must be the other guy."

Teacake looked around the parking area, the driveway, the hillside. "Where's the rest of your crew, man?"

Roberto took a moment. "I'm it."

"You're *it*?" Naomi shouted.

Roberto looked at Teacake. "Why is she shouting?"

"Gunshots. A .45, next to her ear. I think she can hear a little bit in the right."

Roberto looked at the building. "Who's got a gun in there?"

"So far, everybody but us."

Roberto nodded and hoped Trini still knew how to pack.

————

WHAT WAS ESPECIALLY SWEET ABOUT THE MINIVAN was that both the side doors could slide open electronically, and the back hatch went up too. Teacake had been singularly unimpressed by the white Mazda when Roberto first led them toward it—"You gotta be kidding me, they sent one guy, and he's in a fucking *Hyundai* or whatever?"—but he'd come around as soon as the doors opened and he saw the array of military crates inside. The first one Roberto opened held one of the hazmat suits, neatly folded, with its dead-faced helmet staring up at them like a *Scream* mask. The next several cases were standard Navy SEAL gear: a tactical vest, Ka-Bar knife, Heckler & Koch machine pistol, sniper rifle, half a dozen breaching charges for removing iron doors that might stand in the way, and a surprising number and variety of MREs. Trini was a mom, and she worried about people getting hungry.

But there's nothing that really catches your attention like a nuclear weapon. Naomi's eyes had fallen on the half-barrel-shaped backpack immediately, and its obvious age, military origin, and strange shape gave it away as the joker in the deck. "What the hell is that?" she'd asked. But Roberto declined to answer right away, arming up instead.

Given all that had transpired in the past four or five hours, they required very little bringing up to speed. Roberto told them what he knew about the fungus, and they were already perfectly aware of its lethality. After Roberto was satisfied that they were both uninfected, there was a brief period of debate during which he unconvincingly offered them the chance to leave. But that argument had collapsed under the weight of reality—there were now as many as seven infected humans inside the storage facility. The three of them out here, three of the only people on the planet who had seen *Cordyceps novus* in action firsthand, were the ones who truly understood the need to eradicate it right here and now. And Roberto couldn't be in two places at once. The only way to pull off his plan was with someone upstairs, making sure no infected bodies left the building, while the others went back down to sub-level 4.

"*Back* downstairs?" Teacake asked. "Are you crazy? To do what?"

Roberto reached in and pulled the pack forward, feeling his back twinge again. How long would it take him to learn that leaning at bizarre angles and trying to move heavy weights was a bad idea, from an orthopedic standpoint? This time he felt the pain shoot out from his sacroiliac and radiate all the way down his right leg, a hot searing feeling that reached his big toe. The muscles of his lower back, having voiced their objection, released their hold on his spine after a few seconds. But their point had been made. Roberto bent his knees and dragged the pack carefully to the edge of the cargo area. He stopped and thought for a long moment. There was no escaping reality. He could bob and weave for as long as he wanted, but eventually it was going to punch him in the face. He decided to stop dancing with it.

He turned and looked at Teacake and Naomi. "You're going to have to place the device."

Naomi, who had most of the hearing back in her right ear, picked up that part clearly. She stared down at the half-barrel shape. "What kind of device?" she asked.

"Think of it as a big bomb."

"How big?" Teacake asked.

Roberto gave it to them straight. "Point-three, five, ten, or eighty kilotons. It has a selectable yield."

Naomi closed her eyes, her fears confirmed, but Teacake went through the motions of pretending he had not seen that one coming. "It's a *nuke*?! A fucking *suitcase* bomb?"

"No, it isn't a suitcase bomb," Roberto said, irritated, as he strapped on the tactical vest. "There's no such thing as a suitcase bomb. What kind of invading ground force carries suitcases?"

"Dude, you know what I mean. It's a—"

Roberto cut him off. "Yes. It is." He turned to Naomi. "You asked if we had a contingency plan. This is it. You saw how that fungus spreads. How fast and how far and how lethal. A group of us have spent thirty years thinking about this. Precautions have been taken. Arrangements were made. This is the only way."

Teacake looked at Naomi, who seemed calm, but he couldn't believe what he was hearing. "You're gonna kill everybody in eastern Kansas."

"We're not going to kill anyone. Detonation will be hundreds of feet underground. This immediate area will be irradiated, and they're gonna sell a lot of bottled water around here for the next twenty years, but there will be no atmospheric fallout, and the problem will be solved. Once everything sorts out, we'll all get awards. Let's just hope they aren't posthumous."

"You're out of your goddamn mind," Teacake said.

"No. He's right."

Roberto smiled at Naomi, strapping the Ka-Bar knife to his thigh. She'd sounded smart when he talked to her on the phone; he was glad it was true. He turned to Teacake and looked him up and down. "How much can you deadlift?"

"I don't know. Two hundred?"

Roberto looked doubtful.

"What? Is that too much?"

"We'll find out," Roberto said. "You two are going to carry this down to sub-level 4 and activate the triggering mechanism. I'll show you how. I'm going to stay up top and remove any infected organisms that try to escape the area prior to detonation."

"'Remove'?" Naomi asked. She knew, but she asked anyway.

"I'm going to kill them," he said. "I'm going to execute people whose only crime is that they were exposed to a deadly fungus. Would you rather do my part of the job or yours?" They didn't answer. Roberto continued. "After you start the timer, you'll have between eight and thirteen minutes to get back up here, get in the van, and get at least half a mile away."

"Eight to thirteen?" Naomi asked.

"The timer duration is unstable without a mechanical wire."

Teacake was aghast. "So it could blow up at any fucking time?!"

Roberto looked at him and repeated himself, keeping his tone neutral. "The timer duration is unstable."

Teacake looked at the backpack, incredulous. "What did they used to say to the poor fucking grunts they sent out with these?"

"'Tell your parents that you love them.'"

"And they still did it? Blew themselves up?"

"No, Travis, no one did it. These were never used. You would have heard about that in school. But people were *willing* to do it, because they thought the future of the world depended on it. Which it does. Right now." He picked up the Heckler & Koch, slapped a fresh magazine into it, and straightened, using every inch of his height advantage over Teacake in an attempt to inspire. "E-3 Seaman Meacham, you're what I've got right now, and frankly it's more than I expected. You were on a ballistic sub, so you're no dummy, and you know at least the fundamentals, if you weren't too stoned in recruit training. I suspect you're a much better soldier than the 'General Discharge, Honorable Conditions' they gave you. C'mon, Squid, why don't you prove it tonight?"

Travis looked at him, stunned. "How'd you know—?"

"We had your first names and your place of business, these aren't state secrets." He turned to Naomi. "I know you've got a child at home, Ms. Williams. But that pack is fifty-eight pounds, and Travis can't get it down the tube ladder by himself, not safely. Can you shoot a gun?" She nodded, sort of. Roberto took a Glock 19 from an open case, loaded it, and turned it around, offering it to Naomi handle first. "Travis will have his hands full, so you'll watch both your backs. You've got a twelve-shot magazine, a trigger safety here, and a thumb lock over there. You need to flip both of them to pull the trigger. Once you've pulled, each shot requires another pull, but the safeties won't re-engage unless you take your finger off the trigger. Got it?"

She nodded, taking the gun. She'd never held one before and had always hated them on principle. She still did. "I'm not going to fire it," she said.

"You will if you need to," Roberto replied.

"I doubt it," she said.

Roberto continued. "When you put somebody down, you aim for the chest, it's the biggest target. Wait till they get close enough and you won't miss. Two shots in the chest, then, once they're on the floor, another one in the head. No more than that. That's four people per clip. Count your shots. If you get below three shots left, you change clips. Understood?"

She nodded.

Roberto looked at them. "You two may have started the night as minimum-wage security guards, but you're ending it as a Green Light Team. America's finest. Now put on the suits."

THIRTY

At that moment, there existed on Earth four distinct colonies of *Cordyceps novus*, each with its own chromosomal characteristics, growth rate, and ambitions for expansion. Deep underground, in sub-level 4, the original colony, or more accurately the original *American* colony, remained in a multiplication phase, though its growth had plateaued since its expansion into the hallway outside the cell in which it had first escaped from the biotube. In terms of organic nutrients, the rats it had infested and fused together were far and away the most abundant source of fuel, but that had been exhausted. The Rat King mass was already in stasis, the precursor to decay and disintegration. A tributary of growth was making its way across the dry cement floor, toward a puddle of water beneath one of the sweaty overhead water pipes that made up the cooling system, but it hadn't reached it yet. Once it did, it was hard to predict the fungus's reaction, since it had never encountered water in its pure form before, only as a component of a human body. Safe to say it was going to like it, but it wasn't there yet.

This colony of *Cordyceps novus* was a bit like Reno, Nevada—popular once, but limited by location and climate, and not anywhere a serious person would want to go.

Aboveground, on the hillside behind Roberto's van, was the second colony, the one C-nRoach1 had founded a little over fifteen hours ago. This colony had begun in the trunk of Mike's car, where it still maintained a strong presence. But after the deer and Mr. Scroggins had taken off, the fungus had to content itself with feeding on old towels, steel, rubber, and other unsexy fuels.

More successful was the outpost begun by Mr. Scroggins when he had exploded at the top of the tree. It had spattered in all directions and fallen to earth as far as seventy-five feet from the tree itself. It currently thrived on the moist, humid forest floor, spreading at a rate of three to four feet per hour. It was a nearly ideal environment for the fungus, but its expansion was held tenuously in check by the lack of carriers with rapid and independent locomotion. The whole area was just one stray coyote or ill-fated squirrel away from boomtown status, but for the moment the fungus had to be content to continue its leisurely but steady growth here. Still, given enough time, there was no telling how far its sprawl would spread.

This colony was similar to Los Angeles— slow, inevitable, and in no one's best interests.

On the main floor of the storage facility,

the third colony was enjoying the least success. Spread out over the cement walls and floor, the Jackson Pollock painting that was once Mike Snyder was now largely inert, at least by human time standards. It wasn't dead or even dormant, but its growth had slowed to a barely perceptible rate. The floor and walls were made of Portland cement, the industry standard, composed primarily of lime, silica, and alumina—about as nutritious for a growing fungus as a sand sandwich. Still, *Cordyceps novus* was no stranger to adverse conditions—it had grown its way out of a biotube; it could certainly handle a hallway. It festered and burrowed and shifted as best it could, but the kind of booming growth it had experienced when it first entered Mike's living body was long over. Maybe it would get lucky, hit a vein of ironstone somewhere in the cement floor in ten years or so and enjoy a comeback, but until that happened, it was going nowhere fast.

In urban terms, this third colony was Atlantic City. Used to be a big deal, dead on its feet now.

As for the fourth colony—that was another story.

In 1950, Shenzhen, China, was a fishing village with three thousand inhabitants. By 2025, twelve million people will live there. In terms of rampant, unchecked, dangerous growth, there's no place on earth like it. Except for what was going on inside unit G-413 at Atchison Storage.

From the moment Mike's wide-patterned projectile vomit had launched from the open doorway, the fungus had found abundant organic nutrients. The spray had landed on all five of the occupants of the locker, but Cedric, Wino, and Garbage had been caught openmouthed. Infection was immediate in their cases, and the fungus penetrated the complex substrate of their biological systems with zeal and aptitude. It produced immediate and exponential growth. Ironhead and Cuba, who had no cuts, crevices, or orifices through which the molecules could enter them without effort, were a few minutes behind. *Cordyceps novus* had to deploy *Benzene-X* to first burn a pathway through their pores, which took a bit longer.

But within minutes there was a fungal party raging inside all five of their systems that could not be stopped or curfewed. The fungus entered the most productive phase in its history, joyfully increasing its biomass through the perfectly balanced human carbon-nitrogen ratio of 12:1. It started with a familiar, if accelerated, growth-expansion-expulsion pattern inside Wino, whose blood alcohol content provided additional glucose. While Griffin was outside the locker door, ordering Teacake to remove the lock, Wino was bulging, screaming, and bursting inside the locker, to the extreme consternation of the others. Cedric and Garbage went in the next thirty seconds, swelling and rupturing in quick succession. Ironhead and Cuba, their systems lagging behind, were left to scream in horror.

But then something extraordinary happened. The growth in the last two human hosts *slowed down*. Intentionally. Perhaps the fungus recognized the limited supply of human tissue and the confined space of the storage locker. Or maybe it registered that the walls of the locker, to which it was now largely affixed, were of limited food value, or maybe it even bore some sort of cellular memory of the successful result of the slowed-down fruiting and bursting process it had gone through with Mike. Whatever the reason, it tamped down its formerly unbridled surge of growth. The processes consuming the bodies and minds of Cuba and Ironhead, the last remaining humans inside the locker, actually decelerated. This implied, if not volition, then at least airborne endocrine signaling—a cell's ability to transmit information and instructions beyond its own walls. *Cordyceps novus* had, for the first time since its initial human contacts in the Australian outback, modified its mechanism of control.

The fungus racing through the brains of Ironhead and Cuba got the message and curtailed its development. Their brains were allowed to retain a measure of autonomous control, but the fungus wiped out massive portions of their amygdalas, home to their fear and panic centers. As a result, they thought everything was okay. They thought they were still in charge.

"All's cool, man," Ironhead said through the door, to Griffin. "Just got a little hairy there for a second."

Griffin turned the key in the lock and unlocked the door.

THIRTY-ONE

A full hazmat suit weighs about ten pounds, the oxygen tank and breathing apparatus another twenty-one, and the T-41 unit Teacake had strapped to his back was nearly sixty. That meant every step he took, he was moving an additional ninety pounds over his own body weight, give or take. His shoulders ached almost right away as the straps bit into them through the suit, his thighs started to burn after the first dozen steps, and by the time they reached the front door of the building the sweat was running down his neck and into the suit. Naomi had less weight on her back, but the burden of being the sole lookout and guard, coupled with the amount of effort it took to keep turning from side to side in the bulky suit, meant she was expending as much effort as he was. The gun in her hand felt like a stone.

They'd gotten into the suits quickly enough, with Roberto's help. The idea of climbing back down the ladder in the bulky things was harder to imagine, but they tried not to think too far ahead. Roberto secured the suits around their

wrists, ankles, faces, necks, and waists, and
showed them how to use the two-way radios in
their headsets. He flirted briefly with the notion
that he could somehow Bluetooth his cell phone
into their headsets but gave up on the idea.
There wasn't much he could have done to help
them from this point anyway. He'd shown them
both how to arm and activate the T-41, which
was fairly straightforward. It had been designed
for soldiers in the field to operate under pressure,
and simplicity was at its core. That, and fissile
fuel that could sustain a nuclear chain reaction.

There was no third suit for Roberto. Teacake
had asked why he'd brought two in the first place,
and Roberto had just looked at him blankly. "For
the same reason I brought two of everything
else. What if one breaks?" Roberto would never
understand some people.

With that he wished them luck, told them to
hurry, and sent them on their way into the building. He watched them walk toward the front
doors the way a parent watches his kid walk into
a freshman dorm for the first time, thinking of
a thousand things he should have said, a million
pieces of advice he could have given, and knowing it was too late for all of that. Roberto knew
he should be the one wearing the pack. He knew
it should be him carrying it down to sub-level 4
himself and, if necessary, waiting there with it to
ensure successful detonation, the way he and
Trini and Gordon had planned and discussed
thirty years ago. And he also knew with complete certainty that he couldn't. Accepting that

reality and trusting two twentysomethings he'd met fifteen minutes ago was the most difficult decision he'd ever made in his life. But he'd had no choice.

Of course, he'd left himself a fail-safe. A contingency for the contingency. He hadn't shared that part with Teacake and Naomi. They had plenty of information already, more than they could probably handle, and the rest would be revealed at the exact moment they needed to know it.

He watched them open the doors and walk into the building, then turned his attention to the parking area in front. Next order of business: make sure nobody goes anywhere. He pulled the Ka-Bar from the sleeve on his thigh and started with Teacake's Honda Civic, parked on the far right side. He drove the blade deep into the edge of the back right tire and jerked it forward six inches. A puncture would take too long to drain the air and was no guarantee the car couldn't limp out of the parking lot, but a slash did the job immediately. The tire deflated, and he moved on to the other rear wheel and did the same thing. The car's chassis dropped a few inches. Anybody who tried to drive it now would be on the rims by the time they turned around, and the axle would snap before they got up the driveway.

The Harleys were easier; he only had to stab and slash one tire on each bike. They maybe could have limped out of the lot with a flat rear, but a flat front would break the fork. Nobody was driving out of this place unless they took his

Mazda, and you can have my minivan keys when you pry them from my cold, dead hand.

He'd slashed four of the bikes and had three to go when his cell phone rang. He touched the Bluetooth in his ear to answer.

"You have incoming," Abigail said.

Roberto straightened sharply and looked around. "Where?"

"Around the corner of the building. Ten seconds. Male, moving fast, major heat signature."

Roberto turned, taking a few quick steps to his left, toward the front door, far enough to clear the sight line between him and the eastern edge of the building. He pulled the machine pistol from a holster on his hip and flipped the safety off with his right thumb. With his left hand he reached up and pulled down his thermal imaging goggles, which activated with a hum and a whir, showing the landscape in vivid purple-and-orange-tinted images. He didn't need the goggles for light; there was plenty to see by, and more streamed around the corner of the building as the motion sensor lights went on, triggered by whoever was running toward him.

What Roberto needed was heat detection. When he'd first put on the goggles and looked at the hillside, the bits of fungus scattered there had glowed a warm red, and traces of that same red were visible in the open trunk of Mike's abandoned car. There was live growth in those areas, and the chemical reactions of the growing fungus gave off heat. If he could see the heat, he could avoid contact with the fungus and could get a quick read on whether a human being was infected. It would be pleasant to avoid killing innocent people. If possible.

Roberto's eyes stung at a sudden blast of harsh yellow inside the goggles, every last cone in his retinas getting a wake-up call at the exact same moment. He hadn't fully adjusted when the figure came barreling around the corner of the building, looking less like a human being through the goggles than a blazing, burning, white-hot chunk of melted iron.

That answered the infection question.

"Get this shit off me!" the figure screamed.

Roberto didn't pause to wonder how the man in motorcycle leathers had come to be completely covered front and back in mutating fungus yet still remain in possession of his faculties. He just aimed the machine pistol, pulled the trigger, and put five rounds in the center of Dr. Steven Friedman's chest.

A Heckler & Koch machine pistol has a short-recoil action, meaning the barrel moves back sharply, rotates the link, and causes the rear of the tube to tip down and disengage from the slide. It's a hard, jerking motion, and its effect on the shooter is usually mitigated by putting a stabilizing hand on the front handle. Because he'd had so little reaction time and he needed his left hand to pull down and activate the goggles, Roberto had been forced to fire the gun with one hand. That in itself was no big deal, all it meant was that his right elbow needed to be snugged up against his right hip to reduce uncontrolled movement. He'd made that firing maneuver dozens of times in the field and at the range.

But he'd never done it at the age of sixty-eight.

His body absorbed the first three recoils without incident, but on the fourth one his back rebelled. The spasm was sudden and fierce, the low back tissues seizing up and sending a red alert throughout his nervous system. The recoil from the fifth shot, which Roberto's brain had already ordered before he could countermand it and remove his finger from the trigger, finished the job.

A blinding pain lit itself on fire in his back and lower extremities, and Roberto's legs went out from under him. He collapsed, hitting the ground just a second after Dr. Friedman did, the difference being that the dentist's problems were over for good and Roberto's were just beginning. He landed on his side and rolled helplessly onto his back, staring up at the stars overhead. He knew immediately, the way you know, that he hadn't just pulled something, he'd torn it in half. Could be ligaments, could be tendons, or maybe he'd ruptured a disk. Whatever it was, it didn't matter.

What mattered was that he couldn't move.

THIRTY-TWO

A few minutes earlier, outside unit G-413, Griffin had removed the lock from the hasp on the door, turned the handle, and swung the overhead door open. He and Dr. Friedman both recoiled, involuntarily falling back a few steps. The visual was bad enough—there were three dead bodies in there, or at least their barely recognizable remains—but what had overcome them was the stench. Intense chemical reactions give off intense odors, densely packed clouds of fetid molecules that invade the nasal passages and cling to the olfactory sensors. The rancid waves of smell that rolled out of the storage unit were dense and alive. They overwhelmed all other senses for a moment.

The now highly mobile *Cordyceps novus*, hitchhiking aboard the bodies of the people once known as Ironhead and Cuba, stepped calmly out of the unit and smiled.

"What up, Griff?" Ironhead asked.

Cuba winked at Dr. Friedman.

The uninfected stared at the infected with horror. Though Cuba's and Ironhead's outward expressions were calm, friendly even, there was no mistaking their sickness. A strange color had seeped into their faces, and the telltale swelling of their abdomens had begun, albeit more slowly and smaller, since the fungus had modified its takeover approach. Still, there were vast and rapid changes occurring in the victims' body chemistry, and beneath the skin of their faces, necks, and hands, there was movement—a seethe, a roiling of their bloodstreams that was visible to the naked eye.

Dr. Friedman, who had seen a lot of rotted gums and decayed molars in his day, had never seen this. He staggered back, screaming. Afraid to turn his back on Ironhead and Cuba, he failed to notice he was moving directly toward Mike Snyder's remains, which were now a viscous, slippery coating on the floor and wall of the hallway behind him. Dr. Friedman hit the edge of the slick and his feet went out from under him. He fell, spinning, and landed facedown in the murk of green. He screamed again, lifted his hands, and stared in terror at the excited fungal residue there. He whipped his hands around in the air, trying to shake the clingy substance off, but it held fast. He slapped his hands back down, right in the middle of it, to push off the floor and stand up. His right hand slipped out from under him, he fell back down, onto his side, rolled over onto his back, and thrust himself back up on his feet.

Now covered front and back in fungus, Dr. Friedman looked up at Griffin and the others, eyes wide, mouth agape, struck mute.

Griffin, who still had his gun in his right hand, swung it around and pointed it at Dr. Friedman, then panicked as he realized he was leaving Iron-head and Cuba uncovered and swung it back to them. "What the fuck is going on what the fuck what the fuck?" was all he could spit out.

Blind with panic, Dr. Friedman turned and ran. The others stood between him and the main exit, but he'd seen both Teacake and Naomi run in the other direction, which meant there was probably a side entrance to be found someplace. He barreled down the hallway, around the corner, and saw a red Exit sign lit up at the far end. He ran toward it as fast as he could. Raising his right hand, he looked at the fungus while he ran. It was on the move too, wrapping around his fingers and penetrating his pores, pushing the openings in his skin wider and wider, clawing its way into his system.

Through bobbing vision, he saw a door up ahead, the one with the hole in the glass that Mike had smashed earlier. He ran toward it, knowing only that if he could get to his Harley he could go someplace safe, somewhere he could wash this stuff off him and figure out what the hell was happening. Maybe he would drive straight to the hospital.

He banged through the door, hit the night air, and felt a tiny bit better. Still moving as fast as he could, he cut right and ran along the outer edge of the building. Motion sensor lights flicked on as he passed them. There was a strange warmth spreading in his chest—maybe it was just the exertion, he thought, but then he got the distinct and unsettling feeling that his scalp was crawling. It was as if he wore a toupee and it had come to life, moving around his head at will. *Yes, for sure the hospital*, he told himself as he neared the corner of the building, *I am definitely going to the hospital—where am I again? which one is closest?—oh yeah, Waukesha Memorial on Highway 18, that's it, I'll go straight there, but shit, I wonder if I can still ride*, he thought as a dizzy fog started to descend on his brain.

He rounded the corner of the building, now certain that he couldn't handle a Harley in this condition—hell, he could barely ride one when he was in full possession of his faculties. So when he saw the guy standing there, the guy with the funny goggles on and something in his right hand, he was relieved—*This guy can help me, this guy can do something.*

"Get this shit off me!" he shouted to the man in the goggles.

Then the something in the guy's right hand spat fire a few times, something heavy and hot slammed into the dentist's chest, and he started to fall. *That's weird*, he thought as the ground came up at him. *I get that I've just been shot, but why is the guy with the gun falling too?*

Dr. Friedman hit the ground, still alive for a few more seconds, and saw his right hand erupt in what looked like green mushrooms. He knew he was dying.

Probably just as well, he thought.

THIRTY-THREE

Teacake and Naomi were halfway down the tube ladder when Teacake realized he was going to have to get the rest of the way there mostly blind. It was too bad, because their entrance into the building and move to the elevator had gone more smoothly than they'd anticipated. Hearing the shouts from the hallway near Griffin's storage locker, they'd cut to the left, gone down a parallel hallway, and made it to the elevator without incident.

Teacake had insisted on going down the ladder first, because the T-41 was a son of a bitch on his back, and his legs were trembling with lactic acid before they got to the first rung. He was by no means confident he was going to be able to make it all the way down without slipping and falling, and the backpack was so large it was pressed firmly up against the wall of the tube. If he fell and Naomi was below him, he would take her all the way down too. Couldn't let that happen.

Everything about the suit made the climb down difficult. The gloves were clunky, and his hands moved around inside them, which made his grip on the ladder uncertain. Shifting his weight from one rung to the next required full concentration and a bit of luck. The pack scraped along the wall as he went down, producing friction that slowed him and made every movement harder than it needed to be. But worst of all was the clouded mask.

The effort of lugging the extra ninety pounds that far had been grueling, and he was sweating profusely by the time they started down the ladder. The sweat wasn't the problem—that was just uncomfortable—but the inside of the plastic shield was fogging up from his labored breathing. The suit's oxygen recirculating system had been designed with some amount of condensation in mind, but not this much. The designers had never anticipated a full-body workout while wearing the suit, and the heat and CO_2 that Teacake was throwing off were more than it could compensate for.

"I can't see," he said to Naomi through the radio.

"What?" she replied.

"I can't see!" he shouted into the mask. *Great,* he thought, *one of us is blind and the other one's deaf. This should be a breeze.*

Naomi, indeed, had problems of her own. Climbing down with two hands had been difficult enough with no suit, but now she faced all the same obstacles as Teacake, plus she was clutching a fully loaded Glock 19. She'd had to climb every rung with her left hand, while her right held the gun free. That meant her left arm, her weaker arm, had been doing all the work, and it already burned so badly she almost couldn't feel it.

And then there was her hearing. She was still deaf in her left ear, and the ringing in the right, though it had abated, intensified whenever the radio frequency was activated. It was as if the suit was deliberately trying to mute everything Teacake said, raising the level of the ringing to obscure his words, then going back down when he was silent.

But his second shouted "I can't see!" had gotten through—clearly enough, anyway—and she shouted back, "Why not?"

"Sweat. Fogged up. Can you?"

"Yeah. Mostly."

"How much farther?" he asked.

She paused, wrapping her left arm through the rungs of the ladder, bending her torso back and to the right as much as she possibly could, and strained her eyes all the way to the edge of her mask. "About fifty rungs. Maybe less."

"Okay." He kept climbing down.

Naomi's left arm shook violently, and she knew she'd have to take a chance and switch gun hands. She pulled her right arm up and reached behind the rungs, to pass the gun to her left. It clanked against the rungs and she lost her grip on it. Her hand lashed out, pinning the gun against the wall. She was no longer holding it; she was just sort of trapping it there with pressure.

Teacake must have heard the clank and he

asked her something in the headset, but it was lost to her under the ringing sound. She ignored him, eyes focused on the gun, still held tenuously up against the cement wall of the tube. She stretched out the fingers of her left hand, got one of them through the trigger housing, and pulled her right arm free. The gun spun over, upside down, held up only by her left index finger. She readjusted her grip on the ladder, now with her freed right arm, and slowly withdrew her left from behind the ladder.

She closed her left hand around the handle of the gun and moved that arm free of the ladder. Blood flowed through her left biceps again, washing away enough of the built-up acid to give her some amount of relief. She closed her eyes, grateful. She looked down. Teacake was about ten rungs below her. She continued her descent.

THIRTY-FOUR

Flat on his back, Roberto stared up at the sky. *This is why*, he thought. *This is why I didn't take the backpack. In case this happened. God, I hate being right all the time.*

There weren't as many stars out as before; heavy clouds had blown in and obscured them, making the night darker. He looked up at the heavens and wondered if the satellite look-down window was still open, if the thing was somewhere overhead right now. Were Ozgur Onder and his girlfriend, Stephanie, watching him at this very moment on Ozgur's laptop, sitting up in bed, wondering why the hell the guy who fired the gun was just lying there on his back, not doing anything?

Being right was little comfort to Roberto, given his current position. Initially, he'd thought he was paralyzed from the waist down, but after a minute or two some of the tingling had eased, replaced by intense, paralyzing pain in the lower half of his body. Getting up was out of the question, as were crawling, rolling, and any other form of locomotion he could think of. He was on his back with his head near the front door of the building, and if he turned it to the left—which was only possible with its own unique hell of shooting pain—he could see Dr. Friedman's dead body on the ground five or six feet away from him.

Okay, Roberto thought. *Okay.* He counted breaths to steady himself. *I'm here now. I'm here now.*

He was still wearing the thermal imaging goggles, and he could see that the dense amount of thick fungus on the dead man's body was very much alive and quite industrious. The churning ooze was already moving off the corpse to explore its environment, but it seemed to have slowed as soon as it hit the gravel on the ground beneath him. Slowed, but not stopped.

Roberto heard a chirping sound from nearby and his eyes searched the area around him. His Bluetooth had been knocked out when he hit the ground, and lay about five feet from him, lighting up with a soft blue glow as it rang. It would be Abigail, calling in to say, "What are you doing, man? Why don't you get up?" But getting himself five feet across the gravel to answer a phone call was beyond his capabilities.

Roberto turned his head again, this time craning it backward, digging the back of his skull into the gravel as hard as he could and rolling his eyes up, to get a look at the entrance to the building. It was upside down, but he could see it. The lights were on inside, and he could hear screaming and shouting. No one appeared to be coming out, at least not yet, and he wasn't sure what he would do if they did.

He looked down at the ground and saw the machine pistol, just a foot away from his right hand. A foot. Twelve inches. That was maybe possible. He dug his fingers into the gravel, summoned himself, and clawed toward it. His upper body moved an inch and a half, and he screamed in agony. His vision blurred and doubled, and he felt himself nearly pass out.

But then it cleared, and he was an inch and a half closer.

He raised his eyes, looking at the three still-operative Harleys, leaning on their kickstands, awaiting their riders.

Nobody leaves.

Roberto dug his fingers into the gravel again, repeated the motion, screamed again, and felt the darkness nearly descend.

Nearly. But not quite. Nine inches to go.

He would get to the gun or pass out trying.

BACK IN THE HALLWAY OUTSIDE G-413, GRIFFIN HAD pivoted from Dr. Friedman as soon as the dentist had disappeared around the corner. He pointed the gun at Ironhead and Cuba, swinging it wildly from one to the other. "Stay the fuck away from me the fuck away from me stay the fuck!" he'd managed to spit out, though they were making no attempt to advance on him.

Cuba raised her hands and spoke first. "Easy, man."

"Yeah, come on, Griff," Ironhead chimed in soothingly. "We're all in the same boat here."

Griffin looked at the locker behind them, its walls, ceiling, floor, and TV boxes covered with pulsating globs of fungus. "What boat, what the fuck kind of boat, what fucking boat are you fucking talking about?! What the fuck is going on?!"

Ironhead took a step forward, his hands up, palms out, and his tone calm. "Definitely some strange what-have-you taking place here, my friend, I know. You weren't even in there, man."

"That was horrible," Cuba added, and she meant it.

It's okay, her brain told her. *Everything's fine. Better if you all just get out of here.*

"What do you say we all get out of here?" she suggested.

"Yeah, no shit we're leaving! You first!" Griffin said, gesturing with the gun. "You go ahead of me!"

"Sure, man, no problem," Ironhead said. He turned and looked at Cuba, nodded his head toward the entrance, and started walking that way. She fell into stride beside him.

Ironhead was cool. Best he'd felt in a long time. *That dude behind you is crazy*, his brain told him. *Don't do anything to upset him. He doesn't know up from down. Let's just go.*

They kept walking. As they reached the corner, Griffin looked back over his shoulder, at the mess in the hallway, and the greater mess oozing out of the storage locker. Forget figuring out what was going on, none of it made any sense, he just wanted to get gone. He turned back to the front and watched Ironhead and Cuba as they walked ahead. There was something on the backs of their necks, or *in* the backs of their necks, maybe. The skin was mottled and moving, pulsating from underneath. He didn't care what they did once they got outside, but for himself, he was getting on his Fat Boy and putting as many miles between him and this place as he possibly could. If anybody got in his way, they were going down.

Ahead of him, Ironhead and Cuba were calm. They weren't thinking much, but the thoughts they had were clean and focused. *Cordyceps novus* was a quick study and had modulated its technique with enormous success in the last twenty-four hours. The singular urge to climb that had been effective as a means of escape from sub-level 4 had proven less useful in the case of Mr. Scroggins, who blew his guts at the top of a tree for relatively little payoff. Mike Snyder, on the other hand, had proven the vastly superior dispersal possibilities available in lateral movement, and the minicolonies of the fungus that had sprung up in human beings needed only to find others like themselves to ensure maximum spread and reproduction.

Though it can't think in those terms, or think at all, per se, a fungus knows what works and what doesn't, and it pursues the former as vigorously and completely as it disregards the latter.

Climbing houses and trees was out. Spreading further into the human population was in.

Ironhead and Cuba were completely at peace, focused on one goal: leave.

Go to town, their brains told them. *Ride out of here and into town. Where more people are.*

They rounded another corner. Up ahead, the fluorescent lights of the lobby were visible. They headed toward them.

THIRTY-FIVE

The floor of the sub-basement thunked into the bottom of Teacake's boot. Didn't see that last step coming this time either. He stepped off the ladder and wedged himself back against the wall of the tube as far as he could get, but it wasn't far enough to clear any room for Naomi to join him. "Hang on," he said into his helmet.

Naomi winced at the screech and crackle in her ear and couldn't make out the words, but she caught the meaning. She stopped and turned, looking down. She could see Teacake at the bottom, but the half-barrel-shaped pack was so big he could barely turn around, much less move enough to make room for her. Opening the pack and activating the device in that tiny space was out of the question.

"You're going to have to open the door," she shouted into her microphone.

An enraged, inarticulate screech came back from Teacake, but she understood perfectly well what it meant: under no circumstances would he open that door. She proceeded on that assumption and replied, "There's no room to take that thing off!"

Teacake looked up at her through the thickly clouded face mask. He could see the white blur of her suit and her arm, extended, pointing toward the heavy metal door. He turned, tried shaking his head in the hope that some beads of sweat would fly off his face, hit the mask, and streak paths through the condensation. It worked, sort of, and a tiny ribbon was wiped clear, just enough for him to get a sense of where the large handle was that would release the door mechanism. He reached out and gripped it. If he hadn't been wearing the hazmat gloves, Teacake would have felt the heat immediately, and there's no way in hell he would have opened the door. But through the thick plastic layer, he couldn't tell there was any difference.

On the other side of the door, the situation had changed radically in the past ten minutes. The trail of fungus that had been creeping across the floor from the depleted mass of the Rat King had reached the small puddle of water on the floor beneath one of the sweaty cooling pipes. Throughout its entire history as a species, *Cordyceps novus*, in all its mutated forms, had never run across pure H_2O. From its birth inside a sealed oxygen tank, through its brief childhood in the arid Australian outback, and even in its recent experiences inside the bloodstream of human bodies, water had been a rare and heavily diluted substance. Even in abundance, inside a mammal, it was corrupted by other elements, its essential power limited.

The moment the fungus broke the surface tension of the water molecules at the edge of the puddle, it had undergone a profound and spectacular blossoming. It bloomed into the puddle like a time-lapse film of a flower in springtime, it shot up the rivulet that had run down the wall within a matter of seconds, and it attacked the outside of the sweaty overhead pipe with fervor. It grew along the length of the pipe in both directions, sprouting and dripping onto the floor in great gobs of living organism. Everywhere it contacted the pipe, it set to work with great industry, deploying copious amounts of *Benzene-X*, now a steel-eating acidic substance determined to chew through the pipe and free the flowing waters within. Once it broke through, it would open the way for the fungus to spread like wildfire through the pipe, into the groundwater and then the Missouri River beyond.

As the chemical reactions raged, the temperature in the hallway had risen. It topped 80 degrees when Teacake turned the handle on the door. The interlocking metal bolts slid out of their guide tracks, and the door swung inward.

"Holy Jesus Christ," he said, looking into the hothouse, now dense with active, visible growth. Aerosolized bits and spores hung and swirled heavily in the air all around him.

Through Naomi's headset, all she heard of his voice was a tooth-grinding shriek. But she saw what he saw and had no interest in pausing to admire it. She spun Teacake around, shouting into her microphone, "Unbuckle the front straps!"

He set to work with fumbling hands to undo the leather straps and get the T-41 off his back so they could activate it and get the hell out of there. The buckles on the bottom came off easily enough, and his shoulders seemed to float as Naomi lifted the weight off from behind. He fell forward, his upper body surging with relief, and for a moment he felt like he was flying. He could hear the backpack thud to the cement floor behind him, and he stumbled forward against the tube wall, staring in disbelief at the gurgling mass of fungus covering the walls and floor of the hallway. He could hear the snap of the leather and the rustle of canvas as Naomi opened the pack in the way Roberto had demonstrated.

"Son of a *bitch*!" she said.

Teacake pushed himself against the wall and turned around. Naomi was on her knees, bent over the backpack. Its top was opened, a tangle of belts, ropes, and buckles dripping off its sides. There were enough warning stickers plastered to the inside of the lid to scare off all but the most dedicated kamikaze soldier. Nestled on the padded bottom of the pack was an impossibly antiquated-looking pair of metal tubes lying side by side. There was a small square box beside each of them, a neutron generator, and a red fitted cap at one end of each, the "bullet" that would fire into the tube's fissile core. There was a snarl of wires that led from the explosive caps to a thing that looked suspiciously like an on/off switch, set in its downward position. It seemed like it could be maneuvered manually if necessary, but it was also connected by a web of wires to a small, square digital timer.

The timer was the problem. It was set at four minutes and forty-seven seconds.

And it was already counting down.

Naomi looked up at Teacake.

"The son of a bitch *started it*!"

THIRTY-SIX

Upstairs, the son of a bitch sincerely hoped they'd reached the bottom, opened the pack, and seen the timer by now. He'd hated to do it to them, but there really was no other choice. They'd looked strong and fit, and if they'd made it this far through the night without dying, he'd figured, it was reasonable to think they'd be resourceful enough to get themselves out in time. He truly believed that.

Or maybe he'd just *decided* to believe it.

As for himself, things didn't look promising. He finally had his fingers on the butt end of the machine pistol, but the darkness kept creeping in around the corners of his consciousness every time he moved. The kind of pain he'd experienced in moving his body twelve inches across the gravel had been entirely new to him, an intensity of discomfort he hadn't dreamed possible. Still, he'd managed to get his hand on the gun, and with one last superhuman effort he brought it up, off the ground, aiming it unsteadily at the last three motorcycles and squeezing the trigger. The Heckler & Koch could hold magazines of either fifteen, thirty, or forty rounds, but Roberto didn't know which was in at the moment. There's no way Trini would have left him with just fifteen, but the forty had an extra couple of inches that made the gun harder to maneuver, so he was betting on thirty.

The first two-shot burst collapsed the front end of the first bike, which toppled over into the second. As the second bike fell away from him, he closed one eye and aimed for its rear tire, but on its side, it now offered a more slender angle. It took three shots for him to be certain that bike was disabled, and when it fell it left a clear path to the third bike. That one was farthest away, and the thermal imaging goggles weren't helpful with no heat coming off the thing, so he sprayed four shots along the length of the Harley to be sure it was left unusable. If his count was true, he had used fourteen shots, which left him with sixteen for anybody who came out the door.

Behind him, he heard voices. He arched his head back again, digging the back of his skull into the gravel and looking at the door to the lobby, upside down through the heat-vision goggles. He blinked the sweat out of his eyes and could make out figures coming this way—a man and a woman in front and someone behind them. They'd heard the gunshots and were running.

The man and woman were infected. They glowed red hot, not quite as vivid as Dr. Friedman had been, but clearly alive with mutating fungus. The figure behind them looked normal, but the angle of his arm suggested that he had a gun. Roberto sucked in his breath, and with a great groan of pain, he flopped the machine pistol over onto his chest. Gritting his teeth so hard he thought he might crack a molar, he slid the gun up the length of his body and over his left shoulder, trying to get the barrel as far away from his ear as possible. That wasn't very far, maybe six inches at the most.

The lobby door swung open, inward. The man was in front of the woman, a blurry red-hot target, almost impossible to miss. Roberto knew that as soon as he fired, the others would start to disperse, so it was going to have to be three very short and precise bursts of gunfire rather than one long one. He squeezed the trigger as the first man came out the door.

Ironhead's chest exploded and he staggered back, into Cuba. That was a bad bit of luck for Roberto, as it meant his aim was obscured and he'd need to take a moment to wait for another clean window. He found it quickly, as Cuba moved to the side, against the doorframe, burdened by Ironhead's weight as he fell, dead, into her. Three shots had been spent on Ironhead, and four more ought to take out Cuba quickly enough.

Two of them hit her, but the gun's recoil triggered a spasm of hideous pain in Roberto's back. His hand twitched and the gun jumped to the side. The other two shots hit the doorjamb, shattering the lower hinge and sparking off its metal surface. One of the slugs ricocheted back at

Roberto, slamming into the dirt just a few inches from his face.

Ironhead and Cuba fell backward, out of his line of fire, but the few seconds he'd used to adjust his aim had given the third guy time to flee. Griffin was on the move, heading for the front desk, and was nearly there already. Roberto sucked his breath in, held it, and fired unsteadily at Griffin as he vaulted over the counter. Roberto counted seven shots, all of which went wide of their mark, smashing through the broken drywall behind the counter but missing Griffin. Somehow, the lucky bastard had threaded the needle; he'd made it over the counter unhurt and landed on the other side, out of harm's way.

Shit. Roberto had just used, to the best of his knowledge, twenty-eight shots, which left just two in the clip. There was an armed man who had taken cover behind a wooden counter that completely obscured him. And Roberto still couldn't get off the ground.

The situation was less than ideal.

Roberto blinked as something pattered onto the lens of the goggles. He looked up at the sky, and a few drops of water appeared in his field of vision, accompanied by a low rumble somewhere in the distance.

It was starting to rain.

Hearing a sound from his left, Roberto turned and looked over at the body of Dr. Steven Friedman. The green globules of fungus were swelling outward off his dead flesh, ballooning up as the raindrops hit them, as if activated. *Cordy-*

ceps novus greeted the rain with unbridled joy. The fungal mass, re-energized, dripped off the dentist and moved, expanding across the gravel driveway on the light carpet of water that the rain was laying down.

It moved toward Roberto.

THIRTY-SEVEN

Teacake and Naomi had both stepped in smears of active fungal colonies when they were in the main hallway of sub-level 4. It would have been impossible not to, even if they had been aware that *Benzene-X* had the adaptive capability to eat through the thick rubber soles of the boots. The bottoms of all four of their boots were alive with that process even now, as they made their frantic way back up the tube ladder. They didn't know it, but they had less than a minute to get out of the suits before *Benzene-X* finished its work and the fungus would be able to pass through and make contact with their flesh.

That wasn't the only clock they were on. As soon as they'd seen that the timer on the T-41 was already activated, the only thing left for them to do was to get the hell back upstairs and get out. Teacake was livid, cursing Roberto with every step, but Naomi saw the logic behind what he'd done. They'd had limited time to do the job, he couldn't take the chance that they'd fail to activate the device correctly, and so he'd made a judgment call. All he really needed them for was transportation and placement of the device anyway, and he'd gambled they had a better chance of getting it down there quickly than he did. And, more important, that they could get back up even faster. Tactically speaking, it made sense.

Teacake fairly flew up the ladder, fifty-eight pounds lighter than when he'd climbed down. Naomi, who still had to hold the gun in one hand, was a bit slower, but only a dozen rungs behind him. She looked up and could see the small round circle of light where they'd removed the manhole cover. They climbed fast, both running mental timers that told them they had at best three minutes to get in a car and get a survivable distance away from the underground blast.

Whatever the hell *that* was going to be like.

Teacake got to the top and pulled himself up through the manhole cover with all the grace of a dog climbing out of a swimming pool. He got the bulk of his body up onto the floor, rolled over on his back, and unzipped the neck area of his hazmat suit, ripping the helmet off his head. The burst of fresh air was great, but having clear vision again was even better. He slid his body over, clearing the way for Naomi to come up through the manhole, and he started wriggling out of the suit, rolling it down over his torso and hips.

Naomi came out of the hole a few seconds later, and the first thing she saw was the moving green ooze on the bottoms of Teacake's boots. She gasped and shouted, but he could only hear her muted voice from inside her mask. He got the gist, though—there was something on his boots—and he didn't bother to look, just moved even faster, wriggling desperately to get the suit and the contaminated boots off him. Naomi shouted louder from inside her mask, and this time he could hear her. "What are you doing?! You can't take it off!"

"We'll never get out of here in these things! Take yours off!"

She saw his point—they were hard enough to walk in, forget running. She rolled herself the rest of the way out of the hole, pulling off her helmet. Teacake, freed from his suit, got the hell away from it and its contamination and moved over to her. Avoiding her boots, he ripped the suit off her as fast as their combined efforts would allow. She kicked the suit away, got to her feet, and they took off down the hallway in their socks.

Downstairs, there was less than two minutes showing on the timer.

But Roberto's voice floated through Naomi's mind as she ran.

"The timer duration is unstable," he'd said.

THIRTY-EIGHT

In front of the building, the rain was falling harder now, and the creeping fungus was bubbling across the gravel in lively fashion, only a foot or two from Roberto. Through the thermal imaging goggles, he saw it as a blazing white foam, headed right for him. He turned his head and looked toward the lobby entrance again. The shooter was still out of sight, hidden somewhere behind the front counter, but Roberto had a more immediate concern. And an idea. His eyes went to the front door, the lower hinge of which had been shot off by the errant rounds he'd fired at Cuba. The glass door was hanging at an angle, held in its frame by just its upper hinge now. The door was designed to open inward, and Roberto was lying directly in front of it. Or at least he hoped he was.

He glanced over at the advancing fungus, which was dancing exuberantly in the falling rain. It was only a foot or so from his left hand now, and Roberto took a breath and dragged his arm closer to his body. The movement produced a stabbing pain that radiated all the way down his left leg and caused his foot to spasm, which in turn produced a fresh round of torment. But that gave him a few more seconds.

He looked back up at the top door hinge, tilted the barrel of the gun upward, steadied his aim on it as best he could, and prayed he'd counted the shots correctly.

He had.

The two remaining rounds tore into the metal of the top hinge, blasting it off the doorframe, and the glass door fell over like a domino, straight toward him. Roberto closed his eyes as the heavy door whooshed downward, slamming into his body hard. He screamed underneath the heavy glass as his body torqued unnaturally, but he made use of the moment of agony, dragging himself to his right as far as he could so that the door settled on top of him at an angle.

Its left edge bit into the gravel; it sloped upward over his left arm, hip, and leg and angled out at its top edge, like a lean-to. It now lay like a shield between him and the advancing fungus.

And just in time. The fungus oozed up onto the doorframe, slithering and spreading over the glass just above Roberto. *Benzene-X* got down to business immediately, trying to decipher this new silicon-based barrier and how it might burrow its way through it.

Roberto hadn't bought much time, but a little was better than nothing.

Inside the lobby, Griffin poked his head up over the counter. Whoever was out there shooting at him, he'd heard their gun go dry with a series of soft clicks. Griffin didn't so much care if the guy lived or died, he just wanted to get out of there before he ended up dead like everybody else. He'd seen the pile of trashed Harleys so he knew that was a no-go, but whoever that was, lying out there, they had to have gotten here somehow. Which meant they had car keys.

Griffin straightened, holding his gun in front of him, and headed for the space where the front door had been. He stepped over the bodies of Ironhead and Cuba, trying not to look at them, instead keeping the gun trained on the figure beneath the glass door. Somehow, the dumb shit had managed to miss him with an automatic weapon, and in his last desperate act the guy had shot a door off its hinges and pinned himself beneath it. *Joke's on you, motherfucker.*

Griffin stepped through the door and looked left and right, to make sure there was no one else outside. He saw Dr. Friedman's dead body, covered with the same bizarre foam that had been spattered all over the inside of the storage locker. Griffin shuddered: Teacake had been right, there was some zombie shit going on here, all right, and he needed out, fast. He double-checked the bikes, confirmed they were all down and unusable, and then spotted the minivan parked a little way up the hill. It must belong to the shooter trapped under the door.

"Hey, fucker!" Griffin said, and Roberto squirmed, turning his head slightly to look up at him. Griffin edged closer, the gun shaking in front of him. He'd kill this guy if he had to;

he'd kill anybody who got in his way now. Griffin came around to the side, staring warily at the green ooze that was moving over the glass, just a few inches above the guy's face.

Roberto looked up at him. His eyes asked for help, but he wasn't saying so. *Wouldn't matter if he did*, Griffin thought. *Fuck* you *I'm gonna help you. This is some every-man-for-himself kind of shit going on here*. He squatted down and shoved his hand inside the guy's right pants pocket, feeling around for his car keys.

Roberto screamed in pain at the movement. Griffin didn't care—the others were all dead, and he didn't plan on joining them. He felt the fob of the car keys and yanked them out. Still squatting, he turned and pointed his gun at Roberto's head. The last thing he needed was this guy surviving the night by some miracle and pointing a finger at him in a courtroom and saying, "That's him, Your Honor, that's the guy who left me to die." Griffin wasn't sure what crime that would be exactly, but why take chances?

"Don't look at me!" he shouted, and stiffened his arm, aiming the gun at the center of Roberto's forehead.

"Griffin!"

The voice called from behind him, a woman's voice, and Griffin turned. It was her, the hottie; somehow she'd come back. She had a gun too, but she wasn't bothering to point it at him, it was dangling at her side. "We have to get out of here!"

Griffin looked at her, cold.

Well, you know what? She was gonna have to go too, and that little shit Teacake along with her, because he wasn't taking any chances with any more semi-infected motherfuckers. Once a life-or-death situation starts, you gotta play it out, all the way down the line. And was she or was she not coming at him with a gun? Those two had to go. If that made him an asshole, so be it.

Griffin started to stand, springing out of his crouch. The barrel of his gun, which had been just underneath the lip of the glass, caught there, just by an inch or so and only for a second, but combined with the force of his rapid rise, it was enough to tip its aim downward, pointing it straight at the ground. The sudden unpredictable movement in his hand caused Griffin to tense up his grip, and he blasted off a shot as he stood up.

Straight into his foot.

Griffin screamed as an angry fire erupted in his foot, and he hopped up, to take the weight off. He lost balance, windmilled his arms, and toppled over onto his right side. His gun hand pinned beneath him, the barrel pressed against his chest, the thick, fleshy weight of his torso crushed his fingers, and the gun fired again. This time, the bullet went into his heart.

In this way, Darryl Griffin became the latest in a long line of *Homo sapiens* killed not *for* being an asshole, but *by* being an asshole.

Teacake turned away and saw the green foam on the glass, just over Roberto's face. He ran to the fallen door, dug his fingers underneath the edge, and flipped it off, freeing him.

Roberto shouted up at them. "Car keys are in his hand!"

Naomi clawed the keys out of Griffin's exposed left hand and looked back at Roberto. "Get up!"

"I can't. Drag me."

Figuring he'd been shot but knowing there was no time to dwell on it, they each grabbed him by an arm and dragged him, screaming, up the short driveway to the minivan. The heat-vision goggles had fallen off Roberto's head, but he didn't need them to see the fungal growth anymore. As they hauled him up the hillside, he could see the forest floor lit up with its glowing green tendrils, spreading rapidly in the now-heavy rain.

They reached the minivan and threw him into the back, producing more screams. Teacake jumped in beside him, Naomi slid behind the wheel, and she started the engine.

Teacake shouted at Roberto, "You started the timer on us!"

"I knew you could get out."

"You did *not* know that!"

"But you did."

"But you didn't *know*!"

"But you did."

Naomi dropped the van in reverse, threw her arm over the seat, and floored it, backing up at top speed. "Guys, shut up." She reached the top of the driveway, spun the wheel, and the minivan slid around, almost knocking Roberto and Teacake out the still-open side door. "How much time do we have?" she asked Roberto.

He turned his head, painfully, and looked at the timer that he'd set on his watch when he first activated the device. It was at −1:07 and counting. "It should have gone off a minute ago."

Naomi dropped the van in drive and they took off, down White Clay Road and toward the highway. For a moment, nobody spoke.

Finally, Naomi did. "Well. The timer is unstable. You said."

"Yep," Roberto replied.

They drove. Still nothing. No bright light, no tremors in the earth, no fire and brimstone. Nothing.

"How will we know if it goes off?" Teacake asked.

"You'll know," Roberto said. He looked at his watch again: −1:49.

Naomi drove, fast. They rode in silence, waiting.

Every second seemed to take forever, and Teacake's vivid imagination went to work. He had time to imagine three possible scenarios, each more vivid than the last. In the first scenario, the T-41 failed to detonate. The pipes in the basement buckled under *Cordyceps novus*'s assault within a few minutes, and the fungus exploded in growth, billowing through the water in the pipes, flowing into the groundwater and eventually into the Missouri River. Within a matter of days, the powerful waterway would be converted to a carpet of solid green fungal matter, which would spread over the surrounding lands, unchecked and unstoppable, rewriting the rules for life on the planet and bringing about a Sixth Extinction, a mass die-off that this time would include all human and animal life on Earth.

So that one was pretty bad.

In the second scenario, Teacake imagined the blasting caps went off and the device detonated as planned. But a few hundred feet underground wasn't nearly deep enough for a nuclear explosion, and in this version, he imagined the explosion erupting out of the ground, billowing up into the sky in a massive mushroom cloud just like the ones he'd seen in movies and on TV. The poisonous cloud of radiation would blow eastward on prevailing winds, spreading death and disease over the eastern half of the United States.

Admittedly, this scenario wasn't as bad as the first one, but it wasn't a lot of fun either.

The third scenario was Teacake's favorite, and it was for this that he now prayed to a God he didn't believe in. In this version, the blasting caps went off, better late than not at all, exploding inward on the metal tubes and beginning the process of nuclear compression. The chain reaction commenced, producing an outpouring of heat somewhere between 50 million and 150 million degrees Fahrenheit. The sub-basement and the layers of rock closest to the backpack would be vaporized instantly, forming a crater into which the entire contents of the storage facility would collapse.

All the unneeded furniture, the contents of homes that would never be reoccupied, the pack-rat hoardings of a thousand unhappy people, the stolen Samsung TVs, Mrs. Rooney's twenty-seven banker's boxes filled with her children's school reports and holiday cards, her forty-two ceramic coffee mugs and pencil jars made at Pottery 4 Fun between 1995 and 2008, her seven nylon duffel bags stuffed with newspapers from major events in world history, and even her vinyl *Baywatch* pencil case stuffed with $6,500 in cash she was saving for the day the banks crashed For Real—all of it, all the junk in all the sealed boxes in all the lockers, some of their contents long forgotten, all the shit, shit, shit, shit—all of it would melt, collapsing downward into the cavity, forming a rubble chimney that would swell upward.

From ground level, Teacake imagined, a perfectly round crater might emerge, sucking the entire facility and the hillside all around down into it in a matter of seconds, as if it were on some giant round elevator, as if God had pushed the Down button and called everything back inside Mother Earth to be reconfigured, repurposed, used another day for a greater end. The fungus itself would be incinerated, Teacake thought, burned off the face of the planet for good, and as the explosion settled, a harmless cloud of dirt and dust would rise up, all that was left of the

Atchison Storage Facility and this fucked-up night.

And in the end, two minutes and twenty-six seconds behind schedule, that was exactly what happened.

AFTERWARDS

THIRTY-NINE

The snow globe was back in the cabinet. Roberto had upgraded the emergency cell phone and given it a fresh charge, just in case. Both were locked away in the secret kitchen cupboard again, and on most days, he hoped they'd never come back out. On the other days, the days when he felt particularly proud of himself, he'd muse about how awfully good he was at his job after all and what a shame it would be to park those skills on a shelf forever.

The government attention had been flattering in the immediate aftermath of the Atchison Event, as it was now universally called in the media. In the first hours after the blast, Jerabek had tried hard to play the traitor/terrorist/rogue-agent card, but Roberto was much too skilled a player to be snookered. The initial white paper he'd written on the fungus had been archived in three separate backup locations, to ensure it could never be destroyed without being widely read and, inevitably, leaked to the press. Abigail, whose real name actually *was* Abigail—huh, guess he didn't know everything—had proven to be a determined truth-teller and a savvy player of government games. Within twenty-four hours the real story was out, and they were heroes. Talk of renegade Deep State actors gave way quickly to serious conversations about planning for potential future hostile biological invasions and a lively debate about real estate values along the Missouri River bluffs. Speculation ensued.

Roberto sat now on the back porch of the house in North Carolina, in the rocker, the one that felt good on his back. He was nowhere near full strength, but at least the surgery was over with, and he was in the sweet zone of his second Percocet of the day, so pain wasn't an issue at the moment. He was watching Annie, who was working in the garden. He loved the wide-brimmed hat she wore in the sun, the one she'd bought on the trip to Harbour Island. He loved the blue Wellingtons she stomped around in, the pair she'd bought at the Clarks on Kensington High Street in 2005. He loved the way she stood back after clipping or weeding a particular area, the way she assessed what she'd done and thought about whether it was good enough or needed more. Invariably, she'd see that it needed a little more pruning, a bit of extra shaping, and she'd keep working. He loved watching her form. Her shape was the shape of home to him, and he never tired of admiring her.

Beside him, his cell phone buzzed. He looked at it and smiled, recognizing the number. He picked it up. "You're still terrible on TV."

"Like, I know, right?" Teacake replied. "I don't even know why I do that shit."

"I do. How much you get?"

Teacake laughed. "Five grand."

"You're selling yourself cheap."

"That ain't what I called about. Fucker, what the fuck is this?"

"You'll have to be more specific."

"Notice of Expungement. I got it in the mail. What the fuck is this, dude?!"

"It's exactly what it says, Travis." Nobody called him Teacake anymore, and he didn't miss it. Roberto continued. "Your conviction has been set aside and your record permanently sealed. It's as if it never happened."

"How the fuck did you do that?!"

"It isn't that hard."

"Well, fuck, man, thanks! Fuck!"

"You have *got* to learn another word. You know, for when you want to emphasize something."

"I've tried other words, man. Nothin' else is as good. Anyway, thank you."

"You're welcome."

"And hey—go easy on them painkillers. I can hear it in your voice. You got the thick tongue."

Roberto smiled. "Will do."

"That's a slippery slope, man. I've seen it."

"So have I, my friend."

"Later, dude."

"Later, Travis." Roberto hung up.

He watched his wife as she worked in the garden.

I'm here now.

———

TRAVIS PUT THE PHONE IN HIS POCKET AND TOOK Naomi's hand again. Sarah ran ahead of them. They were headed for the playground. He glanced over at Naomi, figured now was as good a time as any. He spoke, soft and halting at first, then picking up steam.

"So, like, I gave it a lot of thought, and it's not something I say much or have said much, and I don't want to come off like 'Ooh, I'm this guy who knows all this shit about whatever or what have you,' but, you know, given what's up and how it is, I mean, you prolly know what I'm gonna say, and I can't honestly say that I've ever said it before, or maybe what I should say is I *can* honestly say I've never said it before, you know, anyway, the thing is, I love you."

Naomi didn't respond. She kept walking, looking straight ahead, watching as her daughter ran the last fifty feet of sidewalk and cut right onto the sandy expanse of the playground, toward the big play set in the middle.

Travis stared at Naomi, furrowing his brow. He hadn't expected an "I love you" back, but he hadn't expected this either. Ignoring him? Staring straight ahead? What kind of ridiculous bullshit was this? Had he freaked her out that badly? Then he remembered.

He let go of her hand and moved around to the other side of her, the side with her good ear, the one she could actually hear out of. He looked at her.

"I love you," he said.

Naomi turned and looked back, hearing the words for the first time. "I love you too," she said. She kissed him.

Oh, Travis thought, *how much there is to be said for a sober kiss.*

With her.

ACKNOWLEDGMENTS

Many thanks to all who helped get this book out of my head and into your hands—Brian Murray, Zachary Wagman, Dan Halpern, Laura Cherkas, Miriam Parker, Sonya Cheuse, Meghan Deans, Allison Saltzman, and Will Staehle at Ecco; Mollie Glick, Brian Kend, Richard Lovett, and Danial Mondanipour at CAA; David Fox; Mike Lupica; and Dr. Andrei Constantinescu, who was of enormous help with the science. Anything that is too fanciful here is not his fault.

For encouragement and early reads, thanks also to Melissa Thomas, John Kamps, Howard Franklin, Gavin Polone, Will Reichel, and Brian DePalma. Special thanks to my son Ben, whose dreamy sense of story and vibrant creativity were with me every step of the way; to my son Nick, whose infectious enthusiasm and first look at my earliest pages were invaluable; to my son Henry, for sharing his exuberant love of science in general and *Ophiocordyceps* in particular; and to my daughter, Grace, who's taught me there's a whole other gender out there and they tend toward the awesome. And thanks to all four of you for somehow understanding Dad can do horror and still be a nice guy.